THE COLOR
OF BRANDY

BY RAYMOND SMECKER

The Color of Brandy
by Raymond Smecker

Library of Congress Number: 2017959101
International Standard Book Number: 978-1-60126-552-4

Masthof Press
219 Mill Road | Morgantown, PA 19543-9516
www.Masthof.com

DEDICATED TO

St. Elizabeth Ann Seton,
Major William Wells,
the First Vermont Cavalry, &
the Morgan Horse Valor at Gettysburg

"Look up. Look up, and we'll all get
to heaven on horseback . . ."
- Mother Seton

"Look back at our struggle for freedom. Trace our present day's strength to its source; and you'll find that man's pathway to glory is strewn on the bones of the horse."

- Anonymous

TABLE OF CONTENTS

– A TRIBUTE TO –
General Reynolds and Kate Hewitt

The Fall of Reynolds—The death of General John Fulton Reynolds at the Battle of Gettysburg in 1863, depicted by Alfred Rudolph Waud.

Catherine Mary Hewitt became engaged to future Union General John Reynolds in California in the late 1850s. Since they were from different religious denominations—Reynolds was a Protestant, Hewitt a Catholic—she kept their engagement a secret, even from her parents. Kate and John had decided that if he were killed during the war and they could not marry, she would join a convent.[*]

After he was killed at the Battle of Gettysburg and buried, she went to Emmitsburg, Md., and joined the St. Joseph Central House of the Order of the Daughters of Charity.

Bas-relief of Vermont Cavalry on monument at Gettysburg Battlefield.

---

[*] *Information gleaned from www.civilwarwomenblog.com/kate-hewitt.*

MORGANS IN THE CIVIL WAR

Morgans were a favored mount of cavalry soldiers on both sides in the Civil War. They were sensible under fire, and could march tirelessly all day. They maintained their condition on unpredictable rations, and were loyal to their riders in all circumstances. Morgans recorded in Civil War stories include Philip Sheridan's Winchester (also known as Rienzi), Charlemagne, and Stonewall Jackson's Little Sorrel. Other Morgans included the mounts of the 5th New York Cavalry: Pink, Betty, Cockeye, Prince, Frank, Mink, Mollie, Jack (#1), Topsy, Nellie, Jack (#2), Dunlap's mare, Sukey, Black Dick, Brydon's Nellie, Charley, Jane, Pomp, Wyman Horse, June, and Lucy. A monument was built to honor Pink, and a marker was made for the grave of Billy. Betty Root served under Lt. Trussel in the 1st Vermont Cavalry. Old Clem was owned by Colonel Lemuel Platt who organized the 1st Vermont Cavalry. Clifton was ridden by Dr. William Capeheart of North Carolina until he was killed in action in March 1864.

The following regiments of the cavalry were mounted on Morgans when they were first organized. As horses were killed in action they were replaced by government-owned mounts which varied in quality:

FIRST MAINE CAVALRY

SECOND MICHIGAN CAVALRY

THIRD MICHIGAN CAVALRY

FOURTEENTH PENNSYLVANIA CAVALRY

FIFTH NEW YORK CAVALRY COMPANY H

FIRST RHODE ISLAND CAVALRY (Morgans and French-Canadian horses)

FOURTH VIRGINIA CAVALRY COMPANY H—Also known as the Black Horse Cavalry or the Black Horse Troop, this unit created panic among the raw recruits of the Union Army at the First Battle of Bull Run or First Manassas.

FIRST VERMONT CAVALRY—This unit received shipments of more Vermont horses during the war; 200 of the original 1,200 Morgans used to mount this regiment survived the war. They inspired the following remarks:

"The mounts of the First Vermont Cavalry were decidedly the best I had ever seen. Everybody was attracted by them. I have heard both General Buford . . . and General Hatch . . . say that the mounts of this regiment was the best in the army. General Buford . . . also told me that he would as soon have this regiment of Vermont volunteer cavalry as a regiment of the regular army."

- Charles Tompkins, Captain,
U.S. Army

"The other day, a very fine horse being offered at the Inspection Ground, I bought him. He is a chestnut horse about 15.2 hands high, five years old, weighs between 1,000 and 1,100 and is pretty as a picture. He is of the Morgan breed, proud and high spirited, yet fearless. He will stand within four feet of a puffing locomotive and never thinks of being frightened. He is deep-chested and has very powerful and muscular limbs. Built for strength, speed and endurance. He has a very fine head and ears and a neck that might serve as a model in painting. In fact, he is a prince among horses, and I doubt not that I shall be envied my treasure when I rejoin my regiment. I ride him a little every day and enjoy it hugely. It seems good to be once more in the saddle. On the street his proud bearing attracts much attention and the rascal gets more admiring glances than his rider."

- Captain William C. Hazelton,
8th Illinois Cavalry,
letter to his mother, June 3, 1864

"Dad fought in the Civil War and saw a lot of that company from Vermont that had all the Morgan horses. Dad was with the artillery. Six horses were needed to pull each big piece of equipment and Dad got two of those Vermont Morgans for his lead team. He sure thought a lot of them and according to him there wasn't anything they couldn't do. They were constantly in demand to move pieces of artillery that were mired and other teams had failed to move."

- A. G. Maier,
speaking of his father and
his Morgan horses in 1950

Information on pages viii and ix gleaned from the Vermont Historical Society, UVM Morgan Horse Farm, and the Morgan Horse Museum.

BATTLE OF CEDAR CREEK

Rienzi (a.k.a. Winchester) was ridden by General Philip Sheridan to rally his Union troops and was commemorated in the poem and painting, "Sheridan's Ride," written by Thomas Buchanan Read. Winchester is preserved and is at the Smithsonian Museum. Sheridan's ride at the Battle of Cedar Creek on Morgan Winchester. Credit: Library of Congress.

Lithograph by J. G. Fay (1877). Traveller, the war horse of Robert E. Lee, and Little Sorrel, Stonewall Jackson's horse. Little Sorrel was a Morgan ridden by Confederate General Stonewall Jackson in his Civil War campaigns.

Charlemagne was the Morgan mount of General Joshua Chamberlain.

General Joshua L. Chamberlain acquired Charlemagne as Confederate contraband. J.L.C. paid the government rate ($150) and Charlemagne was foaled in the spring of 1860. He was shot down three times under J.L.C. Once the same bullet passed through the neck of the horse and hit J.L.C. in the breast. He was brought back to Brunswick where for many years he was the idolized pet of the family. He was buried on the grounds of the family's seaside cottage, Domhagen.

PART ONE

Overlooking Devil's Den at Gettysburg Battlefield

GETTYSBURG, A MEADOW NEAR BIG ROUND TOP

"Claret is the liquor for boys; port for men
but he who aspires to be a hero must drink BRANDY."
- SAMUEL JOHNSON

The melon moon and his mother were the first to see his soft wet body.

His equine mother licked the residue that was sticking to him, and then she stood up and ripped the grey shroud from his clammy body. She nickered softly and nudged him gently—all of the night creatures whispered, "Welcome to life!"

This newborn colt was the color of a fine French brandy.

Overhead the stormy clouds shifted and flashes of lightning lit up the Adams County, Pennsylvania, landscape. The peaceful farmland looked like a battlefield.

Thunder rolled down the cloud banks and the lightning darted violently through the whites of the dark grey billowing clouds illuminating the quilt-like landscape. Lightning bolts danced randomly through the moonlit skyline; one sizzling bolt crashed into a nearby tree splitting it while the sprouting vegetation crackled in its wake.

The other horses nearby in the fields scattered and headed for the shelter of the nearby weeping willows. Brandy's mother stood over top of the newborn colt, attempting to shield him from the cold rain falling from the steely sky. She was weak from the new birth but she lovingly straddled him while rivers of rainwater rolled down her forelock and into her large brown eyes. The rain felt cool on her body and she hung her weary head over the colt's exposed body.

She shielded his face and the newly born colt huddled and cuddled underneath her wide bay body. The rain turned to sleet and it pelted their bodies.

Finally, nature turned kinder as the rain and cold front blew ominously out of their pasture and across the oddly shaped hills in the distance . . . and on into the small town of Gettysburg nearby . . .

GETTYSBURG &
JAKE RANDOLPH

T he morning sun jumped over the horizon, burning off the mountain mist that shrouded the bucolic farmland as the farmer and owner of this peaceful Adams County horse farm, Jake Randolph, reined in his plowing Morgan mare, Belle.

"Well look at that," he said to his dew covered horse. "Brother Seth was right. That new Morgan mare he sold me was a good deal. Two for the price of one. This colt looks just like Figure and his famous sons—Sherman, Bulrush, and Woodbury—just like brother Seth said he'd look!"

Jake's brother's words rang in his ears as his black mare lifted her beautiful head and finally stopped, imbedding the head of the working plow into the rich damp soil.

"Take this one to Pennsylvania with you and put some more Vermont Morgan blood into your stock. She will purify your bloodlines . . . " his brother had encouraged. "Vermont Morgans will do the plowin', pullin', prancin' and dancin' you in a fancy way all the way to town! That's what a Morgan will do for you! And they won't even get tired if they do it all day. Won't be hard keepers like those big plowers are, and they'll be prouder doing it all. And when the work is done, hitch 'em up to the fancy buggy and they'll pull you all the way to the local dance and never miss a step."

As his mind recalled all the discussions he had had with his brother, he watched the colorful newborn colt get to its feet, but the protective senior mare flicked her head and sent out a warning scream.

"Ok, ok . . . I'm not going to hurt him," rolled out of his lips which were surrounded by a stubby beard.

Jake lifted his injured left leg up on a sod clump and then watched as the cold and wet dark green hayfields swayed in the morning breezes.

Their whimsical tips wavered showing the lime color of the emerging buds while the stems matched the terra cotta earth shades. The trees that edged his pastures and the barren surrounding fields were also budding and some even matched the color of the new colt. The forests that ran from the edges of his fields into the nearby tree topped hills pushed out their leaves matching the skyline—all were blending with the same colors Mother Nature sent this time of year.

Jake finally pushed on his Morgan horse and she turned and headed back down the furrow row that ran the edge of this fertile field while the plow heaved and cut into and then carved its way.

He watched and thought how good it would be for him to be able to add more cash income studding out another Morgan stallion. Since leaving his father's Vermont farm and landing in Pennsylvania, life on this farm along the Emmitsburg Road was getting more economically difficult. Good Morgan stock was so hard to find and it seemed that since the country was split on the slavery issue with an ugly Civil War brewing, the best Morgans were being auctioned to the highest bidders—the military!

There was a current agrarian high that was fueling an increased demand for good horses and the Morgans, around the country, were bringing very high prices. His native Vermonters were concerned about the possible depletion of their state's own fine breeding stock. But many of them could not resist selling their Vermont-bred Morgans for the higher prices just to help pay off their mortgages which enabled them to send their children to better schools.

Many Union officers had been scouting around and buying up all the good stock and driving up the prices in this area. Jake was so grateful that his brother and family were still steadfast Vermonters and that they were still holding on to their good mares and stallions and breeding their own quality stock.

This Gettysburg to Emmitsburg Road area was a peaceful and safe place to live and if a war did start Jake felt that this area would be one of the safest for his growing family. Thankfully, his two daughters were schooled several miles down the road at the Daughters of Charity School in Emmitsburg under a barter system.

He praised and loved the Sisters in the Emmitsburg, Maryland, school and they were very good to him, especially when they learned of the loss of his wife Emily. In spite of all the hardships he still managed to send his daughters, Catherine and Sarah, to their church school and he still had hired help to do the Spring planting and breeding.

"Hey Jake, nice colt." The voice startled him from his daydreaming and he looked up to find his hired hand, Rafael, approaching.

"You better stay away, Raff. That senior mother is very protective!"

"What a color! I've never seen it before," said Raff.

"Color of a fine French brandy . . . the stuff those Army officers drink down at the town tavern," echoed Jake.

"If that colt's half as good as that stuff, he'll be talked about in this county! Soon the cavalry officers will be coming around and after him," continued Raff.

"He won't be for sale, not at any price. He's a rare one with Figure blood in him. We'll stud him and he'll help me keep the farm."

"Oh, I don't believe that. Army fellas are pretty sharp . . . they'll hear about him at the tavern and be out here fixing to give you a good price."

"Not for sale . . . never! Now let's let them graze and we'll furrow this field back to the barn and get some lunch."

BURLINGTON, VERMONT
& SETH RANDOLPH, JR.

The forested hills and pastures of beautiful Vermont and New England were once the only homes for the proud Morgan horse. The demands from the pioneers moving westward dug deep into their heritage Morgan herds and all of this sent the supply and demand and prices for prize Morgan bloodlines higher each passing day. Their beloved horses had been driven West years before by the westward moving pioneers and transient Vermonters, and by the mid 1850s farm journals as west as Ohio had been listing Morgan virtues and values. They were being used to pull stagecoaches, do light farmwork and also as buggy horses. Many of the Vermonters were warned not to be tempted to sell all of their prize stock. They were instructed to retain their best lines to imprint the Morgan image and then to be able to continue to supply the demanding markets. They also had to maintain the integrity of their breed from the not-so-honest horse traders who were soon claiming Morgan ancestry for horses that had no Morgan bloodlines at all in their "phony" pedigrees.

The Randolphs' Vermont farm had been in the family for three generations and now that his Uncle Jake was in Pennsylvania and his dad Seth, Sr., was getting older—the farm would pass down to him. It was a wonderful feeling to carry on the tradition, but Seth felt a yearning, a desire to move on, too. His uncle had matched his own dream and landed in Gettysburg, Pennsylvania, on a beautiful farm. He wanted to move, too, and his dad knew that!

Westward was what he was thinking when he read in the paper one evening that "In the U.S. census of 1850, Vermont had the highest number of its native-born citizens living outside their native state—OVER 40%!"

Now here it was 1863 and he was still entrenched with the urge to leave and at his age of twenty—he was ripe for a change. Seth sat back and looked out the nearby window and yearned to be a pioneer; be one of them moving West, but he could not disappoint his father, and besides his new wife Betsy was a Vermont homebody and had no desire to move West. So he had to find another way to satisfy his yearning for adventure . . . to satisfy that restless Vermont blood running through his veins.

He put down the paper and passed through the kitchen, giving his new bride a big hug saying, "We'll need more supplies from town, Betsy. Grab your bonnet and get ready while I go to the barn and hitch up the wagon."

On the way out he passed by his father who was setting on the porch. "Dad, I better head into town and get the supplies we need. Betsy is fetching her bonnet. We'll be back before dark."

Seth's dad smiled and reached for his hat and said, "Ok Seth I'll bring in the horses and make sure they are all fed."

Seth reined in his handsome Morgan in front of the hardware store where several of the townsfolk were gathered around a military officer tacking up a white poster on the outside of the hardware store. He tied his horse to the hitching post and helped Betsy down.

"I'm going to shop for a new bonnet and some notions and will meet you back here in a bit," replied Betsy.

The sign on the outside of the town hardware store wall read:

> TOWN MEETING TODAY
>
> U.S. Congress passes a CONSCRIPTION ACT. ALL MALES between the ages of 20 and 45, including aliens with the intention of becoming citizens, MUST REGISTER by April 1, 1863!

Seth entered the store that was filling up with locals and a sharply dressed young cavalry officer with a curled-up mustache was seated at a table talking to a group of anxious young men.

"Afternoon," remarked the military man to Seth.

"Afternoon," replied Seth as he strolled over to the table that was filled with military hats and gloves, a riding crop, and a bugle.

"About to give a talk . . . just set down with the other fellows."

Seth smiled cautiously and pulled up a chair as the dust jumped off the arms and fluffed into the air.

The cavalry officer doused his half-chewed cigar and then started to give a speech. The room was filled with young men pressed up against the backdrop of the hardware shelves as pungent smoke from the doused cigar nagged at everyone's eyes and throats.

"I'll give all of you a cigar when this is over," said the cavalry officer as he stood up and went to the front of the store. With the "Notice" in hand he started his speech, "U.S. Congress passed a Conscription Act. All males between the ages of 20 and 45, including aliens with the intention of becoming citizens, *must register* by April 1, 1863!

"When the Civil War began we only had six regiments of United States Cavalry. We had some dragoons and some mounted riflemen, just a few good officers and leaders and then some of our best just quit and went to the other side—to the Confederacy!

"Our Commanding General Winfield Scott felt that our Northerners and our weapons were not good enough for a cavalry. So we only had a few cavalry regiments when we got into this war. President Lincoln then called for more volunteers, but he only authorized *one* regiment of cavalry!

"In '61 McClellan took command of the Army and that idea was changed and he made Stoneman Chief of the Cavalry, and then we got about eighty-two Union volunteer cavalry regiments signed up and fitted, but we didn't have the best weapons and our boys were badly trained as riders, and worse yet . . . we were short of good horses!"

He took his yellow neckerchief from his pocket and wiped the sweat from his brow and continued in a sharp-tongued way, "McClellan didn't make us a very pretty cavalry like the enemy—they had a lot of dash and dignity—but he put us into the infantry—in the Army—where we were just to be used in escort and messenger service duties."

The flashy officer then stopped talking and he swiveled his burly shoulders upright and then watched as Seth and the others intently leaned in to listen to his colorful and patriotic recruitment speech.

"Now we are building a big cavalry depot down in the District of Columbia at Giesboro Point, across the eastern branch of the Potomac. It's going to be the largest in the world!

"Now I'm a Vermonter with the cavalry and ride one of our best bred Vermont Morgans . . . so I'm here to challenge and recruit with the authority to form a Vermont Cavalry Unit! The other side has been unstoppable! The other side has been unchallenged! The other side is always upsetting our Union commanders! And now some of their leaders are riding Morgan horses!"

He kicked the floor with his boot and the fellows around jumped.

"I'm here to show 'em what a Vermont Cavalry can do on a Morgan . . . 'cause they got this dandy fellow named J.E.B. Stuart. Remember that name! He's a West Point graduate and an old Indian fighter from the Western frontier.

"He's a daring Confederate dandy in this war. He dresses with a wide-brimmed hat worn tilted to an angle and he has an ostrich feather in it with a gold star!

"He wears a flowing cape and a red-lined jacket. He puts a yellow sash around his waist and sports long trousers tucked in his shiny boots. He sparkles and jingles when he walks with golden spurs in battle!

"If that's not enough of a show—he also puts a red rose in his button-hole! Now I'm not a flower dandy like him and my name is First Lieutenant Baker, but I am a Vermonter!"

And with that word he raised his riding crop and the crowd let out a resounding cheer.

He continued by saying, "My commander is also a Vermonter from here—Major William Wells from Waterbury! Major and his three brothers joined the Army. He was just like all of you who are going to sign up when I'm done. He enlisted as a private and then helped to raise Company C of the 1st Vermont Cavalry. Very soon after he was promoted to First Lieutenant and then Captain and he was in one of the thickest battles at Orange House in Virginia. After that he was promoted to Major! He doesn't wear a rose but he's been in the Shenandoah Valley. He campaigned at the 2nd Bull Run and he just eluded some captors and now we're all recruiting for the Second Battalion of the 1st Vermont Cavalry!

"We are a Vermont fighting force for the Northern Cavalry and we have a new leader named Alfred Pleasonton. He came by horseback from faraway out West in Utah all the way to Washington to volunteer and they made him commander of our reorganized federal cavalry corps."

The crowd gathered around started to buzz their approval and he continued, "This here's the start of '63 and the South has its rose-toting cavalry leader! But we have some colors, too—the Northern Cavalry," and he threw down his crop on the table and picked up his cavalry hat and put it squarely on his head. Raising his voice he said, "They travel light and live off the land. Stuart and his boys are ranger units that always roam and raid our own Union camps and our supply trains for their own supplies to feed themselves!

"The North is starting to turn the tide now. Most of us carry our own sabers, but we like carbines and pistols. All our cavalry commanders have learned

to use their horses for moving swiftly and not head-on attacks. We go up close to the Southern lines and often dismount. Then we go into action. One of the four cavalry soldiers in our group then sets and holds all of the horses."

The confident recruiter halted his speech and watched the faces of the men in the room. Smiles flicked onto their faces as the emotions of the moment and the sweaty smells ignited the charisma of the recruiter and he now moved into his yarn-spinning part of the speech trying to win over the gathered audience of perspective Vermont recruits.

"We are to get breech-loadin' carbines!" and with that he picked up one from the table nearby and lifted it high into the air and plopped it back down making a cracking sound. He continued, "We will have a Blakeslee for our Spencer rifles known as the Quick Loader! You can shoot 14 to 20 rounds in a minute while most of the Southerners are still using their old-fashioned Enfields and Springfields! So now we have a new kind of cavalry—a new breed!"

The recruiter's eyes sparkled in the midst of the smoke and silence that permeated the room. His audience was focused on his hand as it went for his saber while the other hand reached for his service revolver. He pulled out both and raised them high above into the air as he pitched the scene: "We have leaders now to match rose-wearin' Stuart. Aggressive leaders like Kilpatrick and Pleasanton and a long-haired dashing Staff Officer named Custer on his faithful Morgan horse named Dandy!

"And one of these days ol' J.E.B. Stuart is gonna meet up with us new Vermonters on our Morgans! I'm here to sign up volunteers or it's the Conscription Act for all males between the ages of 20 and 45!

"Now you can register or volunteer . . . but most are signing up as a volunteer to join our new cavalry unit to follow Custer and Vermonter Wells on our own Morgans here in Wells' Vermont!"

He raised his voice higher and then pointed the revolver above his head and pulled the trigger—it was empty!

"We got something those Southern boys don't have! We have the best horses on the ground—Vermont Morgans! Our procurement officers are out now getting the best Morgan mounts and Canadian horses. They are all smaller, easy keepers and we've sent thousands of Vermont Morgans to this Civil War. Many of them are carrying us and some are pulling the artillery and many already have died for our country.

"The First goes into battle on Vermont Morgan horses. We are Vermonters on Vermonters! The horses are saddled and ready to go . . . are *you*? Are *you* ready to join the best of the best—a new breed of cavalry—the First Vermont Cavalry?"

The room exploded with cheers and all of the men in it raised their hands and rushed up to the front table. Seth Randolph was first in line and shouted out loud, "Where do I sign, sir?"

BRANDY IN GETTYSBURG

Seasons passed and Brandy's first birthday came and went through a typical sweltering July 1860 Gettysburg summer.

The landscape then turned colors as the cooler and shorter days of Fall moved in and Brandy changed like the seasons. The yearling look quickly passed. Everything around him but the distant rounded mountains remained in constant flux while his own body got muscular, longer, stronger and wider and like those round-topped mountains, nature never seemed to be quite satisfied with the final images.

The months passed and his head reached farther up his mother's flanks and by the time of the next Spring he had shaded into a deep brandy hue. Winter had gone and blown into the distant past just like the snow disappeared on the mountain slopes; his own moods and instincts changed too, just like the images of the passing humans who often mingled in his foraging meadows.

His coat and personality and character all were changing again as the winter snows melted into the swollen meadow stream that next Spring. The cold clear waters flowed down from the melting mountain foothills and ran into the meadows of his flourishing pasture, helping to alter the view and helping nourish his Justin Morgan bloodlines that were now maturing and chiseling his own muscular neck and body.

His mother no longer defended him around the other horses and she grew very impatient when he was around. The insecurity forced him to become totally independent and to wander alone for longer and longer time periods.

Then one late Spring morning there was another foal at her side and she screamed at him and chased him away. He was now totally alone!

The daily drama and dependence on his own well-being set forth a two-fold conflict within him—one of total independence followed by the scourge of jealousy for the other tiny one now enjoying the fresh and sweet juice of his own beloved mother's teats. Now he had finally felt the end of something that he only knew well, for something completely different—fear of the unknown. He felt loneliness. He felt unhappiness but he realized the best of all—he found freedom.

Summer passed by quickly and so did the two-legged creatures who continued to stand around the outside fence perimeters of the meadows where he frolicked, nearby the foothills of the odd-shaped round-topped hills around his pasture areas. The humans always pointed things at him and shook their heads. He trusted them like the snakes that sunned on rocks near the flowing stream below. Eagles often soared overhead and landed in the treetops, and the rabbits and deer and flashy squirrels often stopped when he approached them. Life in the natural world was getting uneasy in the agrarian world around him.

Brandy's world had always been filled with abundant wildlife and peace and he gleefully enjoyed the new instincts, and didn't even mind when a two-legged creature put a thing over his head and let him walk freely while a long thing kept him from running away. It only lasted a short time and then he would be released back to the coarse grasses which always satisfied his appetite.

After that routine he would buck and jump and run freely and follow his routine that led him up the creek into the lush and greener higher pastures near the placid pools where he spent the really hot summers. Water and food was plentiful and the nearby deer herds and other animals all wandered around the lush plateau feeding freely and living in harmony with all of nature's creatures.

Then one day it all ended as a two-legged creature put that thing over his head and led him out of the pasture and into a large open space area with two-legged creatures surrounding it.

"C'mon Brandy . . . let's show 'em all what you look like! Time to meet the guys with their mares!"

SETH AND THE FIRST
VERMONT CAVALRY

I t was a long and sad ride back to the farm with Betsy as he explained what he did and watched her tears flow. "Look Betsy, I had to volunteer or register for a conscription . . . one way or another I have to serve just like all the others who signed up. I'll be back!" But when he left her with his dad, standing pitifully on the front porch outside of their Vermont home, reality set in—he might not be coming back!

That scene with those raw emotions kept flashing back and forth in his mind so often as he trained in his new home with the First Vermont Cavalry. He realized that much of their teachings he had already known as a Vermonter, all except how to deal with missing his wife. The letters back and forth did not help . . . besides they were few and took a long time to pass between them.

"The most important thing to every cavalryman," the cavalry officer said, "is your horse! Keeping that horse in top condition is the ultimate goal. If your horse is killed—a replacement is hard to be found."

To him the most important thing was not his horse it was his Betsy, but she was home and he understood the difference between the military and civilian lifestyles. Now his most important thing was his horse!

He trained well at his new occupation and learned that one half of his cavalry did not have horses, yet alone replacements, and new ones were of poor quality. Where were all of the Vermont-bred Morgans?

The officers told him that the Southern soldiers brought their own horses so when they lost a horse it was far more difficult to replace it and that was a reason they were known for their horse marauding tactics. If a Southern cavalryman lost his horse and could not find one he was put in the infantry.

In his disciplined training sessions he was issued a saber and a neat pistol, but no Spencer repeating rifle that held seven rounds of ammunition or a multi-shot breech-loading carbine Blakeslee Box to affix to the left side of his saber belt. They told him that the "Rebs knew the Yanks could load their carbines on a Sunday and shoot them until the next Sunday!" But where was his?

15

The trainers explained, "This pistol gives you a greater advantage over the rebel enemy. You can carry it on your saddle with a tent, raincoat, blanket, canteen and rations stored in your saddlebag while your rebel counterpart travels a lot lighter." The enemy used a shorter muzzle loading carbine that was not a breech loader. "Guard your weapon—the Rebs love to capture the Yanks' weapons in battle and use them as their own."

Seth was a quick learner and most things came natural to him. His superiors quickly recognized that and leaned heavily on him to help educate the other trainees. They guaranteed that he would quickly be an officer in training.

His officers told him Southern arsenals tried to make breech-loading carbines but could never get it right. They had trouble producing the casings for the ammunition and their arsenals could not live up to the skill of the Northern manufacturers.

"Seth," his instructors told him, "Southern counterparts prefer gallant charges with cumbersome sabers and you understand that we will win because we can outgun them, overwhelm them with numbers and they will run out of horses. And you agree that like John Buford it's only natural that we should dismount to fight the Confederate Infantry as we have the weapon advantage against their conventional tactics and poorer weapons.

"The Army of the Potomac's Cavalry Corps under General Pleasanton had three divisions with two brigades of horse artillery and batteries with backup horses for drivers and gunners alike. All three brigades joined in line with the remainder of the Corps and many acted as scouts and escorts and couriers, especially when they were on the move in a campaign.

"In contrast, the cavalry led by General J.E.B. Stuart had one large division fixed into brigades with six batteries of horse artillery. Stuart was a budding legend with his cavalry leaders and he ran daring exploits around our slower-moving forces. They even have songs and poems about him and they enjoy an extremely high morale and fancy themselves as superior horsemen! They brag openly that twenty Northern horsemen were no match for a single Confederate Cavalryman!

"We are now using that as our own morale booster! We can thwart them with our Union Cavalry Regiments which are better armed and led by experienced officers who have learned some of their tactics. We can open and then close the battle by dismounting and breaking their desperate late charges to push through our Union positions. We want to change the face of the cavalry so that it is never the same . . . and that's why we are looking for you to move up.

"Overall, the mission is to outsmart their greatest commander J.E.B. Stuart and ensure that his downfall will lead to the collapse of the mighty Rebel Cavalry and eventually to the restoration of our great Union."

Seth took his training seriously and was moving up the ranks in the First Vermont Cavalry, but his letters to Betsy were slow and his heart was yearning to get one chance to see her.

He loved his cavalry and understood his mission, but poor Betsy. *I wonder what she is doing right now?* He missed her every day. *What would she do if I didn't come home?*

BETSY IN VERMONT

Betsy was really excited; it had been a long trip to Brattleboro to the photo shop of a man who, like her husband, had to pack his things, leave home and go off to the Civil War. Only he was a professional Civil War photographer.

He was a friend of their neighbors, born in Putney but had lived most of his life in Brattleboro. Everyone in Vermont, like Houghton, was helping the North's cause in their own way.

He had been an accomplished photographer in Brattleboro before the war, and like so many others and her husband did, he enlisted. Unfortunately his health was not very good so he went and followed around the troops, especially her husband's regiments of the First and Second Vermont Brigades. Some of his photos were left in his office and she saw some of her husband's First Vermont Cavalry. He wasn't in any of them, but it made her feel closer to him. She could feel his presence!

They managed to make a photo of her in a fancy costume and now she was so excited to send the miniature to him.

The trip there and back was long and bumpy but Seth's father was so anxious; he surprised her with the special trip to Houghton's old office and he too wanted to surprise Seth with the photo. He knew what it was like to lose a mate, after all his wife had just passed away last Fall and he knew what it was to mourn an endearing wife. This also helped to soothe his own heartache. He prayed neither Betsy nor Seth ever felt the pain of such a heavy loss. He often heard Betsy at night, crying in her bedroom down the hall.

Betsy wiped her tears and some dropped onto her finished letter:

June 1st, 1863

Dear Seth,

Dad and I are so excited to be able to send this image of me to you.

We saw some images of the First Vermont that Mr. Houghton had taken and are at his office in Brattleboro.

Dad arranged for me to go there and have this image of me made for you.

I would love to be in your arms, but since I can't, this image is sent with all my love and you can keep it near your heart; just like your image is seared into my heart. I have sealed this with my own tears . . .

Always Your Loving Betsy

SARAH AND BRANDY
ALONG THE EMMITSBURG ROAD

The old farm wagon slithered along the tree-lined road with Brandy in the lines. The landscape released the mist forming out of the nearby Tom's Creek. Jake Randolph's daughter Sarah was guiding Brandy with the reins as she read the signpost along the route from her home in Gettysburg to the Daughters of Charity School in Emmitsburg, Maryland. It indicated that the school and convent were nearby.

The late June sun was now heating the chilled morning dew causing droplets of water to roll down the white oak leaves giving off ghostly images that rose high into the blue sky evaporating into the billowy clouds that cascaded above the Catoctin Mountain in the distance.

The air was cool and purifying and the increased oxygen levels served as a motivator to all the living creatures that wandered the landscape. In the distance the Catoctin Mountain touched the sky and the Emmitsburg Road looked like a dead snake wrapped around the tree and rock strewn skyline. They had travelled almost seven of their eight-mile journey so far and were now nearing their destination.

Only this time there were other creatures and other figures that now cluttered this usually peaceful valley. It looked like an army of two-legged blue creatures covering the entire landscape and the roadway. There was a horde of the blue soldiers up in the bell tower of the distant Daughters of Charity convent and on the roofs of the surrounding buildings. Blue soldiers had invaded the entire landscape—it was the Army of the Potomac encamped at the Daughters of Charity homestead!

White tents were pitched in neat rows and the horses with blue soldiers on their backs moved back and forth and up and down the Emmitsburg Road, scurrying helter-skelter. They had completely surrounded the convent.

Sarah could see the Sisters in their black and white outfits moving among the army of blue soldiers. It looked like a giant moving anthill of blue and black and white objects.

The squeals of the iron wheels tearing at the hardened roadbed made whining, sardonic sounds as Sarah watched in sheer amazement and then her field of vision filled with soldiers in blue uniforms on horseback. She murmured in utter shock and amazement, "It's the cavalry!"

Point riders from the cavalry unit on sweating and panting horses encircled her and the wagon, quickly surrounding her. A handsome young man with a cased sword dangling from his side smiled and reached for Brandy's head yelling, "Halt, ma'am! Pull over ma'am! Sergeant Jackson of the First Vermont Cavalry, ma'am . . . " the stoic voice rolled off the lips of the blue-clad soldier on the lead horse.

"Gotta stop here ma'am . . . Confederate Army is roamin' round in the area. Too dangerous for you out here. Our cavalry units are scoutin' for them Southern boys all around and the Army of the Potomac is movin' in, too. Gonna have to quarantine ya and the horse over at the town inn until we're outta here and the area is cleared!"

Sarah smiled peacefully and pulled hard on the reins making Brandy's head jerk on his strong neck and he held it up high from the bit pressure.

"Proud lookin' Morgan ma'am. He for sale? I will pay top dollar for him. We always need good mounts."

"This is my father's stallion, sir. He's not for sale. He's top of the line blood stock from Vermont Morgans. Will you tell me what is going on around here? Why are all of you around the Sisters' convent?"

"Whoa," said the sergeant as his mount pushed on Brandy, "well we are the First Vermont Cavalry and I thought I recognized a Vermont Morgan in your lines. Gorgeous animal! Just can tell you that Confederates were sighted in the area. Some say a major battle could be brewin' somewhere in the area. You're on the perimeter of the camp of the Army of the Potomac. We're a scouting party. What are you doing out here on this lonely road?"

"We live on a farm outside of Gettysburg. I'm taking some crops to the Sisters. Father barters crops and then we came to school here for free. I come two times in the summer each week to deliver their vegetables."

"Please fall in behind me ma'am, if them Rebs catch you they'll steal your stuff and take that horse, too. Confederate troopers supply their own mounts and often supply their own food, unless their horse was killed in action. They do not get any financial assistance for replacements. They have to buy a replacement, capture a replacement from the enemy, or become a member of the infantry and *most* cavalrymen *don't want to be a foot soldier.*"

A CHANCE MEETING

"**Y**our horse looks like a born and bred Vermont Morgan horse," said a dashing young lieutenant from atop the porch of the Moritz Tavern in Emmitsburg as Jake Randolph's daughter Sarah and the blue-coated sergeant and cavalry unit entered General Reynold's headquarters billet.

"Fact is ma'am," continued the lieutenant with blue eyes that matched the color of his dusty uniform, "your horse looks like some of our own stock from our Vermont farm."

"My dad hails from there, sir. He got Brandy's mother from his brother. Sent her down to us in Gettysburg. She was in foal. His brother said it was 'two for one,' and that's a family joke. This here's the other one and we named him Brandy. He sure is a gem. Dad's gonna use him for stud to help us keep the farm."

"What's your name?" asked the lieutenant who was now at the side of the wagon and offering her his hand as she climbed down.

"Sarah Randolph, sir. Sarah Randolph from Gettysburg, sir."

The young lieutenant smiled introducing himself, "Well how do you do Sarah Randolph? I'm Lieutenant Seth Randolph, Jr., of the First Vermont Cavalry. I believe we are cousins!"

TO MOUNT ST. MARY'S
CONVENT

"Captain, my religious belief teaches me to feel as safe in battle as in bed. God has fixed the time for my death. I do not concern myself about that, but to be always ready, no matter when it may overtake me. Captain, that is the way all men should live, and then all would be equally brave."

— STONEWALL JACKSON

Brandy watched as the sounds from the humans and the movements of the creatures surrounded him. He was very sweaty after this long journey and they weren't taking off the cumbersome objects that keep him from running away from that noisy contraption that follows behind him. In fact they were climbing back into that strange thing and leading him to turn around . . . and now they . . . "Get up Brandy, we're heading over to the convent with Cousin Seth guiding you!" Sarah said with a smile. "This is the surprise of my life, cousin!"

Lieutenant Seth shook the reins high and headed Brandy and the wagon with his cousin beside him saying, "Please, take me to the Convent of the Daughters of Charity nearby and I'll deliver their supplies."

"That will be fine," said Seth, "but you must stay there for your own safety. There is too much going on around here. It's too dangerous for you to return home at this point . . . "

"Dad will be worried if I don't return tonight."

"Don't worry, does this horse ride? Is he trained to saddle? I'll leave the wagon with you and ride him back under my saddle. My horse was shot out from under me last week. I came here to Emmitsburg with a troop from my regiment to pick up a new mount, and to deliver a dispatch from my commander Major Wells to Major General John Fulton Reynolds. I just caught up with them here. They also had a special mail package for me from Vermont to pick up. I have it here in my saddlebag. I was about to open it on the porch when I saw you pull in with the sergeant and the troop. If you hold the reins I'll open it now and," he started to unwrap the outside package and then he saw the return address from his wife, "oh wow. This is something special from my wife!"

Seth tore off the outside wrapper and opened the sealed envelope and lifted it to his face, smelling the inside of the sealed wrapper. Smiling happily he said, "Still smells like her . . . " and then he opened the letter and sat back, a loving smile mirrored across his face while tears dripped from his lower eyelids.

"Cousin, I want you to meet my wife, Betsy. This is my beloved wife . . . she sent me this photo of herself!"

"She's beautiful," Sarah exclaimed to Seth.

"I'll put this picture in my breast pocket near my heart just like she writes in the letter. . . . We better hurry now and get you safely to the convent. Has Brandy been under a lot of heavy saddle?"

"I trained him myself. Dad has an old worn-out cavalry saddle in the barn and I ride him all through the hills around Gettysburg. He was born in the pasture below a hill called Little Round Top and for the past year we have been racing all around. Brandy loves it. I often take off his saddle and ride him bareback. No one around can beat him in a buggy or wagon and especially on the road. He never gets tired. He goes a place once and knows his way home. Just give him his head and say *home* and he'll lead you right to the farm."

"I'll take him back to your farm tonight, Sarah. Your dad will be shocked just as much as I am. This is just so strange . . . what a chance meeting," explained Seth as Brandy headed up the dusty, well-travelled road leading to the convent.

"See Seth, he's taking us right to the convent. He knows we drop off the produce and I went to school there. It's his routine. He'll take you right back to our farm. With no buggy behind him and under saddle and with your soldiers and horses he'll just love it! It's the first farm off this road that meets up with the Gettysburg Road. There's a big stone barn with a sign saying 'Randolph's Place.' You can't miss it! Brandy can do it blindfolded!"

"Good, we'll head out as soon as we drop you off. We'll unload the wagon, leave you and the wagon here, and head back right away and get there before nightfall. Are you sure you'll be ok?"

"I'll be fine Seth. I'll be in a helping stage of Sister formation here at the convent. The Sisters at first stage are called Novices. Daughters of Charity do not make temporary and final vows. If I do decide to enter here at the convent in a vocation, on that date I could become a full member of the

Daughters of Charity. It takes about five years after that vocation date, when one takes a Daughters of Charity vow. My older sister Catherine did that. Then they renew it every year after that. I've been considering it. This will give me more time to spend with the Sisters here to make up my mind. You are in service to our country; they are in service to our Lord."

SETH ON THE
EMMITSBURG ROAD

Seth set out with a scout and sent his Company to secure the area with orders to check out the western wing of the Army of the Potomac that was now coming into Emmitsburg to camp. He advised he would return by 5 p.m. the next day and they all would meet at the white house at the Daughters of Charity Convent with the Regiment of General Farnsworth. He had been alerted that there were reported skirmishes in Fountaindale and Fairfield, and General Meade had received dispatches from General Buford reporting that Confederates were already in Chambersburg and Cashtown and heading south-southwest.

"We might be heading into the heart of the Confederate Army on this mission, but I want to scout the Gettysburg Road area," he instructed his squad as they headed out.

Sarah was right, all he had to do was give Brandy his head and he started for home. Brandy did not hesitate and went quickly under the saddle loaded down with all the cavalry equipment—a tent, raincoat, blanket, canteen and rations. A horse was a horse to many but to a Vermont cavalryman the Vermont Morgan was a highly desired horse. It was hard to get, but already building a reputation in this Civil War. The First Vermont Cavalry, mounted mostly on Morgans, was already gaining a widespread reputation as a respected fighting unit. Even the Southern boys were touting the Morgan fame as their own Stonewall Jackson was riding a horse named "Little Sorrel" which they "supposedly" claimed was a Morgan.

As Seth rode he was amazed how Brandy responded to his knees and a light rein on his mouth. Sure he was smaller than most of the Southern cavalry horses who were usually judged superior to Northern horses, but that was mainly because of the Southern appetite for racing. Most southern towns had a racetrack, which helped to create a superior stock of pure-blooded, nimble-footed animals, but war wasn't a race for the North and those in the North loved the stocky, strong draft horse types like the smaller Morgans. But overall, Northern horses were much more prized by their cavalry because of their ability and willingness to work long hours, and they didn't mind pulling cannons!

Brandy was a good example. He had just worked most of the morning pulling a wagon with a load down the ten- to twelve-mile track from Gettysburg to Emmitsburg and now here he was carrying Seth and his gear on his back and he wasn't even breathing heavily. This was one fine horse.

While his mind was working the horse angle, his eyes were watching for any slight movement, especially anything grey-colored riding a long-legged horse. The sun was starting to set as he leaned back in the saddle. He felt the object in his breast pocket and touched it—it was Betsy's picture—she was now riding with him. He touched it again and put his bare hand up to scratch the itch under his nose and he could smell her . . . the smell from opening that envelope . . . her smell . . . sweet Betsy . . . his wonderful wife.

And then he smelled smoke, no it was the smell of burnt gunpowder somewhere out in the distance. He could smell the faint aroma wafting down the air currents; sucked in by the night wind that was starting to blow into his face. He stopped Brandy and looked at his aide, "There is something going on somewhere out there."

His First Sergeant came racing in on his horse, "Get into the trees, Sir . . . Confederate Cavalry coming down the road! Sir, it's J.E.B. Stuart and the whole damn Southern Cavalry!"

"Sergeant, you take the Company back to the General's headquarters and report this. I'll get into that tree line over there and dismount with the scout and we'll see what is going on. Then I'll send the scout back and head to Gettysburg myself to observe and see my uncle. I will report back with more details of the Gettysburg area around 5 p.m. tomorrow."

"Yes, Sir," said the sergeant and he assembled the troop and headed back down the Emmitsburg Road at a full gallop.

"Let's get our horses into that tree line, dismount and get them down on the ground as those Southern boys are pretty sharp."

The tree line was filled with scrubby cedars backed by large white oaks and some fallen hickory so they found a hole in the break line to the road and waited.

"No matter what happens Private, don't fire. Our orders are not to fire on any enemy and start something!"

The scout got on the ground behind his prostrate horse that was laying near Brandy and Seth and reported, "I once met one of their outriders on our Northern flank. I was in a cedar grove and I knew someone was out there 'cause my stallion knows when a mare is in heat and this fella was riding a long-legged mare. I figured he must have spotted me so I dismounted and stripped down my stallion and turned him loose. And just as I had trained, he went struttin' out into the nearby clearing. That fella's mare let out a scream and they came bustin' through the brush out into the open. He musta thought he just got himself a rogue stallion for his lookin' so he got off and my stallion stood still. Well Sir, let's just say that boy quietly sunk into the bog behind the open meadow. I stripped his horse and he and his stuff were sinking in the soggy bog behind while his heated mare was runnin' out there somewhere lookin' for another stallion. I waited near the road and saw them Confederates galloping by in a real hurry.

"I served with J.E.B. Stuart in the Bleeding Kansas Border War—he joined the Confederacy and I joined the Union Cavalry. I served with Horner's Company, under Commander Captain John C. Horner during the summer of 1862. Captain Horner retired from service and I heard the Vermont Cavalry was looking for volunteers so here I am Sir, proud to be servin' next to you! I am one of those native Vermonters who moved west. My momma was half Mohican and my dad was an old Vermonter and my horse is a proud Vermont Morgan . . . got him from the quartermaster's lot . . . he was somewhat of a runt but look at him now!"

"That's some story trooper, glad to have you by my side. I hear them coming . . . "

"That's him Sir, . . . that's J.E.B. out front," whispered the trooper to Seth as the small portion of the Southern Cavalry charged handily down the Emmitsburg Road.

"Soon as they pass trooper you head back and report to General Reynolds and advise what we have seen. I'm going to Gettysburg to see what is going on down there."

"But Sir, it's almost nightfall and you don't know where you're going without a scout."

"Don't worry about me, my horse, or my uncle's horse, knows the way home. I'll just give him his head just like you did with your horse. He's a Morgan, he'll take me right to his home and my uncle's farm."

SARAH IN EMMITSBURG

S ister Angela met Sarah as soon as she dropped off the supplies at their pantry saying, "Thank you Sarah. It is a blessing that you showed up with your supplies as we Sisters have been feeding the soldiers encamped on the grounds. So many are hungry and Sister Mary Jane is afraid that there will be no bread for the Sisters for breakfast. When she comes in now to the bakehouse, she'll find your supplies and your baking goods for tomorrow's meals. It just did not simply multiply, you have brought us more!"

Sister Angela went on to explain, "We cannot continue your lessons today as The Brick House on Tollgate Hill and our rectory have been requisitioned for military headquarters. A General Howard is there at the rectory and he is surrounded by soldiers. We all sense that a battle may be brewing so we Sisters prayed that the conflict would not be fought on our land.

"We are Daughters of Charity founded by our beloved Mother Seton and our mission is to seek out and serve persons in need, especially individuals and families living in poverty. We did not expect what is happening all around but we pray that God's providence will prevail in a peaceful way.

"You and your sister are fine examples of what we do here—teach children who don't have educational opportunities. We also care for sick or dying persons lacking care. We are not just a cloistered or contemplative congregation, we, the Daughters of Charity, understand that at times the urgent needs of poor persons do come before all other things, even prayer. But we have been praying all night!

"We strive to see God in whomever we serve and do relate to the earlier days of our hospital experiences," she quickly added.

Sarah looked lovingly at Sister Angela saying fervently, "Thank you Sister and that is why I may want to join your Order!"

JAKE IN GETTYSBURG

The sun faded over the now purple-colored round tops and the crickets started to do their thing as Jake worried out loud, "Where is Sarah?"

In the distance, in the direction of Gettysburg, he could see blue-clad soldiers moving along the road and buggies and cannons and riders with their horses moving swiftly up the nearby roads.

"What the heck is going on?"

Jake went out on the front porch and paced up and down. He walked to his stone barn, looked at Brandy's vacant stall and when he turned around to leave he heard, "Hello Uncle Jake!"

A Union Cavalryman appeared atop a sweaty Brandy who was panting heavily but flicking his head up and down in a greeting manner.

"What . . . where is Sarah and the wagon?"

"Don't get too excited Uncle Jake, I'm just as shocked as you are. I am Lieutenant Seth Randolph, Jr. It's a long story. Sarah is safe in Emmitsburg with the Sisters there. Let me dismount and get Brandy unloaded and put away and we'll talk in the house."

Jake was in mild shock. *So this is young Seth or grown-up Seth,* raced through his mind as he watched Seth take off the bridle and cavalry equipment and finally put Brandy in his stall.

"No water or food, son, I mean Seth," said Jake.

"No sir Uncle Jake, won't do that . . . let him cool down first. He's had a long day, but he just won't quit. I had a hard time when it got dark and there weren't any signs, but your Sarah said he'd bring me right home and he did!"

After a handshake and a family hug both men turned and walked gingerly to the farmhouse. Climbing the wooden front porch and entering the terra cotta colored fieldstone farmhouse Jake reminisced, "Really dark night . . . no moon out . . . wasn't like the night that Brandy was born." As he offered a seat to Seth he added, "You set down and start talking and I'll fix some coffee or do you prefer some brandy?"

"Brandy first to take off the chill and then some coffee to go along with the story. I'm just as shocked to be here as you are to see me. But, I never question providence and in this case what a great way to meet you! You had left Vermont before I was born and all we have are a few letters, but now we have enough to fill my Civil War diary and this war is far from over!" said Seth.

The coffee flowed and so did the tales. Soon the sourdough biscuits left over from the breakfast that Sarah had made disappeared. Jake fried up some eggs and ham while Seth brought him up to speed on all that had happened.

"I was getting closer with our movements around Gettysburg with the Confederates and when I met Sarah in Emmitsburg . . . I just had to test providence and come out here to meet you."

"It sure is an historical meeting for me too, Seth. And it looks like there is going to be a monumental battle here as Union troops approached Gettysburg today. I noticed Union Cavalry approaching from the south past my farm and a substantial U.S. force in or near the town. I thought that was just our Pennsylvania militia. I really don't know what is going on, but you can check it out in the morning. They have a cavalry post set up in town. I was there this morning and it looks like they are setting up lines on Cemetery Ridge, which is the high ground around here, except for the Big and Little Round Tops in front of us. Sure looks like something bad is gonna happen. This house and the barn are stone so if something does happen I reckon they all will be fixing to use this place for safety somehow!"

"And with that, Uncle Jake, there is something I want to ask of you. I need a new mount. I can get one from the quartermaster but we've been sold a lot of decrepit horses by unscrupulous horse traders who just want to profit off the government. We now don't have many good Morgans left. It's been a chronic problem with our Vermont Cavalry because we only ride Morgans. I would love to use Brandy since he knows the area and there is not a better looking mount in the cavalry than him. I'll take care of him best I can. We don't ride headlong into the firing line like the Southern Cavalry. We dismount and hold our ground and he's got a better chance under me than those guys. And sadly, if the Confederates are in the area and see him they'll probably steal him from you! When the war ends I'll give him back to you."

"That makes perfect sense to me, Seth. Gettysburg has always been a small, quiet and safe place. We are so remote who would ever think we have the Union Army filling up the town of Gettysburg."

"And the other half is down in Emmitsburg where Sarah is and the Confederates are reportedly moving in the area. J.E.B. Stuart and his cavalry are circling out round the Emmitsburg area and where J.E.B. Stuart is General Lee and his army are not far behind! Our brigade has mainly been patrolling against the Confederate Cavalry raiders like their General Mosley and other guerrillas. I was down there on patrol when providence set me up with your daughter Sarah. I'll head into Gettysburg in the morning and get as much detail as I can, and then ride on back to Major Wells and Farnsworth's brigade headquarters."

"Now that your belly is full, let's go out and bed down Brandy. He can eat and have water now. He sure is a magnificent Morgan. Looks just like old Figure . . . and better he be prancing and dancing around with you on his back than some grey-suited cavalry officer. Besides, he's too small for them. They like fancy and fast 16-hand long-legged horses."

"Oh, don't you worry. Brandy can do anything they can do and do it better—he was incredible under saddle for me today!"

BRANDY AND A FARM
AND LADY PROVIDENCE

"Morgan horses are known to have been used in both the Union and Confederate armies. Due to the quality of the Morgan horses and their physical attributes, they were in high demand. They were hardy and their thick winter coats enabled them to survive without shelter during bad weather, they were able to survive on scant forage, their resilient skin reduced saddle sores, and the Morgans were highly trainable and willing to please."

Brandy was snoozing. His knees were locked and his head was arched and he let out an occasional snort, but he was still aware of any danger that might be in the area. He always slept standing with his head facing out towards the barn door; he rarely went down, only when it was completely dark.

He flinched and arched his head up and stood erect as Seth and Jake came through the old pine front door of the red fieldstone barn. The light glared in his eyes and a strong hand caressed his neck as a bucket was being filled with fresh water from the nearby pump.

Jake pumped and the water flowed swiftly from the end of the squeaking old faucet. Seth filled the old tin bucket and then walked over and poured it into another receptacle that already hung in Brandy's stall.

Brandy watched as Jake headed over to his feed bin with a large scoop of grain. Water and grain flashed through his horse brain . . . so he started to munch on the grain first as a clump of freshly cured hay dropped at his feet. Then he switched to the hay.

"He sure is hungry and thirsty," said Seth.

"See how smart he is, Seth He won't drink that water . . . even though he's been setting hours since you brought him in. He went for the grain first then the hay. He's actually smarter than his keepers. He'll drink the water in the end.

"Morgans are really smart and self protective. They also have a 'short back' which means a good wither that extends well back just like his. Look at his wonderful sloping shoulder. His ribs are well-sprung and arching down to his flank. The fellas around here can't wait to breed to him. Good for your type of saddle, too. He has a really short coupling, and no doubt one less back vertebra. Not like those bigger rangy Southern mounts. And because he is only 15 hands with this muscular build and is somewhat smaller that other horses he is better at carrying heavy weights for long distances. Some of the horse traders say that most horses have 24 vertebra but a Morgan only has 23. I don't know where they get that . . . I never read that," Jake explained as Seth got a curry comb and brush, grooming Brandy while he was eating.

"Look at this color, he is handsome. Just proud to be on his back," echoed Seth.

"See Seth, you can groom him, lay down in front of him, make all kind of action around him while he is eating and he just keeps on doing his thing. He doesn't get excited about nothing. Does what he does and is the gentlest creature in the area, even though he's not cut. And when the ladies come around in heat he just walks up to them and whispers and blows in their ears."

"Morgans are the ideal horse for the cavalry," said Seth as he picked up Brandy's front foot and cleaned out the hoof. He's got the best feet and the walls are so strong."

"Never need to shod him. His feet are like iron," said Jake. "This has been a wonderful evening for me Seth, having you, my brother's son here with me. I don't have any sons. My firstborn was a boy but he died in child-birth and Emily then gave me two beautiful girls. Catherine is now working in a hospital in Philadelphia with the Daughters of Charity and, well you know where Sarah is. She, too, may join the Sisters; both of my girls had free schooling at their place in Emmitsburg. All I had to do was barter with produce and some crops and they educated both of them. I'm really happy for them, but . . . "

Seth looked up as he finished cleaning Brandy's back hooves, "But what Uncle?"

"Well," said Jake as he went over and put his arms around Brandy's head stroking his short muscular neck, "it's a little like the color of Brandy. I have a rare request.

"Soon all I'll have here on the farm is Brandy, and you're now going to take him and I think you should for his sake. If something happens to me . . . well, the farm will . . . well . . . who will help the girls take care of the farm. I've worked all my life. Look, you take my horse for safekeeping. That way I know you'll come back here with Brandy. Kinda give Lady Providence something to help guide you safely through this Civil War . . . and for me to share in my heart while you two are out there in harm's way."

Seth backpedaled and grabbed the white oak beam that was supporting Brandy's greyed stable side walls. "That is such a humbling request Uncle. How can I say anything but yes! I've grown extremely fond of Pennsylvania and especially this farming area.

"This is a beautiful place. In our grammar school they often quoted George Washington, 'By the all-powerful dispensations of Providence, I have been protected beyond all human probability and expectation; for I had four bullets through my coat, and two horses shot under me, yet escaped unhurt . . .'

"I have already had one horse shot out from under me, and I pray that God will protect me and Brandy and that we both shall return here."

SETH IN GETTYSBURG

The rooster crowed and there was an early knock on the farmhouse door. As Jake opened it Seth was behind him when a soldier appeared in the entrance and saluted and said, "Sir. We have *urgent* orders from headquarters. Sarah gave us the directions and it was easy to find your stone house and barn in daylight, but we had to dodge some Rebs on the way up here. The Third Division of the Cavalry Corps and our First Vermont Cavalry were moving up behind us into Pennsylvania around Hanover when they heard cannon fire. The Eighteenth Pennsylvania Cavalry met J.E.B. Stuart's Cavalry as they approached the town of Hanover. Our Vermonters engaged them and chased them exhausted Rebs causing them to break off and they headed southeast not able to hook up with Lee and his army. That's when we saw them coming so fast past us," explained his First Sergeant who was standing at the front door of Jake's farmhouse.

The First Sergeant continued, "The Regiment just left Hanover where the Confederates shelled some of the Companies but the ladies were good to the boys. Had some cake and wine . . . even got some brandy . . . nice town. All eight Companies are spread out and headed to Adamstown where General Kilpatrick and the Third Division are now heading. They are all spearheading this way with the possibility of deploying around a place called Big Round Top. Our Company and Company F and D and K will rendezvous north of Gettysburg . . . looking for Stuart and his boys. They had a nasty engagement on the 30th getting out of Hanover. There's been no sign of Lee and his army. We are to meet up there today. We had an urgent order to evacuate the convent in Emmittsburg and head to Gettysburg.

"Your orders are to report immediately to Colonel Nelson of General Buford's command at the Lutheran Seminary Tower in Gettysburg."

BETSY IN VERMONT

Home life on the farm in Vermont with her husband so faraway was very difficult for Betsy. She was fortunate to have enough money from Seth's pay as a lieutenant and also the security of living on the farm with his father. She was so much better off than many of the other ladies in town, especially those who were now war widows. It was so sad to know so many local widows as the First Vermony Cavalry did have many casualties. These thoughts were racing through Betsy's mind as she sat rocking on the front porch with Seth's father.

"I wonder what Seth is doing now, Dad?" she asked as a cool Vermont breeze blew across the very hot front porch. The lemonade on the table beside them tasted sweet and added some zest to the calm scene. "Lemons . . . what a delicacy for us in Vermont."

"Yes it is Betsy, and I'm sure Seth and the boys are drinking some southern lemonade somewhere down in forsaken Virginia! This here war is a lot different than the Revolution, but you know the Vermont tradition!

"The Green Mountain Boys of the American Revolution started our patriotic military tradition of sending a significant portion of eligible men to the war effort!

"And this war is especially close to the heart and tradition of the Vermont citizenry as slavery was abolished here in 1777, a year after the Declaration of Independence! *We* were the first state to do that!

"The slave trade is horrible and some of the earliest abolitionists were from our state. We Vermonters voted heavily to elect Abraham Lincoln and that Buchanan from Lancaster didn't help and most of the politicians failed in an early peace conference.

"The newspapers have reported that our governor said, 'Vermont will do its Full Duty.' Seth is just one of many officers from our state who are serving in the war. He's doing his duty and we have so many generals in this war, many already have been honored for their bravery . . .

"I'm so proud of him and I know you are, too. I know it's harder on you than me, but we just have to endure and trust that Providence will return him safely to us."

As Seth, Sr., finished his last word a rider appeared at the end of the lane. He was trotting up on a gorgeous black, high-stepping Morgan. Betsy saw him and immediately got up and looked at Seth's dad saying, "Oh Dad . . . oh Dad that's a cavalryman on that horse. He's not in any hurry. Oh Dad I'm scared. What does he want . . . you don't think . . ."

"Wait Betsy, I know him. He's Brett Macinrow; he signed up at the same time as Seth. In fact they left with the 'First' on the same day. Look he's waving and smiling . . . he can't be bringing any bad news with that grin on his face."

Seth, Sr., stood and he and Betsy moved to the front of the porch. The cavalryman dismounted and tying his horse to the white picket fence he quickly walked over to greet them. "Hello Mr. Randolph. Hello Betsy. Don't look so upset, I'm just here to bring you news on Seth. Last I saw him he was heading out to find the Confederate Cavalry."

"Welcome Brett. Come up and set down to talk. It is so good to see you."

Brett took off his hat and set it on the railing and pulled up a seat.

"Betsy will get you some lemonade, real lemons . . . yup we have some real lemons," said Mr. Randolph. "The paper reported that the availability of lemons with its ingredients is helpful to us; they wrote that lemons are the favorite of the South's famous Confederate General Stonewall Jackson. My Seth loves them, too. But he's only a lieutenant in the Vermont Cavalry."

"That he is Mr. Randolph, and a dear friend of mine," Brett continued as Betsy quickly returned and handed him a glass.

"Set back and enjoy the breeze," said Betsy. "Tell us about Seth. I'm so excited to hear! We don't receive many letters, and I can't wait until he is setting next to me and I can hand him a lemonade. He loves it. I got a recipe from Godey's *Civil War Recipes* book that we purchased in Brattleboro. That is where I had a special picture made of me and then I sent it to Seth."

"Not much time for writing Betsy. That's 'cause we're on the move a lot. Not much time for anything and especially not an officer like him. He is so dedicated to his men. We were serving in the Shenandoah Valley and they sent me back to Vermont as a representative of the First Vermont Cavalry because we have a very difficult problem: a lack of serviceable mounts and especially good Morgans.

"With over 900 men in the regiment we only had a little more than 100 usable horses and about 250 that we could not use! Many unscrupulous purchasing agents were buying bad horses and selling to us for a profit no matter how good they were.

"We did get a good supply of replacement horses from Vermont in the first of the year, but now due to attrition we are strapped again. By early Spring we had two men for every one horse and many were forced into a permanent dismount role and they sure don't want to end up in the infantry!

"Seth was mainly patrolling with a mission to defend Washington. Those who had horses guarded the supply trains and some rode out against Confederate raiders who were ravaging our supply lines.

"J.E.B. Stuart's causing a lot of damage but Colonel John S. Mosby is a rogue and a really big problem. We managed to catch up with a lot of Rebs in Virginia in May. We did spend most time at one point in camp situations mainly because of poor leadership and Seth was sent off for more officer training. He don't much believe in 'Cavalry Charges' and did speak out but he was only a junior officer at the time. They like him and some of the big generals met in secret with him.

"I just arrived in Vermont and want to sleep in a real bed and enjoy lovely Vermont. There's no war here! They gave me some extra leave as a bonus 'cause I enlisted again back in January. They do that to get us veterans whose enlistments are running out and it worked for me, but I would've done it anyway.

"I reenlisted as they do need me. I am departing for the front again and fighting off some depression that haunts me with all the deaths I've seen around me. We lost many great Vermonters and our infantry is suffering even more. But you know we Vermonters stay the course!

"I will visit some of the widows of our cavalry which adds to my depression. Knowing their losses increases my depression but the bounty helps my wife and kids, as the government promises about $30 per month. Getting this leave and a promotion under your husband boosted my spirits.

"Lieutenant Seth is a smart leader and he like the other officers were a little crazy about General Kilpatrick's methods of using headlong attacks that earned him the nickname of 'Kill-Cavalry.'

"Lieutenant Seth lost his Morgan mount in one of those headlong attacks but he managed to survive the ordeal. The last time I saw him he was looking for a horse.

"He knew I would be in the area and told me to stop to see you and tell you he was fine and that he was going to try and see his uncle who lived on a Gettysburg farm. He wanted to see if he had any good Morgans before those Southern boys who were moving North got to them. He said he would write soon and hopefully have good news."

"Thank you for stopping Brett," said Seth, Sr., "and tell him we are thinking and praying for his safe return every day."

Betsy got up and shook Brett's hand and with a simple smile said, "Tell him I love him!"

Brett gave Betsy a hug and shook Seth, Sr.'s, hand then sauntered down the porch, mounted his horse, and galloped down the lane.

Seth, Sr., looked at Betsy saying, "You sent Seth a picture and I think it's time to take you to see my brother in Gettysburg. What do you think?"

"Dad, I've always been a homebody . . . but you have changed my opinion with our trip to Brattleboro. I really loved it. I think that I'm getting more adventuresome, too. This is exiting! I'll write Seth tonight and tell him we are coming to Gettysburg. I'll send him the letter with a kiss to seal it. Hopefully we will all arrive at the same time!"

"There is something that I've been working on with my brother Jake in Gettysburg. He sent me a letter a while back about his neighbor offering him the farm next to him. My brother is going to buy it and he wants me to move to Pennsylvania—next to him! He said he could get it for a really good price. Seth is not interested in the farm here . . . and the price of farms here have really gone up. A local general affiliated with the new military hospital in Brattleboro has offered to buy our place and our Morgan stock; he wants to make a Morgan breeding farm here. He offered me a great price. I have really been hesitating but . . . "

"Dad, that's wonderful . . . why didn't you tell me?"

"Look Betsy, you have enough to worry about . . . "

"Nonsense Dad, you contact that general and make the agreement. Let's go to Gettysburg! Take two of your best stallions and four of your best mares and me and buy that place in Gettysburg. You send a letter to your brother and tell him to buy that farm. I'll go anywhere with you and my beloved Seth. This is so exciting . . . when can we leave?"

"I'll see my lawyer in town tomorrow and have him set it all up with the general. The general told me that he can get us special travel arrangements and handle it through a telegraph. I don't know what he is talking about. He said he could make all the arrangements and he'll advise all by a 'wire' with the good news."

SARAH STILL IN EMMITSBURG

"Now Sarah," the Superior explained, "I have lost track of the time but the Union Army troops came the other day and they all surrounded St. Joseph's. They were very kind asking permission to stop here on our site.

"Of course we said yes. They asked if their head general could have his headquarters in the Sisters' house and if another general and his officers could stay in the other house that we used as an orphan asylum.

"They told us it was a must because 'the Southern Army' was close by and moving in. They said that the Union officers would station guards at the perimeters of our place and that was why one of those guards stopped you on the Emmitsburg Road and escorted you in here.

"One of their French generals told Mother he would pray to St. Joseph and ask him to keep us safe and not have any fighting here. He didn't want any battle to take place at our precious convent.

"They were all still here yesterday when Father and other visiting priests were hearing confessions of those who were Catholic. We ran out of holy medals and scapulars for those who asked for them.

"We were all in the kitchen slicing up the leftover meat and buttering bread. They also needed our help filling canteens while drinking the little coffee and milk we had. Those poor soldiers were ravenous."

"Yes Sister, my escort told me all that and that he was in the long lines of soldiers outside. He said they were ordered to line up by squad and to be polite and only take what was offered. And to be ready for a quick movement if and when ordered, as Confederate pickets were spotted in the area, too."

"Yes Sarah, they were well behaved and some broke our hearts. Some were so young, too young to be away from home. We did have a fair pantry then, but have much more now with the rations you have just brought us. Providence sent you at the right time."

"But Sister, my escort said that they were all packing up as I arrived because they had an order to 'break camp and march north up the Emmitsburg Road' to where we live. He said it was better I stay here."

"Look out there now; the lawns are empty. St. Joseph must have answered all of our prayers. They are all gone!"

"My escort is gone and when he left they told him to 'fly' as one of our priests was stopped by Confederate pickets asking about the soldiers at our convent. Do you think the Confederates will stop here, Sister?"

SETH TO GETTYSBURG
HEADQUARTERS

S eth dismounted Brandy as his aide held the reins and took control, leading him to a nearby holding shed where other officers' horses were gathered.

He straightened his hat, dusted off his boots and tried to look professional; he had urgent orders to meet with a Colonel Nelson of General Buford's command.

"Lieutenant Seth Reynolds reporting as ordered, Sir." Seth saluted and stood at attention.

The stubby-bearded colonel saluted back and sat down. "Set down, lieutenant. You're a hard officer to track down!"

"Sorry Sir, my aide and I encountered J.E.B. and his cavalry on the road outside Emmitsburg yesterday and I was meeting with my uncle to get a new Morgan mount."

"And how did you do?"

"Mission accomplished, Sir! He gave me one of his finest Morgan breeding stallions, actually his own stallion."

"Gave you . . . you aren't paying him?"

"It's not like that Sir, it's a long story."

"Well lieutenant, congratulations on another fine job. Actually we've been watching you for some time. You come with pretty high recommendations; especially from some of your home state generals who are patriotically serving in this Civil War."

"Well Sir, thank you, but . . . "

"I'll come to the point lieutenant. General George G. Meade took command of the Army of the Potomac several days ago and we are making some major changes and he realizes the need to change the 'Cavalry Charge' mentality. Also General Lee has invaded Maryland and Pennsylvania and J.E.B. Stuart and his cavalry are around somewhere. General Meade quickly drew up a defense plan. We had a line of troops starting at a town in Maryland and north and General John Reynolds and his First Corps made up the middle, about 80,000 troops that were in Emmitsburg are now moving north . . ."

"Yes Sir, we were there."

"Right," said the colonel, rolling out a map and motioning Seth over to review it with him.

"Now here's where our line starts and ends and that's Lee, we think, here. General Reynolds' headquarters is here where we are . . . and General John Buford and his cavalry are here. Your First Vermont Cavalry is here.

"We are to hold these heights here and to the south of the town and we will put up roadblocks if necessary here in Gettysburg. We *need* and *must* hold the high ground if they choose to do battle here!

"Now your Uncle Jake's farm is here, right smack on the defense line. And here are the Round Tops nearby—the highest grounds in that area. This is his stone house and it's strategically located with a small fortress of a Pennsylvania stone barn. We want you to go there and set up a defense, on your own. That barn has queer long slits, great for snipers. Secure it and wait for further orders.

"Now there are two reasons for that. First, protect that stallion you're riding and get him into a safe environment. You are going to need him. Second, you're being promoted to captain with the assignment of assisting our quartermaster's unit to produce and to procure quality horses, especially Morgans. As you know the First Vermont is only half staffed with not enough good horses. Also, we have a seasoned Vermont general who personally bought your dad's Vermont farm and most of his fine Morgan stock. Your dad, your wife and two pair of horses are going to show up at your uncle's place depending on how fast and safe we can get them here. Your uncle purchased the farm next door to his for your father yesterday! Your dad is in partnership with him to raise Morgans. He and your wife are moving to Gettysburg . . . they are en route now!"

Seth looked up. "Thank you for the promotion and . . . "

"Captain, you've been a rising star in the military staff and you deserve this promotion. Your dad has produced some quality Morgans for his own use. We could not say a word as the whole plan has been a military secret and it has finally been given our approval. We are sending over snipers to assist you in your plan. Now get back to that farmhouse and secure it the best you can; that spot could be the most strategic point if a battle is fought here. Captain, if the Confederate Army moves like we think they will we will *all* have a bigger surprise than what I just told you. We will have more to deal with than the lack of Morgan horses!

"We just received information that a few days ago J.E.B. Stuart moved through the southeastern corner of Carroll County in Maryland. He had many Confederate troops. They were attempting to tear down our telegraph lines and destroy part of the B&O Railroad tracks. They supposedly raided a local cotton factory removing the belts from the factory's machinery to repair the soles of their worn-out boots. But you know how reports are.

"Major General Sedgwick led the Sixth Corps through some of the small towns nearby in a ten-mile dusty road trip in this scorching summer heat. The Second Corps is coming in through Taneytown to join up with the Third and Twelfth Union Corps.

"We have our Signal Corps all set up with their flags by day and flares by night system and we have been in constant contact with Lookout and Indian Lookout and we're hooked all the way to Washington in our communications lines. We're up on Big and Little Round Tops here and our line is complete. The Confederates have nothing like that in place.

"Our communication lines are important and we want you to also have a small cavalry contingent to protect our Big Round Top contingent that is located above your location in that stone barn.

"On the 30th our troops engaged Stuart's cavalry with a small Delaware Cavalrymen Unit in a light delaying encounter in Westminster. Stuart's cavalry fled and 'appears' everywhere. If Lee is in the area he must be pulling his hair out as he uses Stuart to be his eyes and ears. He relies on manual communication and outriders. Thank God we have this telegraph and the Signal Corps . . . we *have* to keep these lines open at all times.

"General George G. Meade's first plan was for the Sixth Corps to head to Manchester then on to Hanover. But with the recent sightings around Gettysburg, we are now switching to redirect all troops to Gettysburg. Our Sixth Corps is along the Littlestown Pike and are being slowed down with miles of wagons. They are hurriedly on their way here.

"Their horses, soldiers, cannons, and wagons are moving through the county towns causing the locals great concern as we keep our troop movements in flux; especially with our great communications. Lee and his army must be going by the seat of that old general's pants!

"We did capture one of their couriers. They blindfolded him and some of the men rode him out to a remote location, releasing him to try and fool him about our movements. He was probably one of General J.E.B. Stuart's communications scouts. Our system of intelligence tops theirs.

"One of our Indian scouts from your First Vermont Cavalry, a Delaware scout, managed to locate Stuart near a grove of cedars standing up against a tree. He said he watched him for awhile and then he had a messenger ride in and he then mounted giving the order to move out. We get so many stories . . . which are true is anyone's guess.

"Our scout was so brave and was able to get so close he could hear Stuart say that the new Union Commander, General George Meade, is a dandy and they were trying to get his location. He told them they had to tear down some of those newfangled poles with the wires to break the Union's new telegraph communications. Lee probably thinks Lincoln knows almost daily what is going on because of the new Signal Corps. His orders were to disrupt us when they can.

"The scout managed to melt into the night and make it back here to headquarters and give us the details. He's outside and I'm assigning him to you."

"Thank you, Sir. My other scout is part Mohican and from Vermont. They should work well together."

THE RANDOLPHS LEAVE
VERMONT

Seth, Sr., watched as the soldiers led his two stallions and four mares out of his barn. It would be the last time they would be walking on their native Vermont soil and the last time he would see them until they were transported by the military to his new Gettysburg farm.

He didn't ask how they would get there but his general friend told him they would use every means available and ensure their safety, informing him that so much corruption had been in the rail industry it forced legislators to enact the Railways and Telegraph Act of January 31, 1862. This legislation allowed the President to take control of railroads—to continue running them and preserving public safety. The War Department now could supervise any railroads taken over by the government.

He told Seth, Sr., that a few Northern railroads were seized under the Act and organized into the United States Military Railroad (U.S.M.R.R.). Railroads now supported and fell in line with this new law, to aid in the Union war effort for fear of being seized.

This had stopped a lot of the profiteering and corruption immediately and trains began to move in an expedient way. And since the Army of Northern Virginia was reportedly moving north into Pennsylvania, some of the Northern railroads were seized to adequately and efficiently deal with the threat posed by General Lee.

The general told the Randolphs that they and their supplies and horses would be under their care, as their mission was necessary too, as so much profiteering and fraud was in the "horse trading" industry that this was one of the new endeavors to help curb the problem. This would not be a "90-Day Volunteer War" as thought!

"Thank you and have a safe trip. Godspeed and protect you all the way to your new home in Gettysburg," said General Harold Simpson.

Seth, Sr., handed the special pass letter to Betsy saying, "We're off Betsy and the general said this was our pass to Gettysburg."

"This is really an adventure Dad. I mailed a letter to Seth, but what if we get to our new Gettysburg farm before the letter?"

"Oh Seth knows we're coming Betsy. The military has informed him of our move. Plus there is another big surprise, he was promoted to captain and head of a new procurement program.

"We will be starting our new Morgan horse breeding program down in Gettysburg with my brother. Our farms will be side by side. Our farm is not much good for farming as it is pretty rocky, but it is great for raising horses with open meadows and streams and a place nearby between Big Round Top and Little Round Top. It's very scenic and my brother said there is a place with huge boulders that they call Devil's Den. Some call it Devil's Cave.

"He said there are apple orchards and wheat fields and a stream called Plum Run that runs north to south with brook trout, but overflows with heavy rains. It will be a good place for the horses we're gonna raise for the U.S. Government and the cavalry.

"He also said there is a train station with a depot platform in Gettysburg that we will be arriving at! We are all so excited to have our family together again! We will be Vermonters in Pennsylvania—in one of the most peaceful places he has ever seen!"

"Oh Dad, this is so exciting! I'll finish packing and then we'll say goodbye to the Vermont we love so dearly by looking out for a final view from the front porch."

SETH HEADS BACK TO
JAKE'S FARM

The road out of Gettysburg very early July 1st was filled with incoming parts of the Union Army. Some were setting up barricades and checkpoints, and as he passed the Lutheran Theological Seminary he noticed Union soldiers in the cupola set up a signal station similar to what he saw up on Little Round Top. Seth felt good, the new officer assigned to Buford's cavalry that he met seemed to reassert the fact that the Union's communications were far better than the enemy's.

The Union had a new Signal Corps Division and were also using that new telegraph, although the Southern boys were doing their best to tear down the lines and poles as fast as the Union was erecting them.

In Seth's last staff meeting with General Buford, all the officers were briefed on the approval of using the Signal Corps in the field because it was a different asset and a unique auxiliary tool. The Corps would use those powerful glasses from strategic lookout points, especially when they had nothing else to use.

As Seth and his aide reached a checkpoint a lookout came running down and reported to the officer in charge, "I was told to watch out for enemy campfires last night and any movements this morning. It looks like a small part of the Rebel Cavalry is watching us too, from somewhere down on the Chambersburg Pike. We have to report this to General Buford now."

Seth looked at both of the officers and saluted then took to a full gallop with his aide beside him, while the other two officers headed for General Buford's headquarters.

The mist was melting off and they had difficulty maneuvering among the soldiers, wagons, and horses coming in from the opposite direction. Then they saw a group of Union Cavalry officers heading their way at a full gallop.

"Wow, that's General John Reynolds!" Seth shouted as he and his aide stopped and saluted.

"You're going the wrong way captain. My corps is coming up behind and parts of the cavalry are skirmishing with the enemy down that road. We're headed to see General Buford," stated General Reynolds.

"He may be in the Lutheran Seminary cupola, Sir. They've spotted something."

"Thank you captain. You two better get back to your cavalry!" They saluted while General Reynolds and his staff burst into a full gallop towards the quaint town of Gettysburg.

"Sir, there is a secluded back way that we tried when we came to find you. Sarah told us about a secret way into her dad's farm, one that Brandy knows well, and it was a shame we didn't have him. She told us to try to find it ourselves, by picking up the creek bed where it crosses the pike and heading up it about a mile."

Seth reined Brandy to a stop then took him through the brush and onto a secluded path. "Yes Sir, this is it. It's a maze and it took us a long time to get through as we followed the trail along the Plum Run. It is quite rocky and brush and pines cover a lot of it. We got lost a few times. This is where we got lost and went back onto the road where we came in."

"Ok, let's see what Brandy can do. Brandy, go home boy!" Seth shouted and gave him his head. The reins went limp in his meaty hands.

BRANDY HEADS HOME

"Look Sir, he's been here before! He turned right when we turned left and had to come back to this point. See our hoof prints in both places. We had to backtrack, but he knows right where to go! We got off that pike just in time Sir. Look, there's the corps heading up in quick step and I can hear gunfire in the distance."

"Something's brewing private, good thing we have generals like Reynolds and Buford in the action. I'm sure they'll figure it out and we'll get our orders coming down the line. General Reynolds," continued Seth, "is from nearby Lancaster and he knows the area well. He's not married like me, doesn't have to worry about leaving a widow behind. Some say he's engaged, but it's only hearsay. My wife's back in Vermont, but she and my dad are heading down here to Gettysburg."

"Did you get a post when you were at headquarters?"

"Not that kind of post. It's a long story . . . a good story. My dad bought the farm next door to my uncle. This may be a part of it; I don't know the boundaries yet. The Plum Run flows tranquilly through parts of it. It straddles my dad's new farm. The old owner sold out and is heading west for some new gold strike out there. He said it was too boring and quiet here!"

Brandy felt the loose reins and recognized that he was in familiar territory. This was where he roamed with the other young horses following his mother and often stopping to drink from the cool pools along the creek as a youngster. Now he had this new human on his back but he had bonded to him, there was something about the special closeness of this human. He crossed the stream and leapt over a log while Seth held on with his legs. He recognized the open field and raced across it to the edge of the white oak trees and red cedars.

As they rode, Seth's aide remarked, "Sir, those officers were on the road and really far off. How did you know it was General Reynolds from that distance? You have a sniper's eye!"

"During a special cavalry officers' class they told us, 'During this young Civil War, some of the cavalry officers from Vermont were refraining from wearing colorful and distinguishing insignias as Confederate snipers are most often on the battlefield. They like to single out and pick off the leaders . . . snipers could be anyone and anywhere nearby!'

"So far we haven't had any of our senior officers killed like the Southerners have, but it's just a matter of time. Being a brave officer is one thing, being a target is a military risk. My recruiter informed me of J.E.B. Stuart and how he wears all this fancy stuff, including a rose in the field. You can spot him . . . it's a wonder one of our snipers haven't singled him out yet. He's very smart and he did devise a new piece of cavalry equipment, a saber hook, which was a better method of attaching sabers to belts. I don't know if he has one for attaching a red rose or a sniper-proof uniform.

"I'm a Vermont officer and don't believe in all that fancy stuff. Like my Morgan I like to stay close to the ground, nothing fancy. A Morgan's about 14 to 15 hands and stocky and lower to the ground. Those Reb officers who ride on fancy 16 or 17 hand high trotters put themselves up more into the line of fire. We were taught that the less of a target the better and to stay low. I also don't subscribe to the charge tactic exposing my horse and men to open fire from infantry, most of whom are good shots even though they don't have the repeating weapons we have. One good shot will kill you and your horse. I lost my horse with a lucky shot. He died, but I lived. I don't think the shooter knew I was an officer so he shot my horse out from under me. I'd surely be dead if I was wearing flashy rankings and a sash or red rose like J.E.B.!

"Horses and cavalry and being dashing and daring are a big part of the Southern charm and rightly so with George Washington's legendary bravado on horseback in colonial history records. He had many horses shot out from under him, but he rode those large Southern horses and always survived. Robert E. Lee supports the Southern side of this conflict and did not side with Lincoln, quite unlike his father who was summoned by President George Washington to suppress the Whiskey Rebellion in western Pennsylvania, which is not too far from our current location.

"This war is unlike any seen and the North versus South presents different strategies. Our cavalry pale to their dashing heroes who lead their divisions, but things are changing and changing fast."

"Sir, listen to that gunfire . . . that's not far away!"

Seth stopped his discussion as Brandy stopped abruptly and set up and threw his head to the East as a volley of gunfire sounded.

"Something is starting out there on the road and I can see the barn in the distance. Let's stay to the inside of that woods line and then race to the barn. I see some movement of our own troops out in the corral.

"Our snipers should be in Uncle Jake's barn by now and I hope they do not mistake us for the enemy as we are coming out of the shadows of Little Round Top. We don't want to be killed by friendly fire. Blue and grey uniforms look the same in dark shadows in a wooded environment so stay low!"

THE STONE BARN

"On the 1st of July 1863, the two armies met near Gettysburg, a large town in Pennsylvania about ten miles north of Emmitsburg. They fought until the evening of the 3rd, advancing by their movements more and more towards our peaceful vale, so that our buildings and very earth trembled from their cannons. That night the rain fell heavily and continued to do so all the next day, Saturday."
- DAUGHTERS OF CHARITY, Civil War Annals, 1863

Jake was pacing back and forth as the old white oak floorboards creaked beneath him. He watched the Union snipers up in the rafters of his barn. The sweet smell of oats and sour air of drying manure permeated the barn and it provided a conflict of odors, while outside sustained gunfire continued in the distance.

"Things are heating up," stated the First Sergeant of the First Vermont Cavalry. He then announced, "There he is Mr. Randolph! Your nephew and his aide are moving cautiously through that woods line." He shouted up to the snipers, "Captain Randolph and his aide are coming in from the northeast. Give them cover if you see any grey uniforms in the area. There are snipers up on that ridge to the north."

"Yes Sir," came the response from the rafter above. "Sir, I've been reading our Signal Corps Unit message flags up there on the Round Top and there is really bad news."

"What is it?" the First Sergeant shouted back.

"One of our officers fired on a Confederate Division while Major General Reynolds was out front leading the Union 1st Corps and was shot off his horse by a sniper. They moved his body off the battlefield very fast Sir . . . but he's dead."

The barn door flung open and Seth came running in, his aide took Brandy and his own horse to the back stalls.

"He's dead, Captain. Major General Reynolds is dead. Just shot down off his horse out there on the Chambersburg Pike . . . and the 1st contingent is now under siege from a large Confederate force. They are falling back to

Gettysburg at Cemetery Hill, south of the town. Our sniper/signalman just read the message going down the Signal Corps line to Washington. President Lincoln will know this very soon."

Seth took off his hat and held it tightly saying, "Oh my . . . headquarters' worst fear has come to haunt this once peaceful place. The Battle of Gettysburg has begun."

BETSY ON THE WAY TO GETTYSBURG

The troop train crossed the Mohawk River, leaving Albany, New York. Betsy and Seth, Sr., sat in the rear, separate from the troops who were bound for the war effort. They were riding in the special car their general friend told them would get them and their Morgan horses to Gettysburg safely!

They were told by those on the train that thousands of volunteers arrived early to Albany when the war started, long before President Lincoln had requested them. The conductor told them they were to stay on the train and not to get out for a comfort stop in New York City as President Lincoln and much of the Republican congressmen were deeply worried as many veteran troops, whose terms of enlistments had expired, were now pressing for an end to the Civil War, so a controversial conscription law to draft soldiers was set.

"A Draft Week" was scheduled to take place in New York City shortly. Anticipating some opposition to the draft, President Lincoln was contemplating sending several regiments of militia and volunteer troops (many of them were now serving in the Army of the Potomac in and around the Gettysburg area) to keep the peace. The President feared New York City riots would break out because many were angry that wealthy men could buy a human replacement if they were drafted.

Except for this situation, the overall trip was fine. It was cumbersome by rail, but Betsy enjoyed seeing so much more than the usual mountains and fields of rural Vermont.

The stop in Albany had been an incredible experience. Overall the citizens seemed to be aligned for the Cause and flags were flying from most places including public buildings, church steeples, school houses and universities, people's homes, and commercial enterprises. There were many soldiers in the streets, sadly some had lost limbs and their war wounds were evident as the cost of the war showed on their faces.

The visit to the Army Relief Bazaar was rewarding and Betsy did manage to get some special trinkets to adorn her new home in Gettysburg. It was truly amazing to see the Patriotic spirit and how each of the sellers there were all competing to raise the most money for all the humanitarian causes, especially for those who suffered the most from this terrible war. They even had a War Trophy Area where they were selling autographs from many military generals.

SARAH AND SISTERS CLIMB THE POINT

"I should spare some of that talk for describing the battle of Gettysburg as seen by us from Indian Lookout. We had a clear view of the field and could see so as to make the men in their lines, attending cannon, the cannon themselves, making charges, officers riding along about their lines."

- A.B.J., Mount St. Mary's College, July 1863

It was common practice for the Daughters of Charity to walk to the Mountain Church on Indian Mountain every Sunday to sing at High Mass and support the Sunday sermon; and often there was a large procession. There was a creek to cross and when it rained heavily, the creek level rose forcing each to cross one by one on horseback. Today it was dry so Sarah and some Sisters crossed by hopping from rock to rock and they had one of the experienced climbing priests along to lead.

But today was Thursday! They were on a mission to climb to the top of Indian Lookout—to personally see what they could hear from below—the sounds of cannons and gunfire that was coming from far off in the distance.

They carried a packed lunch and some dried meat for dinner in baskets. They were all so intrigued, and for Sarah this was a new experience getting to see Gettysburg and her home from the top of Indian Lookout. The Sisters had plenty of glasses or small telescopes, while some had opera glasses to use.

The higher they climbed the louder the noises got. What was going on? They had experienced the encampment by the Union Army on their peaceful property. It was a harrowing experience and their prayers were answered as no battle was fought at their place.

The Sisters and Sarah chatted as they wound their way up a trail following the priest. He often stopped and then decided which was the right path, for in the past some of the Sisters had gotten lost and had to return to the convent unable to find their way to the top.

It was hot and when the sun peeked through the treetops it shined in their eyes and reminded them just how hot it really was with no shade. They stopped once to drink from an old canteen; the water was already losing the coolness from the flowing creek below.

Finally they reached a clearing where a few of the locals from Emmitsburg were gathered, all setting on downed trees. Nearby was a panoramic and clear view of the scene taking place way off in the distance. They watched through their "helpers" with amazement as men in uniforms could be seen in faint lines. They could see the cannons flaring and emitting smoke and flames, and then they would hear the booms echo soon after the flashes. The sounds were muffled. Their special lensed devices allowed them to distinguish officers riding along their lines with flags swaying.

They witnessed the movements of the two armies locked in combat—one inching one way and the other countering and moving slowly the other way. It was surreal to see how many men and animals were dying right before their very eyes. The small group of people who were perched on top of the mountain had the horror scenes painted on their faces. How long could this go on?

It was well known by all in the Emmitsburg area, that Indian Lookout was a landmark. And now that the news of the ensuing Battle of Gettysburg was taking place the locals started to make the trek up the mountain to take in the spectacular view.

Sarah watched in horror as thousands of men in different color uniforms and so many horses were dying in the fields about ten miles away. What she was witnessing now had a more personal connection for her as right in the middle of all that fighting was her home with her dad and her Cousin Seth and her beloved horse Brandy.

As the Sisters watched, unable to eat their packed lunches, a young man from Emmitsburg hiked up and said, "My friend told me as I was coming up the mountain with him that his neighbor saw some flags waving from the top of a mountain west of town yesterday. He got curious so a bunch of the boys went up to an old farm and they met some Union signal soldiers. They were taking signals from the Gettysburg battlefield. One of them had a terrible look on his face when he turned around and announced to the others that a 'General Reynolds had been killed.' I don't know anything more."

Sarah looked at the Sisters and almost fainted; the heat was unbearable up on this mountaintop. "Oh my," she said. "If a general got killed how bad must it be for everyone else down in those open fields?"

"Oh Sarah," replied the Sister, "we'll soon find out as tomorrow Father said he was taking a wagon full of medical supplies and many of us to help the poor victims. Who knows what carnage we will see in the next few days. Let's leave now and return to our peaceful place. We must do God's work and try to help those poor soldiers."

BETSY AND SETH, SR., TRAVEL TO PHILADELPHIA

As their troop train approached the intersection of Washington Avenue and Broad Street, a railroad passenger station for the Wilmington & Baltimore Railroad appeared in sight. Large locomotives could enter Philadelphia easily and get passengers directly into the city. It was sheltered and had a 400-foot long train shed that housed 8 tracks. As they approached the station the conductor told Betsy and Seth, Sr., "This is a significant departure point for Union troops headed to support the Civil War effort. Major General George G. Meade is the Commander of the Army of the Potomac and that's where you are headed as Seth, Jr., is a part of the First Vermont Cavalry and part of that army."

He went on to say that after the war began, many Philadelphians shifted their opinions and were now in support of the Union, with over 50 infantry and cavalry regiments being recruited in part and from local areas to support the effort.

"The city is the main supplier of the Union Army uniforms. Besides providing significant manufactured weapons, warships are even being built nearby along the Delaware River port.

"The war effort is also supported by local armories and those troops you see gathered outside and at the entrances and exits are guarding against any Confederate Army attempt to attack. They were advised this morning that a major confrontation was happening in Gettysburg. They are even building entrenchments and getting prepared for any advances on the city.

"Because of that they will be sheltered here temporarily, until the all clear is given by the Army to proceed to Gettysburg by horse and wagon with a military regiment going out there to join the Army of the Potomac.

"They have your travel arrangements to Gettysburg and the sergeant will be here to advise you as you gather your travel bags."

Betsy and Seth, Sr., sat tiredly listening to the conductor as a cavalry sergeant entered the cabin with a huge smile on his face.

"Welcome to Philadelphia," he said with an Irish accent. "I'll be your guide here in the City of Brotherly Love until we can get you on the first supply train out to Gettysburg. Your horses are very far behind on the trip because we don't want any shipping disease. But have no worries, they are being taken care of by some of our finest groomsmen in our Quartermaster's Equine Division.

"Most military travelers of prominence stayed at the City Tavern that was established in 1773. Unfortunately it suffered severe fire damage and was torn down in 1854. It had the reputation of being the 'most genteel tavern in America' according to President John Adams. Our Founding Fathers and many members of the First Continental Congress said that it was their favorite meeting place.

"It had a rich history, but now is just a vacant lot. I will take you past there to one of my favorite spots that opened up in 1860, the Olde Ale House. Of course you can tell why I like it—it's an Irish inn. Many of the locals and Vets love it. It has a washroom in the back alley and a good house to stay for a few days. It's close to Independence Hall and the Liberty Bell, as well as the Delaware River and all the old colonial houses are within a nice carriage ride."

"Thank you Sergeant," said Betsy. "I'm anxious to see everything and we are both happy to get off this train and get a chance to see the Pennsylvania countryside."

"You will leave here and travel up the Old King's Highway into Lancaster and then on to the railroad station in downtown Gettysburg. There is a carriage waiting outside the station with two handsome old war horses. They are wounded but now healed Vermont Morgans. They are a matching pair and get the best treatment. They are survivors of the Second Battle of Bull Run in 1862."

PART TWO

THE FALL OF REYNOLDS.

THE SCENE AT
THE GETTYSBURG BARN

Jake was swirling with anxiety as troops were whirling in and out of the barn, climbing in the rafters, hanging from special vantage points, and peering through the slits of the old stone barn.

The soldiers had cleaned out all the hay and flimsy burnable objects and placed a lot of the older wagons and tools out near the split rail as blockades. They did everything they could to fortify and secure the place just like they were ordered to.

He was thrilled to see his nephew and his aide galloping in quickly on his beloved Morgan Brandy with Seth, Jr., low in the saddle and his aide covering his back side. He now knew they were safe, but he was wondering what was going on with his daughter, Sarah, who was still in Emmitsburg.

The horrific sounds of warfare echoed all around and below the nearby Round Tops. The fact that the First Vermont Cavalry was supposed to come in for support in the area was more comforting.

Jake watched one of the other officers stand with Seth and talk strategy. He was new and was explaining how he could read what was going on by watching the signal flags on the nearby Round Tops. The signal flags were serving the Union by observing the positions of the armies on the battlefield in Gettysburg and communicating via the flags to the Union officers.

The Signal Corps also had a communication center in Gettysburg where they were using a telegraph to forward dispatches for the entire Union Army. The Corps used Jacks Mountain, Indian Lookout on the Catoctin Mountain, Emmitsburg and Monterey Pass and South Mountain as part of their system—all the way to President Lincoln!

As the battle raged outside and in the area, Seth and the younger officer pulled up a table and started looking at a map of the area. Seth waved saying, "Come over Uncle Jake. You may as well know what's going on. You are stuck here and together all of us and the courier from Gettysburg headquarters and some of the First Vermont Cavalry will discuss our strategy." They all gathered around the map and sat down and planned.

"This is an update from headquarters," explained the harried courier. "On June 28, 1863, General Meade replaced Major General Joseph Hooker as Commander of the Army of the Potomac. General Meade took a day to develop a plan to confront Lee, who was already crossing from Maryland near Williamsport and now is around Gettysburg.

"J.E.B. Stuart and his cavalry were spotted and engaged and chased by the First Vermont Cavalry outside Hanover where the First secured the town and took some prisoners. Now Stuart is loose and somewhere out there in the perimeter. Thankfully the Union has General George A. Custer and his first cavalry troop trying to find them. And we in the First are helping.

"Yesterday a Reb division was coming up the Chambersburg Pike to Gettysburg when they clashed with part of General Buford's cavalry division. Captain Randolph you saw some of that! Other units heard the sounds and went to the scene and by noon the conflict was raging. General Reynolds came back after speaking with General Meade at headquarters in Gettysburg and hurriedly returned to the scene. Unfortunately he was out front of his unit and was killed by a Reb sniper!

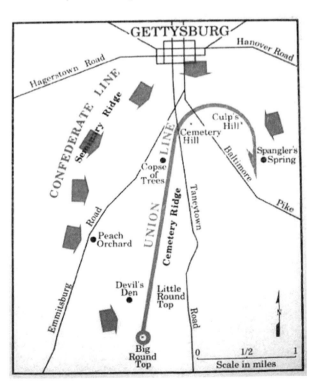

"The Confederates started to push us back and by last night our troops were really exhausted by the onslaught forming up on the high ground in the southeastern part of Gettysburg. General Meade had them form a three-mile long defensive line that looks like a giant fishhook!"

Looking at the map, the courier pointed to the fishhook and the exact location of the barn. Pointing out key spots on the map he said, "Now the line runs from here at Culp's Hill, to down on the right flank with our troops defending Cemetery Hill here and the Ridge line here, and then running all the way down here to Little Round Top.

"Now Lee's forces are pushing hard at us . . . we are ordered that we have to hold this barn! It's on the outside of the end of that fish hook. We are one of the last stone bastions before they can get around us to higher ground. We must hold this at whatever cost!"

BATTLES ALL AROUND

It didn't take long after his enlistment for Seth to realize that what the recruiter had told them all at the Vermont store about getting breechloading carbines and Blakeslees for their Spencer rifles . . . was a lie!

At this point in time, few of them had those weapons. Sadly, with all the different weapons they were using, they had been winning some but losing more skirmishes with that Southern guerrilla John S. Mosby. But now the Vermonters were a part of Elon Farnsworth's First Brigade under Judson Kilpatrick's Third Cavalry Division. Things were getting somewhat better . . . younger generals like Custer were truly inspiring!

He realized that the Vermonters only had two battalions of light cavalry and most were still carrying a mixture of Colt and Remington revolvers with sabres, and only a few men had Sharps carbines. The Third Battalion was a dragoon battalion and the men carried carbines, but this battalion was detached to the headquarters of the Sixth Corps.

Seth, and especially Major William Wells who commanded the Second Battalion and the First Vermont Cavalry, was in command of the two battalions with the regiment. He was pushing to get the entire regiment Spencer 9 shooting carbines, which could be reloaded as quick as a one-shooter carbine. This was inspiration to Seth as Major Wells was his "ideal" cavalry officer.

Some of the newer recruits would eventually be given the Burnside carbines, but all in all they had a munitions problem because of the many different types of weapons they were using. Seth was upset with those facts and that he lost his own horse prior to the incident in Hanover. Good Morgan horses were so hard to find, and those "buying and selling" them didn't understand a good Vermont Morgan horse if they saw one.

He was thrilled with the assignment to help the procurement officer with the Quartermaster Corps; now he could do something about the horse problem! He was sure Major Wells would handle the munitions problems; he'd find the Morgan horses. They were wrong about this war only lasting 90 days—no end was in sight! He could also start to breed now that they had two local farms. But first he had to survive these horrible battles that were taking place all around him.

This stone outpost was out in the open and hard to defend as the Confederates were just about everywhere. As he looked out the barn slit on its north side he could see the top of Little Round Top and some signal flags went up and then down. He could hear the terrible volleys from all over the hill and the cries of the wounded.

As Seth met with his staff in the barn the courier who had successfully been able to return from General Meade's headquarters now was reporting that, "July 1st had started normally but in early a.m. General Buford met and delayed two brigades of Confederates with brave Union cavalrymen who all dismounted with General Reynolds; but the loss of General Reynolds was a terrible price to pay. As the morning faded into the sweltering afternoon, Union reinforcements arrived to form a semicircle that ran west to north of Gettysburg.

"Then the Confederates commanded a massive assault from the north, attacking from Oak Hill while another Confederate division attacked right across the open fields north of the town. There were massive losses in both Union and Confederate lines and miraculously we somehow managed to hold the high ground!

"But the Rebs didn't quit; they regrouped and sent a second wave attack from the north with heavy reinforcements from the west. We had fierce hand-to-hand fighting in a woods by the Lutheran Seminary where we had posted our Signal Corps in the bell tower.

"Our retreating troops fled through the town. We suffered many casualties and the Rebs captured some of our boys. Our retreaters finally stopped to hold ground. We set up good defensive positions along Cemetery Hill and were waiting for their next move when it got dark. All night we could hear the moaning and screaming of those who were injured and left to die on the battlefield. It was horrible and simply awful.

"My trip here," the courier stopped to get his composure, "well Sirs, it was . . . it was a terrible scene and there were snipers firing at me as I sped here. My Morgan is smaller than most and thankfully misty grey-colored and a smart one; she ran here like she was running home."

Jake stopped him for a minute, "That's one of my mares soldier. I recognized her as she came in. She's one of Brandy's stable mates. Look how they are together back there in the barn. That's what horses do. They know their home!"

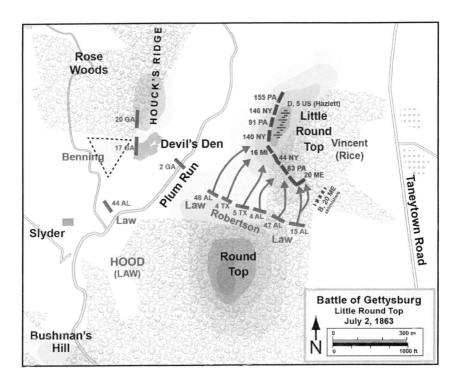

"She saved my life, Sir! I've never been out this far and she seemed to just know where she was going. She matched the morning mist and cloud cover that shrouded my trip—that's how I got here! I have to tell you all, she is so sure footed. It was very hard to get around all the bodies that fell and were lying everywhere, but she did a respectful job.

"And, when General Meade realized that those hills up there were strategically important he sent out another weary courier who reported back that the little hill up there was not being defended! They quickly moved in a division along with Colonel Joshua Lawrence Chamberlain's Maine troops to defend Little Round Top. He was told to hold it at all costs, so thankfully they had a lot of sharpshooters who took up strategic spots like you have here and many had breech-loading rifles.

"The Rebs just kept coming up the hill at them, all taking horrific losses, but they just kept coming—so much so that our troops were almost out of ammunition! They expected another assault up the hill so the men under Chamberlain's command chose to do a charge down the hill. Colonel Chamberlain ordered fixed bayonets with a rush down the hill in a sweeping motion to the right. When he gave the word he was out front leading the charge down the hill in a counterattack. They told me there was so much yelling and shooting and carnage.

"Headquarters says there are so many heroes on that mountain and in the battles yesterday. It is awful . . . and the enemy is still lurking. Headquarters is waiting for Lee's next move. So your orders are the same as Colonel Chamberlain's were—*defend and hold at all costs!*"

BRANDY AND CAVALRY
HORSES IN THE BARN

The inside air of the old stone barn was not as hot as the air outside. Summer in Gettysburg continued to challenge anyone outside with oppressive heat. While the wounded and dying soldiers baked in the sun's blinding rays, the dead just bloated and were in various stages of rigor mortis. Stray bullets and shrapnel had marked up the outer walls of the barn, while some metal fragments were embedded in the soft cement mixture that held the stone wall together. But the wall was not alive. It was dead, like so many in and around the Gettysburg battlefields.

The humans and horses inside the stone barn were lucky; unlike the dead or dying outside that littered the once placid and beautiful landscape. The local streams and waters were turning red from the dead bodies. It was a horrific scene and just about everywhere you looked in the Gettysburg area creatures were now either dying or dead!

The living moved among the dead; those still alive were taken to the now forming field hospitals. With wounds gushing, the sounds of sawing and screaming were now mixed with the horrible sounds of suffering as limbs piled up outside the field hospitals. War is pictured as a red place— Gettysburg was now a part of hell—with vivid colors of red, white, blue and many varying shades of grey.

Those creatures that were in front of the barrage of warfare and were wounded or maimed survivors of the carnage had no rigor mortis, unlike the bodies that began to rigor within three or four hours after their demise with complete rigor mortis setting in twelve hours. Others who were charging or engaged in a very strenuous activity were stiff immediately. The air was a pale of death.

Some air managed to blow in through the vented sides of the barn. The cavalry horses inside were loose and were allowed to mingle as they ate out of the old planked troughs. Some had water, some hay, some grain—but enough to sustain their equine bodies. Mares and stallions, geldings small and large, some wounded and healing from superficial wounds were all alive and it was a peaceful and moving scene with Brandy in the middle of it all.

They whinnied when the sounds of war battered the barn. Some hung their heads; some just back-ended to the barn walls and snoozed through it all. They were safe in a herd. Few of them knew their way home like Brandy did; most would be lucky if they made it through this battle and only a few would be alive at the war's end. Horses live for the moment of time they are in—their actions are dictated by their surroundings. It was somewhat peaceful in the barn and so were all of them.

The war killed thousands of horses that had no control of their human environment. Good horses were harder to find as the war progressed. Morgans were at a premium and the First Vermont Cavalry prized this herd more as each day passed. The cavalrymen who rode them were thankful they had some good horses. Many of their unlucky counterparts didn't have any horses and were doing the tasks where no horses were required for duty!

SETH, SR., AND BETSY ON
THEIR WAY THROUGH
LANCASTER

The uncomfortable wagon holding Seth, Sr., and Betsy rumbled on the way to their rest stop at Wheatland. A civilian guide started to explain the seriousness of the situation as he bumped up and down with them.

"There were reports a few days ago that about 35,000 Confederate troops were in nearby York, and a Reb division was moving in on Harrisburg. There was a rumor that Lee's army might move across the Susquehanna River, so to stop any attempt to cross the river by Confederate troops the bridge was burned on June 28.

"The Confederates were moving onto the bridge when our Union forces set fire to it near the Wrightsville side. They doused the covered bridge with crude oil from a local refinery. The bridge took fire quickly and it was completely destroyed.

"They say that some Confederate generals wanted to cross the bridge hoping to invade Lancaster in retaliation of what the Union was destroying in their beloved Shenandoah Valley. Some even suggested that Wheatland and former President James Buchanan might be targets for not settling the conflict before President Lincoln was elected. Many are calling it 'Buchanan's War!'

"It looks like Lee and his Confederates are now fighting with Meade's forces at Gettysburg. There is a major conflict going on there. We will be stuck here until we get further orders. Wheatland is still in contact with the headquarters there, despite the constant challenge of having the Union telegraph lines knocked out by the Confederates.

"Sadly, this mansion does need some renovations but the guest quarters are still in good condition. They still entertain some 'special' visitors like you, but they stopped the civilian visitors once Buchanan retired from his presidency."

He handed Seth, Sr., a stack of local newspapers from the past few days saying, "You can read these and it will bring you up to speed on what is going on. I don't know how much you have been told in transit, especially with all the traveling from city to city.

"While you are here you can stroll the grounds and enjoy the peaceful settings. You will find your stay here peaceful in his beloved Wheatland.

"Enjoy your stay. I will advise you when it is safe for the tugboat, *Columbia*, to cross the Susquehanna River to Gettysburg, where you will be heading right into the heart of this Civil War. The destiny of our nation hangs in the balance at your destination!"

EARLY MORNING
JULY 3RD AT THE BARN

The morning sun glowed over the horizon as another Union scout from headquarters leapt from his barebacked sweaty horse and barged through the barn door. He was scrawny and dirty and stopped and saluted announcing, "Sir, yesterday was a nightmare!"

With steely eyes he said in a very shrill voice, "During the night of the 1st of July the rest of our cavalry arrived and by the morning we had formed a strong line with General Hancock. In late afternoon we felt the onslaught of their General Longstreet's line of attack. It was a dandy and we took very heavy casualties but held our lines.

"It was all quiet but it looks like they are now going to challenge the center of our line as they are bombarding it with so many cannons it sounds like hell itself has arrived at Gettysburg. If Lee follows his usual course of action we expect a massive head-on assault to our middle. He has done that before and knows it worked in other places because our men have fled and then they crack our lines. But I don't think that will work this time as we have our artillery ready. Plus, if they come up through that wheat field below us there are so many obstacles for their infantry to get over that it will be like a Rebel duck shoot. Our men are on the high ground and set up behind rock walls and fences.

"They haven't seen anymore of Stuart's cavalry in these parts, but there is a huge batch of Rebs out around Plum Run right out there in front of you. There could be another attack coming at you. Your sharpshooters up in the barn are on to them! I saw them checking me out on the way in. I made sure they saw my blue hat! Major Wells with his 2nd Battalion and General Farnsworth in command of the brigade are to be here to offer assistance."

"Thanks for the update and warning," replied Seth.

"Uncle, you better find a safe place back with the horses. We will all take our positions as planned!"

"I'll do my best to keep the horses from trying to get out when the fighting picks up and if they fire the barn I'll open the back doors and let them out; better they die in the line of fire than inside this place."

"I don't think those Rebels will kill loose horses; they'll try to capture them if they get a chance."

"Don't worry about me Seth. I dug an underground tunnel with a huge chamber and there is even a small spring that trickles through. I can hide down there or go out through a tunnel that leads to that small clearing behind us."

LATE AFTERNOON
JULY 3RD AT THE BARN

It was extremely difficult for the newly-promoted Seth Randolph to be inside instead of out in the action while the fierce battle was taking place on all sides of the barn. The snipers were trying to pick off the leaders in the Reb lines of attack and had been successful, but the Rebs just kept coming.

General Kilpatrick and the cavalry had finally made it to their rescue after encountering so much Reb resistance. The right flank around Gettysburg soon drove the enemy's skirmishers back from their main lines with the rapid responses by Companies A, D, E and his old Company and he was pleased to see that they were dismounting– his favorite tactic. Now they were out in front and spread out behind rocks and boulders, as some men had revolvers and some carbines.

"Looks like they are fixin' to charge, Sir!" said a sniper from above peering through a slot. "Sir, it looks like General Farnsworth is commanding the brigade and now they are mounting, fixing to charge.

———————

Several hours later as the sun was setting and the smoke started to clear, the sounds of the battle out front subsided as another lookout from above shouted, "One of our scouts coming in . . . don't shoot!"

Captain Randolph met him as he dismounted and quickly came in the bullet-riddled front barn door.

"Sir, we held their siege and General Elon J. Farnsworth . . . well . . . he got shot off his horse and died under that nearby tree. He was leading a charge through the intense fire that seemed to be . . . the whole Confederate Infantry . . . and we lost over fifty so far . . . but we held them!

"Major Wells and us men held the ground for hours but were forced to fall back. He then had us dismount and protect the right flank. Major Wells succeeded in rallying so many of us that we all went running from behind rocks and boulders and trees with our revolvers. We were under a nasty line of fire but we were driving the Rebs in all directions!

"We just kept going—running over a stone wall and through the line—charging their Batteries. We got through their other line and dead bodies were everywhere. We met up with the 2nd Battalion and the 1st.

"When we got to that hill out there between them two walls we were met by more of them coming from our right to meet us. Major said later that that's where they were trying to get a foothold. We struggled hard for that hill . . . and our First Vermont Cavalry boys carried the day. We suffered so many losses . . . but we managed to hold our position!

"The Major sent this message, Sir. He said you'd understand."

Congratulations on your promotion. We tried to keep you and your horses safe and you were right about dismounting and fighting on the ground, too. I'll keep pushing for those breech-loading carbines and you keep pushing and producing us more Vermont Morgans. I want the first colt from your beautiful Brandy!

JULY 4TH, 1863
THE RANDOLPHS LEAVE
WHEATLAND MANSION
IN LANCASTER

"It's safe to go now . . . but," said the cavalry officer in the parlor of the majestic Wheatland Mansion, "even though the siege at Gettysburg has ended there is carnage everywhere. The Southern Army is in a retreat pattern and we are in a holding position as General Meade considers the next move of the Army of the Potomac.

"Somehow they have been able to keep the telegraph lines in Gettysburg open. There have been heroics undefinable and undeniable on both sides of this battle and already rumor has it that a female operator is one. She quickly left the besieged Gettysburg Train Station communications center, carrying a telegraph machine to a hiding point and . . . all alone . . . kept the besieged and troubled line open.

"Sadly, Lancaster's beloved General Reynolds was killed on the first day; shot off his horse by a sniper after he gave the command, 'Forward men, forward for God's sake, and drive those fellows out of the woods.'

"A Union Army ambulance arrived quickly and he was taken from the field. His body was shipped to his family in nearby Philadelphia to lie in state waiting for the public funeral services scheduled for today, here in Lancaster. He will be buried somewhere in Lancaster City."

Hearing this news, Betsy pulled out a handkerchief and started to cry. Her father-in-law quickly went to her side consoling her.

"Oh how awful," said Betsy.

"Sadly, there are so many deaths but we just got word that your husband's 1st Vermont Cavalry was fighting gallantly yesterday near your brother's and your new farm. They were trying to stop another attempt by the Southern Army to break the lines and pierce through our defenses. The Rebels continued their assaults and killed another cavalry officer general. I don't have his name.

"They report it was another heroic Union deed done by a cavalry unit on horseback. At one point they dismounted and a major and his men heroically held the line . . . but with many casualties! Our cavalry was very much a factor in the overall defenses . . . but we don't have anymore details right now."

Betsy looked up, "Oh how terrible! Who was the general and is there any word on my husband?"

"Sorry Mrs. Randolph, that is all we have. We can wait for more telegrams and information or we can leave this afternoon on the *Columbia*. We have been given clearance to cross the Susquehanna and proceed with a military caravan to resupply Gettysburg. We are sending in more nurses and doctors from the surrounding area to assist with the wounded and dying. They say there are hundreds of field and other types of hospitals being set up. Some troops that can travel are being transported back over the river to local hospitals . . . they just can't handle the carnage . . . on either side!"

"Let's go now," Betsy replied, squeezing the hand of her father-in-law. "I don't want to be setting on this porch waiting for a sad telegram to arrive like all the poor mothers, families, and widows of dead loved ones. I'd rather go where my husband is."

THE RANDOLPHS' TRIP
TO GETTYSBURG

Seth, Sr., and Betsy swayed in rhythm with the pulling action as the *Columbia* moved their party slowly across the wild and wide Susquehanna. Their horses had finally caught up with them at Wheatland and they had a chance to spend some time with them, bringing back sweet smells and fond memories of Vermont.

The scenery along their trip started to change—some of the rivers were more wild and wider—especially this one between Lancaster and Gettysburg. They looked out at the long covered bridge that spanned before them, scarred and blackened by war, it was unlike the historic and colorful covered bridges in their beloved home state. Vermonters' lives, just like the lives of so many in the nation were now scarred and burnt just like that bridge out there. They would replace that bridge eventually and make it whole again, but that was impossible for the humans and animals and the fabric of the nation—all were scarred permanently—by the Civil War.

"Dad, look at that group of ladies with the large white hats and black outfits. They are all huddled together back by that railing."

"Oh Betsy, they are Sisters. My brother wrote me a long time ago saying one of his daughters was a Sister in a religious order that was near his place at Gettysburg. She was working in a hospital in Philadelphia. Let's go over and talk with them . . . we could benefit from their angelic-looking company."

As the fast currents pushed against the bow of their portaging boat, Seth, Sr., and Betsy swayed back and forth as they slowly crossed the bow to meet the Sisters. Smiling widely, Seth, Sr., addressed the first one who was smiling at him with a big, "Hello Sister!"

"Hello sir and hello to you too, ma'am," said the Sister. "It's really a scary ride on this smoking thing. Last time I crossed from Gettysburg I went over that burned-out wooden bridge. Now we are on this rocking, smoking thing. We don't know how it works but we do hope it gets us across to that shore. We are going to help bind, bandage and give medicine and care to those who are suffering in Gettysburg. So many need help!"

"Oh," said Betsy, "we are headed there, too!"

"It's just terrible," said the Sister. "They are opening so many field hospitals there. We passed some of the ones who were injured early in the battle as they were heading to the hospital in Philadelphia where we work."

"Oh," said Seth, Sr., "we too were in Philadelphia a few days ago. We are traveling from Vermont to our new farm. My brother Jake owns a farm there with his daughters. My son, Captain Randolph, is at the farm now but we had word that the area was under siege by the Rebels."

The Sister stopped smiling saying, "Randolph, sir? Your name is Randolph, too?"

"Yes Sister, do you know the Randolphs?"

"My religious name is Sister Cecilia, but my actual name is Catherine Randolph . . . and my dad is your brother and . . . "

Betsy walked over and hugged the Sister. Smiling and laughing she said, "And I'm Betsy Randolph your cousin's wife. What an act of providence . . . to meet in the middle of this free-flowing river."

"God is wise and good and cleansing," said Catherine as she reached out and put her arms around both of them.

The other Sisters began to wonder what was happening and one of them asked, "Sister Cecilia . . . do you know these people?"

Sister Cecilia, with tears in her eyes lovingly remarked, "Yes I do! These are my Randolph relatives from Vermont. We're all on our way to our home in Gettysburg . . . that is now under a veil of death!"

"Amen," said all the Sisters in a somber tone.

EMMITSBURG SISTERS
TO GETTYSBURG

During the three-day battle that raged at Gettysburg the Sisters prayed for the combatants. Some had even watched in horror from atop Indian Mountain. That was yesterday, Saturday the 4th of July!

What a stark difference from the year 1776, which was printed on the original Declaration of Independence and on the Dunlap Broadside copy of the Declaration which hung in their tiny seminary school. Now, almost a hundred years later the Battle of Gettysburg had been fought. Today was Sunday the 5th and some of the Daughters of Charity Sisters and a priest were packing and preparing for a trip to Gettysburg to render aid.

Reports were flowing in that carnage was everywhere and the local churches and hotels, and even personal homes, were filled and serving as field hospitals for those who were wounded.

"Sarah, you may see your sister in Gettysburg. She has traveled with our Sisters from Philadelphia to help aid the suffering," said the Superior. "Our Sisters from Baltimore are coming, too. When you arrive in Gettysburg, please help to serve the wounded as best you can."

Sarah hugged the Superior goodbye and she was on the road, but heading back home to what? Tears filled her eyes as they traveled up the Emmitsburg Road. Rancid gusts of wind blew slowly into their faces causing them to turn their heads from the horror. Peering out of their wagons they could see men moving on the roadways and fields around the dead who were lying where their last breath was taken. Some men were still in the saddle lying with their dead horses. There were so many dead along the road that the old priest who was steering the wagon had to slow down and carefully wind around the decaying bodies lying askew.

It was a slaughter scene of opposing armies with objects of red, white and blue colors among broken staffs and strewn flags, some riddled with bullet holes just like the corpses. Wounded soldiers limped past, some asking for help, while others obviously maligned with anti-Catholic sentiment turned their heads as the wagons rolled past.

As they rounded a bend closer to the city there was a field hospital set up with a pile of limbs outside of it. An orderly came racing over asking for any bandages or food stuffs. They quickly stopped their wagon and unpacked some of the supplies. He took what they gave him and hurried back to the field hospital where screams could be heard. Their horse-drawn wagon moved on as the priest and Sisters prayed silently.

The town was filled with dramatic scenes of a mortal combat . . . a frightful spectacle of burnt and bullet-holed dead bodies of both Armies scattered helter-skelter, dead horses, bayonets and sabers strewn all about, and cannon and bullet-riddled houses looked like they were barely standing.

There were overturned wagons with separated wheels left behind and multi-colored infantry supplies of blankets, caps, and different uniforms and even body parts strewn all over. It was indescribable.

"This way Father!" came a cry from a field medic. "We need some of your supplies in our field hospital up here. We have set up as many hospitals as possible but we are running out of supplies!"

"Then you must get more," said the head Sister as she organized the supplies to give to him.

"I have seen you Sisters on other battlefields before. Don't you ever get tired of this?"

"This is what we do, sir . . . we are the Daughters of Charity."

"Well, Washington must pay all of you very well! This is just so horrible and difficult and so awful to deal with . . ."

"This is what we do."

"Oh Sister, we have Confederates here, too. Do you only help Union soldiers?" asked a passing Union doctor.

Sister Ann looked at him sympathetically saying, "We make no distinction sir, they all need help!"

THE RANDOLPHS' RENDEVOUS AT GETTYSBURG QUARANTINE FACILITY

Typhoid fever kept the Randolphs from continuing on to their home farm and meeting up with Seth, but the military said they were arranging for Seth to come to them instead! The shooting was over, but now a typhoid epidemic had to be stopped.

The doctor at the staging area leading into Gettysburg explained to them, "There have been so many cases of typhoid fever in the Union Army during this war. Contaminated food and water, as well as flies, contribute to it. It already killed two out of ten affected soldiers in 1861 and now it is close to six out of ten and the 'after the battle' chances of contracting it are higher than the chance of being shot! Typhoid fever is very common in Washington, D.C., and last year it took the life of President Lincoln's son Willie. Our soldiers die from two general causes: battlefield injuries and disease."

Seth, Sr., Betsy, and Catherine listened and then were directed to a special room near the staging area.

"Over here please. Please come over here," instructed the sharply-dressed cavalry officer in full dress uniform. "We have a special room set up. Captain Randolph has been cleared to welcome you all."

A long table was set for a special dinner with beautiful linens and dinnerware and patriotic Union flags. The officer instructed them to sit at the chairs with their name card and then he left. Everyone sat down, looking nervously at each other. They heard a door open and some muffled talking and then heavy boot sounds.

The cavalry officer stepped back in announcing, "Ok, I will take you outside where we will wait for Captain Randolph to arrive. He just left the screening tent and his military escort and should be here in a minute."

They all got up and followed the officer through the back door of the room to a cleared grassy field. They saw a uniformed rider coming into view at a full gallop. "That's my son!" yelled Seth, Sr.

"Oh Dad, oh Dad . . . that's my beloved Seth!" screamed Betsy.

"Praise the Lord," whispered Sister Cecilia.

THE RANDOLPH REUNION

S eth looked dashing as he stood smiling in front of his family, with Brandy slowly bowing. They all ran to them. Betsy, with tears in her eyes, threw herself into Seth's open arms; he felt her pressing against the metal-plated picture of her near his heart as they kissed.

Seth, Sr., and Catherine rushed to Brandy and he lifted his head, whinnying softly as they hugged him. Catherine smiled saying, "Thank you Lord" and her large white hat glowed brightly in the sun, matching the gleam in all of their eyes and hearts. They had all waited so long for this meeting.

They moved silently back inside and sat in their assigned seats with Betsy and her beloved Seth at the head of the long table. After they were all seated, there were two empty chairs that remained. Seth stood up quietly announcing, "Two of our family are missing . . ."

"Oh, I believe they are here now," said the officer near the door as in stepped Jake Randolph and his daughter Sarah.

THE RANDOLPH
CELEBRATION

The Randolph reunion carried on into late afternoon. Eventually Seth brought them back to reality saying, "It is not safe for the ladies to go to the new farms, their health will be in jeopardy! There have been some local cases of typhoid and the Plum Run is still not cleared to drink. The local spring at the farm is ok, but the area is in a temporary quarantine. Plus the local Devil's Den is not a sight for the ladies to see.

"My dad and Uncle Jake have to go sign some military papers to complete the sale of the Vermont Morgans who are now in the quartermaster's stable and ready to be chosen by a few select Vermont cavalrymen who don't have horses.

"Sarah and Catherine are rejoining the Sisters of Charity to help in the local field hospitals, while Betsy and I will travel to York tomorrow for a special vacation and a gala called, 'The Confederates Are Gone.' We will be hosted by a prominent doctor who treated some soldiers from the Battle of Gettysburg.

"The Army of the Potomac and the First Cavalry selected me to speak at the special gala hosted by local dignitaries to show them that we now have the Rebels on the run and how our cavalry plays a big role in the Union Army. I will be assuring them that the Army of the Potomac is now taking the offensive.

"From June 28 until the 30th, York had been overcome and occupied by the Confederate Army Division of Major General Jubal Anderson Early. The town of York was forced to grant the Confederates their ransom request, sparing their town. They yielded to and supplied Major Early's demands of needed food, supplies, clothing, shoes, and thousands of dollars from the citizens and merchants before his troops departed westward to be a part of the Gettysburg Campaign.

"On the morning of the 29th, a Rebel cavalry unit burned all the bridges that led to York. You all saw firsthand the burned covered bridge on your trip across the Susquehanna!

"They want me to remind the town and the locals that Pennsylvania is still a vital part of the Union. Pennsylvania is a raw material source and recently was the target of several other cavalry raids by J.E.B. Stuart. But he was unsuccessful to cut off that source.

"They want me to parade through town on Brandy to boost morale, flying the colors of the First Vermont Cavalry assuring them that we have good officers and generals leading us.

"We want to inform the area residents that the Army of the Potomac is on the move . . . York is now a safe place for all its citizens. The Rebels are moving back to where they came from!"

Betsy proudly looked at him. "Oh Seth that will be wonderful. Dad and I spent some time in Philadelphia strolling around in the evening seeing the historic sites. But now I can stroll around the city of York, walking hand in hand with my handsome, cavalry officer husband!"

SETH AND BETSY IN YORK

There had been a lot of firsts in the historic town of York. It was the first town west of the Susquehanna River, with the first hall for public entertainment where famous actors presented plays to substantial audiences. It was also the first Capitol of the United States, but for the Randolphs it was the first place to romantically celebrate their reunion in Pennsylvania where they would start their new lives.

"Oh Seth, I'm so happy and so proud of you! I'm so lucky to be your wife . . . and I'm so in love with you!"

Seth blushed under the lamppost next to the building where famous actors performed romantic roles on stage. They were not famous actors, nor were they were on stage, but they were humbled to be married and alive and together again.

"Evening Officer, evening Ma'am," and "Congratulations Captain," were some of the pleasantries the citizens spoke as they passed them on the street. As they strolled arm in arm, heart to heart, the evening air brushed off any previous worries and cares.

"We are so fortunate to be together . . . providence has been good to us," said Betsy as she reached up and kissed him. "I've been wanting to do that in public for years honey!"

Seth blushed again then reached into his breast pocket, pulling out her picture that he was carrying. Showing it to her he remarked wistfully, "Before you came, I kissed this picture of you every time I got a chance and you rode with me on every mission. You are much more beautiful in person . . . oh Betsy, I have missed you!"

"When we married I was a real homebody. I was never going to leave Vermont. But look at me now, standing on a cobblestone street in a city named York, with a handsome cavalry officer and going to live on a farm in a town called Gettysburg."

"I can't wait Betsy, but the quarantine still is in effect and my headquarters sent me orders to attend a 'special celebration' in nearby Harrisburg. They said to enjoy our stay and then go to Harrisburg and do what I did here in York for the troops there. Hundreds of thousands of troops have been going through Camp Curtin in Harrisburg. It's our largest Federal camp of the Civil War. There are major railroad lines running in all directions and it is a strategic way of moving our troops and needed supplies to our armies in the field. It's also a major supply depot, and their hospital is helping with our wounded.

"They want me to get more training in my newly added procurement duties and they want Brandy and me to rally the troops that keep coming from Maryland, Michigan, Minnesota, New Jersey, New York, Ohio, and Wisconsin. The news of the win at Gettysburg has prompted some of the patriotic Morgan horse owners from the northern and mid-western states to start sending us some of their horses. Many have read about the heroics at Gettysburg and how great our cavalry performed. They know that many good horses have already died, but are willing to send some of their best stock for the cavalry to use. They have learned about the First Vermont Cavalry and our Morgan mounts. They are setting up a 'special horse sale' and they want me to give a talk about our unit. Headquarters updated my orders by telegraph and my commander said, 'Enjoy that beautiful wife and horse . . . we need more of both!'"

"Oh Seth, anywhere I am with you is wonderful!"

PART THREE

SARAH AND CATHERINE– THE DAUGHTERS OF CHARITY

"Of all the forms of charity and benevolence seen in the crowded wards of the hospitals, those of some Catholic Sisters were among the most efficient. More lovely than anything I had ever seen in art, so long devoted to illustrations of love, mercy and charity, are the pictures that remain of these modest Sisters going on their errands of mercy among the suffering and the dying."
- ABRAHAM LINCOLN

The line outside the Theological Seminary Hall in Gettysburg was long, and the sun sweltering. Sarah and her sister Catherine sat in a room before the priest from Emmitsburg.

"Our Sisters are doing so many wonderful things in our Lord's garden, but we are all overwhelmed. I have both of you here because there have been so many requests from ladies about helping with the carnage. So many want to know about your Order and we even have some war widows and mothers of dead soldiers here. We set up this meeting and I have chosen you two to give a talk once we get them seated.

"Despite its ugliness, this war is producing so much goodness from the people like those that are in the line outside, and like you two, and all those who are out there assisting the doctors and others with the thousands of wounded and sick . . . despite the prevalence of that dreaded aftermath of this carnage called typhoid!

"They have so many questions and I know you two in your various levels of formation can explain how the Order was founded by Elizabeth Ann Seton. Explain how her struggle through severe personal losses and difficult years led her to finally accept the invitation of the Church and move to Emmitsburg, Maryland, to establish the Saint Joseph's Academy and Free School.

"Now before you start, there is a distressed lady in that room over there. She is quite distraught and a family member told me this story about her and her fiancé. He was a West Point graduate and they had exchanged rings from him to her, and a medal and a ring from her to him which he had been wearing around his neck under his uniform. They found that on his dead body and that is when the family found out he was engaged! They tell me that he was going into battle at Gettysburg with her saying that if he was killed she would enter a religious order. Sadly, he was killed.

"I would like you two to console her and tell her about your Order and how Mother Seton lost her beloved husband . . . keeping in mind that her grief must be unbearable!

"God does work in strange ways and I found this story so heart wrenching. Sister Cecilia is your Order's name, but your mother and father named you Catherine. Sarah told me she always called you Kate down on the farm. Interestingly I met this grief-stricken lady and she said, 'Hello Father, my name is Catherine but most people just call me Kate!'

"Please talk to her . . . she is in your loving hands and in God's loving ways. Such a sad story! Let's hope it has a happier ending."

SARAH AND THE DAUGHTERS OF CHARITY

Sarah had been raised on a farm with wonderful parents and educated by the Daughters of Charity. She had already seen so much sadness, but she had never heard such a compassionate story like the one about the beautiful lady and her beau who was shot off his horse at the Battle of Gettysburg. Her cousin was a junior officer and he had survived so far and now was with his beloved Betsy. Somehow their fortunes had aligned them and they were together.

She had witnessed a very rare human love like that between her mother and father and the tragedy of her father's loss last year made her afraid of dealing with such a loss and it had helped her to understand the difference between a vocational love and a marital love. Something was tugging at her heart and she was still trying to grapple with which vocation to choose—Sisterhood or motherhood?

Her sister Kate was so happy in her religious vocation, and her Cousin Seth's wife Betsy was so happy in her marital vocation. Oh, the sight of Seth and Betsy together and then seeing that poor woman who lost her beau . . . all of this tugged hard at her heart. She often thought about it as she dressed the wounds of those who survived the carnage of war and struggled with the healing process.

Today her sister Kate was leaving to go back with some of her religious Sisters and some inquiring ladies that wanted to visit their convent at Emmitsburg—and the lady named Kate was going, too!

The quarantine had been lifted at the farm and she would finally be able to go home to see her dad. She longed to see his smiling face and to spend some time with him and her Uncle Seth from Vermont. It was such a happy time—the two Vermont brothers finally back together.

> Come see us as fast as you can Sarah. The quarantine is lifted and we will enjoy some lemonade on the front porch while Cousin Seth and Betsy enjoy their time together on the road. Love, Dad.

She pushed the note back in her packed bag and started to walk out the front door when a cavalry officer with red hair to match the cavalry patch on his uniform limped towards her and stopped her asking, "Hello Sarah. Do you remember me?"

"Oh, hello. I recognize that you are with the First Vermont Cavalry."

"Yes, I was promoted when your cousin made captain. I was under his 'wing' and in training when I saw you in Emmitsburg. I was the one that put the saddle on your horse for your cousin after they took him out of your wagon's lines."

"Oh," replied Sarah, "where in Vermont are you from?"

"Burlington. They told me you were nursing here with the Sisters."

"Oh I'm here to help, but I am just assisting. The Sisters are going back to their convent in Emmitsburg for more supplies. I'm leaving right now to go to our farm in Gettysburg. My Uncle Seth just bought the farm next to ours and he can finally get on to it. There was terrible fighting around my home, near Plum Run and the Round Tops."

"I know where that is. I was there with the First and it was an awful fight. It took a while but we finally broke through the lines of those boys from Texas and I think Alabama. We're still trying to figure out who they were that fought so gallantly. So many of us are lucky to be alive . . . sadly for me they broke my leg really bad. The doctors said someday I should be able to ride a horse again, but not now and I am definitely not fit for the infantry . . . maybe a desk job. They are checking on further treatment at another place."

"Oh my," replied Sarah.

"I was lounging here in the parlor and saw you coming. I have this leg wound healing and I was told to find a quiet place to rest and relax somewhere in a better area while they check . . . "

"Oh lieutenant, I'm leaving now for just such a place. You can come and meet my relatives from Vermont and have some lemonade on the porch. I'm sure my dad and uncle would be glad to meet another First Vermont Lieutenant. Cousin Seth will be glad to see you when he and his wife return."

"Sarah, that would be great. I'll check out . . . listing you as my nurse and your home as my next quiet medical place so they can update me on any further treatment."

"Oh, I'm not a nurse lieutenant, and I don't even know your name."

"It's John . . . John Reynolds . . . but they call me Jonnie back home in Vermont."

SETH AND BETSY
IN HARRISBURG

"That's one of the finest looking Morgan horses I've ever seen, Captain. You take care of him as well as that McClellan saddle you have on his back. The colors almost match . . . how do you get that saddle up to that beautiful color of your horse?"

"Thank you, sir! McClellans are standard issue, Morgans are not. Saddles are easy to come by and I'm finding out in my procurement assignment that Morgans aren't. Our War Department made the McClellan a 'standard issue' for our cavalry horse's mission. Our First Vermont Cavalry made the Morgan our horse of choice!

"Funny how this standard issue saddle and our cavalry manual were developed by a man who wasn't even in the cavalry. Same with the man who first bred the Morgan—he was a school music teacher.

"The McClellan saddle is a lot cheaper than other saddles, and it is light and no burden for the horse. The Morgan is a lot more expensive but they are right for us and our line of work, but hard to find.

"Just like our Morgan horse, the saddle is strong enough to support our cavalry riders and our gear. McClellan is made of rawhide while our Morgans are made of horse hide! They just told me at the Procurement Office they are priced right and are available by the hundreds of thousands. We all wished that was true about Morgans and that's why they put me in charge of finding them!"

"And that's why we have come such a long way; some of us wanted to meet you personally. So many of our sons and neighbors are fightin' in the war. Many of us have been holding back on our good stock.

"We get a lot of horse dealers knocking on our barn doors, but they don't know how to choose a good horse. Some of us are ashamed that we sold them 'not so good stock,' but they paid enough and said we didn't have much of a cavalry anyway. They told us most of the horses would be used for guard and scout duties. How were we to know? But we've been reading and hearing about the cavalry and the Battle of Gettysburg. We all get a copy of the *Pennsylvania Telegraph* mailed to us. We sure would be proud to see some of our best stock carrying you Vermont Cavalry boys in it!" said the horse dealer from Ohio.

"There's some good stock out our way, but some use them for harness racing or for pulling coaches because of the breed's speed and endurance in harness. Some have used them as stock horses for riding and light driving work. Morgans popped up in the California gold rush and now the Army is using them very heavily in this Civil War.

"I know some Morgan mares had been brought to points west and interbred and it's hard to really define a 'real' Morgan. That mount of yours we saw in the *Telegraph* is a prime picture of that schoolteacher's Morgan horse named Figure."

"Many of us were confused about the picture of the original Figure, but I've seen a lot in isolated areas like yours," replied Seth.

"Wait until you see what we fellows have brought from our stock. When we saw your Brandy's picture in the newspapers a lot of us said, 'Hey, we got one that looks like him! Almost an exact copy!' Come in the back corral, Captain. Check out what we brought you!"

FIRST GOOD NEWS FOR SETH

P resident Lincoln loved the telegram, calling them "lightning messages." He once sent a terse telegram to McClellan after the Battle of Antietam with this short and memorable line, "about sore-tongued and fatigued [sic] horses," demanding to know "what the horses of your army have done since the battle of Antietam that fatigue anything?"

Seth and Betsy stood in the parlor of the local telegraph office and were amazed how simple that "lightning machine" looked. The operator was frail, bearded, soft spoken and looked more like he could be a doctor. How did he learn to make his fingers work so fast? How did the messages travel so fast? These were all questions that they couldn't answer but they were there to send some really good news to headquarters.

Seth and Betsy smiled and watched the antique clock working its way into noon. It was hot outside and just as hot inside.

"Here are your messages, Captain," and he handed him three messages.

"And here is a reply to their 'Horse Inquiry' one from yesterday. Please send the following message: Procured 200 REAL Morgans from this group and gave them your government voucher number/specifications and they will send you their billing with details. Many of our riderless First Vermonters will be thrilled. On our way to Gettysburg Headquarters."

He watched as the telegraph officer sent the message and gave him his receipt. He thanked him then he and Betsy went back to the parlor and poured some lemonade from the pitcher on the table and sat down.

"Let's see what these messages are about. The first is they received my message. The second is from headquarters with the ok to return to the Gettysburg farm as the quarantine has been lifted.

"The last one is from my dad. It says, 'Quarantine lifted. Come home. Sarah here with a Vermont Cavalry Lt. John Reynolds. Mighty fine fella from Vermont. Says you two are friends. Hurry home. Dad.'"

Seth looked at Betsy. "Hmm, that last one is a little strange. I know him. He's a wonderful officer. We always kidded him how when we went through small towns and the ladies came out to thank us they all flocked around his horse! He never showed any interest! I thought Sarah was heading back to Emmitsburg with the Sisters?"

"Is he good looking?" asked Betsy.

"Never thought about that, but he sure draws the ladies . . ."

"Women love a man in uniform!"

". . . and this man in uniform loves you. Let's head for Gettysburg now!"

IN TRANSIT TO GETTYSBURG

Brandy was getting used to the change in environment around him; his feed and water were always provided, but this constant in and out and up and down in unfamiliar objects into stranger things that closed out the light was hard to get used to. He did not like to be enclosed and especially now he was in with a lot of others like him. They all swayed with the movement of this thing.

"Ok Sergeant, all the horses are here so open the back gate and lead them off one by one. Take that gorgeous stallion over to that lead stall and wash him down and get him into that black spring wagon over there. Captain Randolph will be here shortly with his wife and they will be heading out to Gettysburg. Oh, here they come now!"

Seth and Betsy watched as Brandy got off the railroad car and was led to the nearby shed where they quickly washed him down, groomed him, tacked him and hitched him to the spring wagon.

"Finally Betsy, we can go to our new home."

"Oh Seth, I'm so excited. Look how handsome Brandy is!"

"Oh he's a dandy. I'll always remember going down Main Street to the historic town hall and the Civil War band playing 'Battle Hymn of the Republic.' I had a lump in my throat until I got to the hall and finally dismounted. Did you see him prancing and strutting? It seemed like he knew everyone had their eyes on him."

"And we all did. He made me cry and all the folks were waving flags and a little boy next to me told his dad, 'When I grow up I wanna be just like that soldier . . . dad, get me a horse like him now.'"

"What did he say?"

"He smiled and looked up at me with a big grin on his face. I patted the little boy on the head and thought to myself, 'Someday Seth and I are going to have our own little boy. Will he too want to be a cavalry officer like his father?' Oh Seth, that's what a Vermont wife yearns for . . . that's what this Pennsylvania wife is looking forward to. I can't wait to see this new farm . . . and our new home."

"Oh it's a dandy. My uncle's place is so green and serene this time of year. The front porch of the house overlooks a vast expanse of open land.

Don't know much about what my dad has next door; I know there are a lot of boulders and rocks far off in the distance and it's a great place to raise horses. Brandy brought me in the back way from the Emmitsburg Road at nighttime and I couldn't see much but it was pretty wild and wet. We'll be together on it sometime this evening."

"Ready to go Captain? Your horse is already stomping; he seems to be in a hurry to go where you're heading."

"And so are we Sergeant, we've been on the road since after the battle. It's been so long now that the nights are starting to get shorter."

"Well Captain, it wasn't a pretty sight around here for days and weeks as thousands of dead soldiers and horses littered the battlefield, and a terrible stench was in the town and surrounding farms. We did get some rain days after the battle. Many of the dead were in shallow graves and washed up and the townspeople and local farmers buried and reburied a lot on their own lands. Our Army burial teams were overwhelmed.

"The war is still going on so everyone must help when they can. There's talk of Lincoln wanting a National Cemetery in town and there is a local man with a crew assigned to 'collect' as many bodies to rebury there. Headquarters reports about three to four thousand Union dead and they think about four or five thousand Confederates. It took almost a week to ten days to bury all the dead. Just thought I'd tell you Captain."

"Thanks Sergeant. It's just so sad. This is the first time I've seen the aftermath of a battle. I've always moved on with the cavalry after we had a skirmish. We will be glad to get home."

"Where's that Captain?"

"Along the Plum Run."

"Around Devil's Den, Sir?"

"Well we can see that place in the distance . . . "

"Well Captain, you don't want to see that place now . . . they'll be writing about that place and the Round Tops in the 'history' books."

Betsy sadly looked at Seth as she sat down on the seat of the wagon as the sergeant plopped their baggage in the back saying, "Some of those poor horses and mules . . . and the soldiers . . . just dropped like baggage into shallow graves. Just terrible. Have a safe trip, Sir!"

SARAH AND JOHN
ARRIVE AT THE FARM

"That's a beautiful stone house and barn coming into view, and it looks like it took some heavy shelling," John said to Sarah as the small buggy rounded the bend with the bay horse high-stepping out in front.

"We love it here," replied Sarah. "I was born here and my sister and I played all over the area. Oh look, there are some people out in my dad's field with a basket. I wonder what they are doing?"

"They always come after a battle and it almost never stops. They are souvenir hunters."

"Souvenir hunters? What are they looking for?"

"Remnants of the battle that was fought here. Many people are fascinated and others do it for the money. They better be careful as I'm sure there are still a lot of 'live' shells out there. Not all are exploded.

"I read in the paper the other day that a little farm girl was out playing in the dirt near her house and one exploded. Sadly she died. Killed in the action is not the only way people die from wars!"

"Oh John, how tragic. I didn't see that as we didn't have much time for reading; we spent most of our time trying to heal the injured and maimed."

"Recuperating is resting and reading, if you're lucky. I know that you and the Sisters are well respected. I saw a line of ladies at the Seminary the other day going to one of your meetings."

"I'm not a Sister, John . . . but my sister is. I'm still trying to make up my mind. I am volunteering. We have had so many interested in the Order since the war started; my sister is on the way there now with a lot of lovely ladies who are going to visit the convent in Emmitsburg. I'm just so glad to be home; I want to see my dad. My favorite horse Brandy is also due to arrive with my cousin and his beautiful wife."

The buggy rolled up to the hitching post in front of the farmhouse and Sarah could see her Dad waving from the front porch. "See John, there's my dad. Oh here he comes, that must be my uncle next to him. They look like brothers. My dad is limping like you."

John got down and went over and held out his hand to help Sarah down. "Oh, how polite. Thank you, sir. I never had such a handsome cavalry officer offer me his hand!"

"Don't know why not Sarah, you are very beautiful."

"That she is young man," said her dad Jake as he came over and brushed by the young man, hugging and brushing his daughter's cheek with a soft fatherly kiss.

"Oh Dad, I've missed you . . . that beard still tickles . . . "

"And you still tickle my heart. You are growing into a spitting image of your mother."

"Dad, I brought a guest . . . this is John. He is a lieutenant in the First Vermont Cavalry with Cousin Seth."

"Great . . . was he in the big battle?"

"Oh it's a long story and he'll tell you all about it."

"Oh, I don't mean to be so rude, I'm just so excited . . . I want you to meet my brother, Seth Randolph, from Vermont. He's Seth's father."

They all exchanged pleasantries and Jake picked up Sarah's bags saying, "Let's go up to the porch, it's too hot out here!" Jake started to walk, limping as always.

"Oh Mr. Randolph, I'll take that bag," offered John.

Jake handed it to him saying, "Thanks, this knee of mine's not so good . . . have a bad leg . . . "

John looked at him and started to walk with a limp saying, "This knee of mine's a lot younger than yours, and thanks to Sarah for the invite. Let's see which one of us 'limpers' can get to that front porch first!"

They all laughed and Jake said, "Looks like you got yours in the war; I just got mine from a farm injury."

"You get around good Mr. Randolph. Sarah told me about the lemonade on the front porch. I haven't had that experience since I left Vermont. It's a little hotter down here in Gettysburg, but the front porches all look the same and the shade is still the same. Now I'm with all you Vermonters . . . my heart is yearning for a rock on that old chair to hear your story about selling and raising horses—Vermont Morgan horses!"

"Have a seat . . . you take the big rocker over there."

"I'll make the lemonade Dad," said Sarah.

John got up and asked, "Where is your well? I'll get some cool water."

"It's under that lid there, right on the corner of the porch. Whoever built this house made sure they didn't have to walk too far on a hot sunny day," explained Jake. "Sure comes in handy in the Winter when everything around freezes. We board up those two walls and walk to get the water without leaving the house. We have more shallow wells in the barn. It's easy to dig a shallow well with that Plum Run nearby."

"Yes sir, it's that way around those rocks and walls up there," and he pointed straight out to the hills and dipped out a pail of water.

"Oh, you've been here before then?"

John lifted the pail and walked to the back of the porch where Sarah took it. "Thank you John."

"Welcome Sarah. Oh yes, I was out there with the First in that battle . . . saw your stone house and barn . . . Seth was inside. That's where Major Wells and the First dismounted and we raised our pistols and managed somehow . . . to win that situation. We lost quite a few men. I took one in the leg and the doctor said they would have had to take off my leg if they didn't get the shot out. Thankfully I only got hit by something small and I was lucky they were able to get it out. I have to wait until it heals and then go from there."

"Oh look," said Seth, Sr., "there's a spring wagon coming in . . . "

"That's Brandy out in front . . . look at him moving with his head up high. He's dancing and prancing home! He knows he's home!" said Jake.

"Give Brandy his head and he'll just take you home," echoed Sarah.

RANDOLPH REUNION
AT THE FARM

It was a celebratory time for the Randolphs as it was the first time they were all together at Jake's Gettysburg farm. John sat next to Sarah near the back of the porch while Seth, Sr., and his brother stood and talked and pointed to all the property that Seth, Sr., had purchased. As they talked Seth and Betsy served them tea sandwiches and lemonade.

"That's great Dad! We'll go over there and see it after we eat," said Seth, Jr.

"Good . . . now tell us about your trip or was it trips?" said Seth, Sr.

"We had a wonderful time and it was so much fun to be together. It was a whirlwind of trips. We were in a town called York and then over to Harrisburg . . ."

"And Seth and Brandy were in parades," interjected Betsy. "It was so much of an honor to be treated as we were. They treated us like celebrities . . ."

"And we bought some good Morgans," interrupted Seth as he plopped down in a rocking chair. "I bought a wonderful stallion, almost a cookie cutter of Brandy, except he's black. I bought four bay mares and with the stock you two have we should be able to produce some 'lookers' in a bit. They sold the rest to the military on an open order and are already at the Quartermaster Depot for shipping.

"Our 'stallion and breeding mares' are being brought over by one of the local 'rounders' and he'll give us his bill upon arrival. I figured you both would want them in the stable real quick. They were fantastic lookers and in the prime of breeding years and should not be up for military use at this time.

"We met a lot of horse people from many different cities who all came in and brought us some of their finest stock. They said many had forgotten what a good Morgan looked like until they saw Brandy's picture in their paper that a photographer took somewhere during the Union Cavalry actions. They have some kind of breeder's group they formed and they hope that some of their horses will show up in our Vermont Cavalry. I assured them that they would all go to our men. We would train them and help us maintain our own 'all Morgan' horse cavalry.

"So . . . now that you all have met my friend and Sarah's friend . . ." Seth started.

"Oh, I just met him this morning," interrupted Sarah.

"Really," said Betsy, "and where was that?"

"I was getting ready to leave the field hospital and we bumped into each other and he introduced himself as one of Seth's officer friends."

"Well that was a coincidence," said Betsy with a big grin on her face.

"Well, not really," John smiled and blushed, his cheeks almost matching the color of his hair. "It really was more than a coincidence. I have to admit . . . well, I really wanted to meet her. I saw her in Emmitsburg and . . ."

"And what?" said Sarah.

"Well. Not a coincidence . . . Seth can tell you that when we are in uniform and go through towns the ladies seem to come around me and my horse offering me cakes and cookies and lemondade . . ."

"Like this?" Betsy grabbed the pitcher and started to fill his glass.

Getting redder with each splash of lemonade he smiled and they all burst out laughing. "Look Sarah, you're a lot prettier than all those girls!"

"Prettier?" Edging John on, Jake walked over and asked, "Now what cavalry officer with a war injury would not want to meet my beautiful daughter Sarah?"

John tipped his glass and unknowingly spilled some on the porch. "I'm really a Vermont gentleman and would only approach a lady if I'm really interested!"

"John, I've seen you with all the ladies around you on that beautiful horse. When they hand you that stuff you don't turn red . . . you smile and bow in your saddle, take their offerings and politely pull your horse's head away and then trot on down the road."

"That's right, Seth. But I never met anyone as beautiful as Sarah. I know she belongs to the convent, so I am sorry if I've done anything to embarrass her in front of all of you. She has been so sweet to me and she is so good with her patients. I know she will be a good religious Sister!"

Sarah started to blush and said, "Oh I'm only discerning . . . " and then she looked at Betsy saying, "Betsy can you come into the parlor with me? I want to talk with you."

"Sure Sarah, excuse us gentlemen. We ladies will be back," and they both got up and left for the parlor in the house.

"Wow, I've never seen Sarah at a loss for words. She's never brought a fellow home, ever. You must be special John."

"Look sir, I approached her. I heard she was leaving and I thought I'd never see her again. I just couldn't live with myself if that happened. I don't go around chasing ladies."

"That I can say is very true," said Seth. "We are only teasing you two but I know you, if you weren't interested in her you would have never approached her as politely as you did. That's not how a cavalry officer carries himself. Ladies have a fondness for the uniform. It's a magnet for some."

"Not Sarah," Jake interjected. "She isn't one to look all eyes at a man!"

"Oh really uncle? She's been stealing stares at my red-haired friend and smiling, I've been watching her," joked Seth. "Look, I'm a trained military officer and my eyes are tuned into the things that go on around me. If you have bad eyes as a military officer you are a dead man. If you have bad eyes as a wife seeker you could very well be an unhappy man . . . "

Everyone on the porch burst out laughing and Seth continued, "I've seen that same look in Betsy's eyes, and she's not acting. I saw that look in Sarah's eyes looking at John!"

"Well we'll just have to let the ladies sort this out. Dinner is around eight tonight in the formal dining room. I've asked some of the ladies from town, who are really good at that stuff, to fix us a special dinner. They said they would love to do it. It's a great way to enjoy our evening."

BETSY AND SARAH
IN THE PARLOR

Betsy and Sarah entered the parlor and sat next to each other. "Betsy, can we talk? I've spoken to my sister and now I want to talk to you."

"Sure Sarah, let's talk. This is such a lovely house."

"My sister always knew, even as a child growing up, that she wanted to be a Daughter of Charity. And that is what she is and will always be! I followed in her footsteps as she is such a good role model, especially since mom passed away. I've spent a lot of time with her and the other Sisters in the field doing what they always do. It's fine with me, but . . ."

"But what?" inquired Betsy as her blonde hair captured the rays of sun that peeked through the side window of the parlor.

"It's so hard to find a man like my mom did. I saw that poor lady who was engaged to the general who was killed at Gettysburg. She had made a vow that if he got killed she would join a convent. He was killed and she is really mourning. I see my dad still mourning my mom, I see many mothers mourning; and I've met so many widows that have lost their husbands. I don't know if I could handle that."

"So that's why you want to be a Sister?"

"Oh no . . . you have to be with them and see and do what they do. They are special people who work in our Lord's Garden. What better profession to dedicate your life to than that?"

"I understand what you are saying. I have never wanted to be a Sister because I've always wanted to be married. You know if God wants you in either situation He will somehow instruct you . . . He will guide you. A wife and a mother is a wonderful profession, too. I met your sister and she told me all about their Mother Seton who founded their Order. She told me that Mother Seton was married but her husband died and she was left alone to take care of her children. She was a mother. God worked in her life and she ended up the Mother of their Order."

"When Brandy and I went down to the convent with my wagon and the cavalry escorted me back . . . I saw an officer who . . . well for a moment our eyes met . . . and I felt something I have never felt before . . . then I looked away but his look has been with me since."

"Who did you see? What did he look like?" asked Betsy, by now the sun rays were gone and it was getting late in the afternoon.

"It was John! I was hoping to see him again, but realizing that he was in the cavalry he could be dead. I thought I would never see him again."

"But you are with him now . . . "

"Well, I really was so relieved to see him and when I looked in his eyes I immediately felt a relief. I talked to him . . . he needed a place to relax and recuperate from his injuries."

"But you brought him to your home? There are plenty of rest places you could have sent him to."

"But I trust him. He's a wounded cavalry officer who . . ."

"Who what?" questioned Betsy.

"Well he's a lot like Cousin Seth—a cavalry officer, a handsome, soft-spoken gentleman with wonderful manners—and I feel safe with him. We have so much in common and . . . he's from Vermont."

"It's just like my first impression of your cousin and . . ."

"And what Betsy?"

"And I fell in love with him immediately and married him and we are doing our best to live happily ever after. Sarah, your dad told me we are having a fairly formal dinner tonight, a sort of special evening to share with family, neighbors and friends. My advice to you is—come down tonight dressed in that beautiful taffeta dress that you wore at my husband's dinner and enjoy yourself!"

As they talked the men came in walking and limping. "John can use the back room on the first floor next to mine," suggested Jake. "Dinner is around eight. The ladies from town will be here with 'snacks' or something like that with my wine at seven. See you all then! I'm going to take an after-noon nap."

Sarah glanced at John saying, "I'm going out to the barn with Brandy for a while. If you get a chance come out and see him!"

SARAH, SETH AND BRANDY
IN THE BARN

Sarah was going to a place she loved the most—the barn. It was a special sanctuary for her to clear her thoughts among the smells and the horses that fueled her love of life. She was home and free and somewhat clearer about her emotions and as she neared Brandy's stall he looked up from his feed bin and whinnied at her.

She walked over and stroked him and picked up a curry comb and started to groom him. He was the perfect size for her five foot five frame and it was easy to reach up and scratch his ears. She did and he put his head down for more of it.

"You are home now, Brandy. I am home now, too. When we are away and out of sorts just give us our heads and freedom and we always come straight home . . . and into our barn."

She heard footsteps behind her and turned and saw Cousin Seth carrying a water bucket.

"Oh hello Sarah. I gave him his grain and now I'm going to give him water. He's such a special horse; he bonds . . . if he likes you!"

"Well it's obvious he likes you," Sarah replied back lovingly.

"And it's obvious to me that my cavalry friend likes you!"

"Why do you say that Seth?" Sarah asked in a teasing manner.

"All kidding aside, I have known him a long time. We have been together in battle and in peace. And I've seen him intereact with women. He's like that bumblebee buzzing around and burring a hole in that white pine beam up above you. He is quite focused and nothing, short of hitting him over the head, stops him from his mission. That's John. I've seen him around so many female admirers but he never veers off mission . . . he stays on an honorable course. Now he's injured and healing and I was shocked to see him with you!

"I asked him today about you. He said he saw you at Emmitsburg but was told by headquarters to 'respect the Sisters . . . they are God's angels.' When he was in the hospital he saw you rushing around and he asked one of the Sisters what rank you were. The Sister laughed and said, 'Oh we are not like the military we don't have ranks' and said you were not even a postulant you were just helping. He was satisfied and stayed away. Then one of the Sisters told him you were leaving and going home. He said he approached you because he was interested . . . then he laughed and said, 'I really care about her and well . . . we'll see what happens.' He does have a sense of humor but more importantly—he is an honorable man."

"Wow cousin, that's a lot to absorb."

"Enjoy the time together, Sarah."

"You and Betsy have a special love that I've been yearning for all of my life," Sarah said smiling. She hugged Brandy and then Seth and said lovingly, "I'll see you at dinner Seth. Wear your uniform and I hope John will be in his uniform, too."

AN EVENING CELEBRATION
IN THE FARMHOUSE

"This is quite a party Mr. Randolph," John said as they stood next to the long cherry sideboard in the beautiful dining room of the old stone farmhouse.

"So glad you can be here to celebrate with us John. You sure add a dashing demeanor and the locals are enjoying you. The ladies have told me how gallant you look in your uniform and the color of your hair matches some of the red military epaulets on your uniform."

"This is a great way to rest and recover and now I can heal gracefully, and in a very wonderful place with fellow Vermonters."

Jake looked at John as Sarah came over to offer them something to drink. "We have claret, white wine, lemonade and then this beautifully colored liquid called brandy."

"Oh thank you Sarah. This is a special occasion so I'll have some brandy," said John.

"And you Dad?"

"Oh since I'm in the company of Seth and John, two heroes, I'll have some brandy, too! I was once told about a famous man named Samuel Johnson who said, 'Claret is the liquor for boys; port for men, but he who aspires to be a hero must drink brandy.'"

"I never heard that one sir. But this is the stuff we officers drink in a public house. It is what most of us prefer . . . we officers must maintain our dignity at all times . . . with only a drink or two!"

John was entertained as Sarah, dressed in her beautiful blue and multi-colored dress, returned with some cakes. "It's getting late and the ladies are cleaning up, would you two like some of these cakes before they take them away?" Sarah asked.

"Thanks Sarah." Jake took two and passed the plate to John.

"No thanks, . . . but thank you Sarah."

"I'll see the ladies out Dad. They all had a wonderful time and it's getting late for them."

As Sarah turned and left Jake said, "I was going into town tomorrow to post a new job offer for a manager needed to help on a Morgan horse breed-ing farm . . . but you saved me the trip by resting here. Seth and Betsy will be running my brother's farm and I thought you might enjoy helping Sarah while you are here."

John watched as Sarah moved gracefully to the table near them picking up dishes and carrying them to the kitchen.

"See, she's always doing something homey," Jake remarked, "but not always in that beautiful dress. You should see her in the barn with the horses and hay all over her. She's good with a pitchfork. I'm heading off to bed. Seth and Betsy are out on the front porch enjoying the beautiful moon that shines brightly over the Round Tops. Was a night like that when my Brandy was born. Yes sir, the melon moon was the first to see him."

John got up. "I'd like to take you up on the job offer. That sounds like a wonderful way to rest and relax, but what does Sarah want?"

"She's probably out on the porch and you can ask her yourself. Sarah is always in charge around here when she's home . . . and it looks like she is staying home!" He shook John's hand and politely left the room leaving John alone.

A MOON OVER
THE ROUND TOPS

"was one great hospital of wounded soldiers;
the churches, the public buildings all filled
with the maimed, the sick and suffering . . ."
- HARRIET BEECHER STOWE

John held onto his empty glass and headed out through the parlor door to the front porch where he saw Sarah, Betsy, and Seth talking softly in the light of the full moon. They turned around and said together, "Over here John!"

John slowly walked over, trying not to limp. "Wow, never thought I'd see this view again after being knocked down by that bullet over there on that ridge. What a beautiful sight with the moon shining over those mountaintops."

"That's exactly what I told our visitors tonight," replied Seth. "They were coming to congratulate me about what the First did at Gettysburg near here and I told them I was safe in that stone barn under orders to hold it while you were out there with Major Wells; he was leading the charge and you were there too but took a bullet and got knocked down. I wasn't taking any credit for what the First did that night. I told them to congratulate you, one of the real heroes!"

John started to blush in the moonlight. "Look, he's blushing. Isn't he handsome?" said Betsy. "No wonder all the ladies gather around him."

"John we all were so proud of you tonight," said Sarah, "and my dad and uncle were telling everyone how honored they were to have you as their guest."

"John, hand me your glass. Ladies, hold out yours. I brought a bottle of your dad's best brandy. Please let me pour all of us a drink for a special toast under a Gettysburg full moon!"

They all held out their glasses and Seth poured as John said, "To all those who fought and lived and died at Gettysburg . . . let's drink . . . let's honor all of them and their horses and animals, too!"

They all lifted their glasses and drank slowly. Sarah took a sip and her eyes blinked, and Betsy acknowledged, "That's a lot stronger than lemonade!"

"That's the first time I have tasted brandy," replied Sarah.

"It's what the locals offer us when our cavalry enters their towns. I think they just like uniformed men on horseback," said John.

Seth laughed, "Not all, John." Pulling out a telegram from his coat pocket he announced, "I have some good news from Headquarters! Let me read you what it says, 'Capt. Randolph. Find Lt. Reynolds a place to rest. On October 1st you two will report to Giesboro Point. More details to follow. HDQTRS.'"

John looked at them all somewhat in awe.

"So Lieutenant, I'm following my orders and now giving you your orders! You are confined to the Randolph farm under the care of Sarah Randolph until I can make further arrangements for all four of us to travel to Washington. If we are lucky we may see the famous poet Walt Whitman, or the famous author Harriet Beecher Stowe, or even President or Mrs. Lincoln! Betsy and I are heading off to bed. We are tired from this glorious day and we leave you two to enjoy the rest of this bright moon that we are all blessed to see."

HALF-FULL GLASSES
AND A FULL MOON

Seth and Betsy smiled and put their empty glasses on the nearby table. Saying goodnight they entered the parlor door and disappeared into the house. John and Sarah were left alone with their half-full glasses and the light of a full moon.

"Well, I guess I have my orders!" said John with a smile as he tipped his glass towards Sarah who was relaxing in the cool night air. Soft summer breezes were now starting to move in off the Round Tops.

"I guess we both have our orders," stated Sarah.

John put down his glass on the nearby table and leaned in close to Sarah saying, "Well ma'am, I love my new orders!"

Sarah could smell the aroma of his blue cavalry uniform and breathing in the cool night air said, "Well sir, you also have stall cleaning duty while you await going to Washington, D.C."

John put his arm around her and kissed the top of her head catching the smell of her perfume. "I am so lucky to be alive and to be here with you. We better both go to our rooms. There is a chill blowing in off the Round Tops, but the warmth of this evening is a new beginning for both of us."

Sarah looked up and kissed him on the cheek. "Breakfast is at six Lieutenant and in the barn by seven to feed the horses. I just love it in the barn in the morning."

"Me too," agreed John as he took Sarah's hand and led her off the porch into the house. "Goodnight Sarah and thanks to you and your family this is the most memorable time in my life!"

THE RANDOLPHS AND JOHN IN WASHINGTON, D.C.

"I can make more generals, but horses cost money."
- ABRAHAM LINCOLN

Seth and John peered out in awe from inside their carriage as it passed the White House. Even though there was still construction going on all around and despite the Civil War, it was breathtaking to them.

"Think we might see the President?" John asked as the carriage bumped along.

"That's the White House," stated the cavalry officer who was traveling inside the carriage with them, "and we're about 6 or 7 miles away from Giesboro Point, Camp Stoncham and the Cavalry Depot Headquarters. They will supply horses to the Army of the Potomac. As our army heads into Virginia we'll need hundreds of thousands more horses for our cavalry. The South could still try to attack and we have some intelligence about Jubal Early. Your First Vermont dealt a lot with him and we need that strategy and details, too. They also want you two to survey the area as we loop around and see what other fortifications are needed. With the experience you two have, we can prevent an attack and coordinate your Morgan horse purchasing program with ours.

"As we scout the area you may see the President and his wife Mary Todd out in their carriage visiting hospitals. They go often as there are patients in D.C. being treated at so many hospitals. I've taken them in and out and have seen them both at times with flowers and fruits for the sick.

"Our new Cavalry Bureau is drawing up a strategic supply chain for horses for the entire cavalry, including your own First. Major General George Stoneman chose the farm at Giesboro Point because it is flat and easily accessible to the Potomac River. The government took possession of it on August 12, 1863.

"We seize property for military purposes in and around Washington to thwart any Confederate threat as they are fluid. This is a part of our defense of Washington, always constructed on the high ground.

"We have built wharves along the Potomac shoreline with stables to house and hold more than 25,000 horses or more if necessary. We are building a lot of supporting facilities and buildings, and other necessary infrastructures.

"We are approaching Young's brick manor house and the depot's administrative headquarters. We'll stop back there after you do your rounds. This is the world's largest cavalry depot in the world, so you can see why you are here!

"It's due to open in January 1864 and it's staffed with enough people who will grow their own vegetables, slaughter their own meat supply, and even mill sufficient wheat. We'll need 100 blacksmiths and there is a steam gristmill to grind grain and cut hay and straw—enough for all the horses serviced here.

"In our military design, Giesboro Cavalry Depot is a vital addition to our Potomac Army's cavalry arm. Unfortunately in the past our cavalry was always outperformed by their Southern counterpart.

"When we are finished today you can return to the hotel with your notes and then submit a written report through your First Cavalry Headquarters by mid-November. You will be notified later with more details.

"All this for horses and it all came with enormous expense and as President Lincoln told the War Department, 'I can make more generals, but horses cost money.'"

Seth and John both laughed and Seth responded, "President Lincoln got that right! We try to find and buy the Vermont Morgan horses we ride. We only have half of our cavalry on a Morgan, and we're running out of Morgans and money!"

While Seth and John were on their secret military mission, Betsy and Sarah were enjoying the Capitol scenery in a separate carriage. As they approached their hotel Betsy quietly said to Sarah, "Tonight we are going to a play at Ford's Theater not far from our hotel. They will be singing and portraying 'The Battle Hymn of the Republic' before the featured play! It will be a very special night!"

THE RANDOLPHS AND JOHN
AT FORD'S THEATER

The two couples left the Historic Willard Hotel. Sarah was wearing a cotton homespun white top and black plaid bottom dress and Betsy was attired in an empire waist blue floral cotton gown. John and Seth were sporting their full cavalry uniforms. The White House was in the background and it was a regal scene as they stepped into the two-horse-drawn carriage for the short trip to Ford's Theater.

"I must say, not a prettier scene in Washington, D.C., tonight ladies and gentlemen than you four getting into my carriage," said the driver.

"Well thank you," said Seth. "We're from Gettysburg and we are so honored to be guests here in the Capitol."

"Gettysburg . . . wow . . . newspapers are reporting that President Lincoln is going to be there when they dedicate the National Cemetery in November."

"Oh, we didn't know that," said Seth.

As they pulled away the White House melted in the distance as a soft rising and hazed full moon started to appear. It was a beautiful setting and the night air hugged everyone in a pleasant manner.

"Oh my hair," said Betsy softly.

"Mine too," laughed Sarah as they reached for their matching scarves and gently placed them over their heads. John and Seth reached over to draw down the rolled-up silk blinds.

"Oh, leave them open. Let's enjoy the view and the ride . . . it's as close to being on Brandy's back out in the countryside as I'll get on this trip," joked Sarah.

"It's going to be hot in the theater, so let's enjoy this coolness. This is so exciting that all of us can be together in our nation's Capitol! This is so special and I hope you officers got all your business accomplished," said Betsy.

"Mostly," said John as he finally got comfortable next to Sarah and reached for her hand. "Softest hands I've ever touched."

Seth spoke in an authoritative manner, "We have a report to write and some follow up on the military business and our final report is due later. Did you know that Julia Ward Howe wrote 'The Battle Hymm of the Republic' in the room where John and I are staying?"

Sarah and Betsy smiled while Betsy added, "Our hostess told us that President Lincoln stayed in our room before he was inaugurated. We were amazed, especially because it is more suited for us ladies."

"It is quite Victorian, with a lot of silk . . . not much cotton as we country girls are used to having. But it is gorgeous. We sleep in two huge fluffy beds," replied Sarah.

"We were told that they held the famous 'Peace Convention' on our floor. It was a last political endeavor done in an effort to avert Civil War," added John. "Our two beds are not as fancy as yours are, more like those they have in a country inn in Pennsylvania like where Seth and I stayed in a room together one night. We were lucky to get lodging passing through one of those small country towns. Our horses got to stay in a barn, too. We all had a good night's sleep for a change . . . sure beats the hard ground."

The carriage moved noisily through the mist that was starting to fall from a cloud passing overhead and it wasn't long before they heard, "Whoa, final stop folks. Here's the Ford Theater. You folks will hear 'The Battle Hymn of the Republic' before the play begins. It was performed here first for President Lincoln. This is getting to be quite a favorite place to come."

They exited the carriage with John aiding Sarah and Seth helping Betsy. "I'll be waiting down at the end for you when it's over."

They all smiled and thanked the driver and Seth walked Betsy inside while John and Sarah graciously followed behind. They were greeted and they showed their tickets and were escorted to their seats about halfway down and in the center.

It was hotter inside and Seth jokingly said, "It smells like when you put on some of that fancy makeup and perfume Betsy," and they all laughed.

"Well that's what actors do," joked John. "They don't go on stage looking like us."

"Well the way the ladies were looking at you escorting me down the aisle . . . maybe you should be on the stage," Sarah said in a low tone.

"You two are the most beautiful ladies in the theater. Look at the men staring," declared Seth.

"It's your uniforms," said Betsy. "Everyone loves a cavalry officer in full dress. There's nothing more dashing. And nothing makes everyone feel safer and securer than being under the guard of the Vermont Cavalry! Oh Seth," added Betsy looking faint and raising her hand up to her mouth.

"Are you alright?" Seth asked, turning to comfort her and handing her his handkerchief.

"Oh," and she sat down and put her head forward breathing deeply. "I just need some air!"

"Are you sure you're alright honey? We can go outside for some air."

"Oh . . . that won't help Seth. I think something just kicked me."

"What? It's just the four of us here . . . who kicked you?"

They all looked at her with puzzled looks on their faces.

Betsy smiled and her mouth moved softly as she announced, "Our baby . . . we're going to have a baby!"

The first half of the play was long and they all were enjoying it, but Seth could see that Betsy was tiring. "We're going to leave and go back to the hotel at intermission," he whispered as he leaned out in front of them from his seat.

They all stood up and clapped as the curtain went down. "We will all leave . . . we are getting tired, too," answered John as he yawned.

Sarah put her hand to her mouth and yawned saying softly, "Oh I'm yawning with glee. Seth and Betsy are going to have a baby. Oh how wonderful!"

A MOONLIT NIGHT
IN WASHINGTON

The ride back to their hotel was shorter or so it seemed. "It's always a shorter ride back to anywhere you came from," said Seth.

"Even when we re-trace our steps on a cavalry mission," replied John.

"This evening was so special but Seth, I think I'll just go straight up to the room and you can escort me. We are to depart for Gettysburg at noon. Sarah, you and John should stroll around and enjoy this moonlit night. Look how it is rising above the White House! I'll see you, Sarah, when you come back to our room. If I'm sleeping you can thank this precious baby that is starting to bounce in my belly!"

"Oh Betsy, I love you! That's the best, happiest news we've all gotten in this Civil War. John and I will savor the news and stroll slowly around. Oh look, there is a bench. We'll just waltz over there and bathe in the good news and the precious moonlight!"

"And you and John will be the godparents!" added Seth. "Betsy, you've had this all planned," kidded Seth. "You were just waiting for a very special moment!"

"Come on Seth," Betsy grabbed his hand, "you and I can enjoy this special time alone. Let John and Sarah share this special night . . . alone!"

They both smiled and hand in hand walked slowly and joyfully in the front door of the hotel and disappeared behind its closing door.

"John, look how happy they are. There is a war going on all around them and they are so happy. It was such a wonderful night, and such a wonderful place to hear of their new baby. We need more good news like that in this war-torn world. Wait until our dads hear the news in Gettysburg. They will be so excited. They are probably setting on the porch looking at that moon up there right now!"

John guided her to the bench saying, "This is one of the happiest days of my life. I haven't had a lot of happy days but it's been all happiness since I met you, Sarah!"

"John, that is such a wonderful compliment, thank you. You've brought so much peace and joy into my life, too!"

"Let's set down on this bench and savor the scene. The White House sure looks good in the moonlight. As a cavalry officer it really adds a special meaning to what we are fighting for in this war. We sometimes lose sight of a clear view of life in times of war. I have a focused picture of a future now," and he lifted his arm and inserted his hand under his shirt collar and pulled out a silver chain with a gold ring on it.

"What's that John?"

"Many of us cavalry officers, especially me, carry charms or religious medals or something of special value, always close to our hearts; especially in a battle situation.

"My mom died during my birth. I never knew her. I was raised by an aunt and my dad remarried. He was heartbroken for years and when I joined the First Vermont he gave me my mom's wedding ring and said, 'Here son, you'll be needing this more than me. Your mom was the special love of my life . . . sometimes you only get one chance to find love. I want you to have this. Someday you can give this to that special person who is the love of your life. Choose wisely . . . Mom and I will always love you!'"

Sarah started to cry softly. As the tears rolled down her cheeks the moonlight made them sparkle.

"Sarah, you are that special person in my life. I can't wait any longer to ask you. I have to take my chance just like dad said," and he knelt down on one knee, his blue uniform brushing against her cotton dress. "Sarah, will you marry me? Will you accept this ring and my love?"

Sarah leaned forward and kissed him on the lips. Then she smiled at him and put out her hand saying, "Of course I will Lieutenant!" He slid the ring off the silver chain and placed it on her finger. "It's a perfect fit, John. I love you!"

A MOONLIT NIGHT
IN GETTYSBURG

S eth, Sr., and Jake sat on the porch rocking when Jake asked, "Lemonade? Or would you rather have some brandy, brother?"

"Oh lemonade, let's leave that brandy for those brave soldiers out there!"

"Speaking of Brandy, look at him out there in that meadow with all of those Morgan mares. There's ten of them with him. Those four new ones Seth got are sure cookie-cutter type Vermont Morgan mares. Can't wait to see what Brandy and those mares can do together."

Jake got up and left the porch while Seth, Sr., kept rocking. The moon was now overhead and it was magnificent. The cascading light lit up the shadows of all the rocks and boulders in the far distance. Jake returned with two glasses of lemonade and handed one to his brother. He sat down next to him and they both rocked and sipped.

"What a night. I suppose the moon is shining bright in Washington, too. Bet the kids are having a great night. Bet my son is going to be surprised."

"Surprised about what brother?"

"Oh, before they left Betsy told me a secret. She's going to have a baby. She was going to tell my son on the next romantic occasion in Washington. I bet she told him tonight . . . doesn't get anymore romantic than under a melon moon like that."

"Congratulations brother! You're going to be a grandfather. Sarah is going to be surprised, too."

"About what brother?"

"Just before they left, John asked me for permission to marry Sarah."

"Oh really? Well that happened fast."

"Not fast enough for Sarah. Before they left she felt Washington would be a real romantic place and she was praying that John would ask her to marry him."

"So she didn't know he had asked you for permission?"

"Oh no, I wasn't going to spoil that proposing moment. I just wished them all a good time and said that we old timers would take care of the horses until they got back."

"I'll bet they are both over the moon down there in Washington. I'll bet those two First Vermont Cavalry officers are gonna come back here so happy."

"I'll bet they will break out a bottle of my best brandy . . . that one in there that is the color of Brandy!"

GETTYSBURG–A MEADOW
NEAR BIG ROUND TOP

The melon moon and the mares were the first to enjoy his return to the meadow where he was born. His equine mother was nudging another one of his equine brothers and all of the night creatures whispered, "Welcome home Brandy!"

Overhead the white clouds moved slowly and sparkles of moonlight lit up the Adams County, Pennsylvania, landscape. This peaceful farmland was a battlefield.

Fireflies danced randomly through the moonlit skyline and the crickets sung their noisy tunes. The beautiful Morgan mares gathered around Brandy in the field, including his mother. He watched the peaceful scene and looked out as the moon stood almost overhead of the distant Round Top mountains.

A gust of wind blew softly in and then out of their pasture and across the oddly shaped hills into the small town of Gettysburg nearby . . .

PART FOUR

Front of White House. Color Lithography by E. Sachs & Co., Lithographer. Courtesty of Library of Congress.

BREAKFAST IN
WASHINGTON, D.C.

Seth, Jr., and his wife Betsy, and cousin Sarah Randolph and her new fiancé John Reynolds, gathered for breakfast after the beautiful and momentous evening in the nation's Capitol.

The memorable full moon scene over the White House from the previous evening was gone and a cool wind was blowing outside. They could see the trees around the White House swaying in the wind dropping some of their colorful fall foliage. Inside the Historic Willard Hotel it was cozy where a fire was toasting the chilled air in the breakfast room.

"Coffee or tea?" asked the waitress who was dressed nice enough to be attending a presidential ball.

"Coffee," they all said as they were astonished at the beautiful dress the waitress was wearing.

"I have to be careful, we are serving President Lincoln at an afternoon tea in the Blue Room at noon. We were told this morning that he is having some special guests from Gettysburg, two heroic battlefield cavalry officers and their beautiful ladies. The President often hosts our local heroes when they are in town. The hotel owner said that the special guests are staying in our hotel."

"Oh," said Seth, "that will certainly be a special occasion for those guests."

"We are from Gettysburg, too," said Betsy.

"Yes and we wish them well. We are leaving at noon to return to Gettysburg," said Sarah, adding with a deep sigh, "finally I can announce our engagement to my dad!"

John looked across at Sarah, saying, "He already knows Sarah. Before we left I asked him for permission to marry his daughter and he said 'Absolutely, what's taking you so long to ask!'"

Sarah giggled, "But John, he didn't know what my answer would be."

"Well he said, 'Oh she'll say yes!'"

As they were chatting and the waitress was pouring their coffee a tall cavalry officer with a beard and in his full dress uniform walked into the room and stared at them.

"Oh, there is General Simpson. He's from our War Department and stops in here for coffee, but he looks like he is on official business," said the waitress as the servers were now around their table with their breakfast.

The General came up to the table and both Seth and John got up and saluted, "Good morning, Sir."

Saluting back the General commanded, "Be seated and enjoy the wonderful breakfast. I have coffee here once in a while and enjoy that view of the White House—it boosts my spirits in these dreadful times!"

"Thank you Sir, please have a seat," offered Seth as he pointed to an empty place at their table.

"This is a special set up," said the General, who pulled out the chair and sat down. "I'm General Simpson and am serving in the War Department. We've had some wonderful generals before me in this position. Hard to keep up with the standards they set. We lost General Mansfield who was mortally wounded at the Battle of Antietam last September. He was personally leading the troops when a sniper's bullet hit him squarely in the right chest."

"Oh, how sad," said Betsy as she reached for her husband Seth and gave him a loving touch on the side of his face.

"Which brings me to why I am here! President and Mrs. Lincoln were late last evening for the performance at Ford's Theater. I was there waiting for them and I saw you two beautiful couples walking down to your seats. It was a marvelous sight, and the crowd was in awe of your presence. When I inquired with the owners of the theater they told me you had special seats arranged by Colonel Anderson of the First Vermont Cavalry and that you were in town on military business.

"When President and Mrs. Lincoln arrived I told them all about you and we got to their box late after intermission. When I looked down you were gone. I told the President and he said, 'Locate them and invite them tomorrow for tea in the Blue Room around noon. I want to meet them.'

"Now it his folksy custom to choose who he wants to meet and his protocol is a plain demeanor like you Vermonters know. Don't be alarmed if he addresses each one of you by your first name . . . that's his custom. He's not much for formalities so feel comfortable, just call him Mr. President."

Sarah and John, and Seth and Betsy put down their eating utensils and sat up in shock as they watched the General reach for his poured coffee adding, "So, after the end of the play the President and Mrs. Lincoln left and I went to see the theater owners. They gave me your address here and

I came over last night, but it was late and you were all in your rooms. So I advised the hotel owners to set up this breakfast meeting with an extra seat and advised them of the President's intentions."

Seth and John, dressed in their casual military attire, stood up and both saluting said, "This is quite an honor Sir . . . and we accept. What a humbling surprise and we all will love to attend."

The General smiled and set back adding, "We found out all about you two at the Battle of Gettysburg. We learned by word of mouth what the First did out at that stone barn. The President will be going to Gettysburg November 19th to dedicate the Soldiers' National Cemetery. As the 16th President of the United States and with actions to preserve the Union and end slavery, he signed a Senate Joint Resolution last year to award our country's highest award—the Army Medal of Honor. He is most anxious to talk to as many of our veterans as he can, especially if they are in and around Washington. He was humbled to hear how you two helped to win that Battle at Gettysburg with the First Vermont Cavalry."

The General stood up and placed his napkin on the empty plate. "Now I must leave you. I have a War Planning Meeting with the President at 10 a.m. We will see you at noon in the Blue Room in full dress uniform and you ladies dressed in those gorgeous dresses you wore last evening. I want the President to see what he missed last night. Also, the President wants me to make sure you are all invited and participating at the Gettysburg Memorial Ceremony on the 19th. Captain Randolph, he saw that picture of you and your horse, Brandy, at the Gala in York . . . he wants to make sure you are both out front in that ceremony, too!" He saluted the table, turned and marched stoically out through the back door.

"Oh my," said Betsy as she caressed her belly. "What a surprise and it's either my heart that's beating on my chest or flutters from the beautiful creature growing in my belly. How will we ever get our gowns and uniforms ready by noon?"

"Oh, don't worry about that ma'am," said the waitress serving their table. "The General left orders to have your clothes prepared by noon for the event. We will come to your rooms at ten and pick up your clothes. Our staff are use to handling it. The carriage leaves for the White House at eleven."

DINNER AT THE RANDOLPH FARM IN GETTYSBURG

Seth, Sr., and Jake sat on the front porch, the leaves were almost all brown and the evening breezes were picking up. It was a little too cold for lemonade so they were enjoying some port with their dinner. Brandy was in the nearby meadow with the mares and the new black stallion Seth had acquired was inside the barn. He was a dandy, but very high spirited and still needed some manners.

As they rocked and ate a light meal Jake commented, "The kids said they were leaving Washington at noon by train. I sure will be glad for them to come home."

"Me too. I don't want to see much more traveling for Betsy in her condition. Too much excitement is not good for a lady who is expecting."

"Well, how much excitement can there be relaxing in Washington while the men are handling a military situation?" asked Jake.

"There is something exciting coming up our lane right now. Look at that rider. It looks like the fellow from the town railroad telegraph office."

"Can't be anything that important, he's not coming that fast. Looks like he is enjoying the scenery. You know those guys that work in those offices in town don't get out much. Sure must be a treat. Whoever sent the telegraph for immediate delivery must of spent a lot—that's the manager in saddle."

"Hello Mr. Randolph . . . er Mr. Randolphs. Sure is a lovely evening to be setting on the porch. There's a nice breeze coming off those Round Tops!" said the manager.

"Hello Mr. Phillips," said Jake. "We did not expect a personal delivery of our telegram!"

"We were closing when it came in late and I wanted to deliver it myself. Haven't been out here since they cleaned up after the big battle."

"Well tie up your horse and set a spell. Have some port and let's see what you have for us," said Jake.

Mr. Phillips tied his horse to the white picket fence and sauntered over to the porch steps and ascended in a gentlemanly fashion. "You sure have the best spot out here. Just lovely. Look at those Round Tops . . ."

"Have a seat in the big rocker. There's a bottle of port and some glasses. We were just relaxing. The kids are due back from Washington soon, so that message may be from them."

"No sir. It's from the War Department in Washington."

"Oh my. Let me see it," said Jake as Seth, Sr., got up and looked over Jake's shoulder as he carefully opened the envelope.

```
DEAR RANDOLPHS. PRESIDENT LINCOLN WILL MEET
WITH THE RANDOLPHS AND LT. REYNOLDS IN THE
BLUE ROOM OF THE WHITE HOUSE TODAY AT NOON.
YOUR PARTY WILL BE OFF BY TRAIN FROM WASH-
INGTON TO GETTYSBURG SOMETIME THAT EVENING.
ETA WILL BE CONFIRMED BY THEM IN SEPARATE
TELEGRAM FROM THE TRAIN CLOSER TO ARRIVAL.
GENERAL SIMPSON, WAR DEPARTMENT.
```

"Wow," said Mr Phillips, "now that is exciting!"

NOON AT THE WHITE HOUSE

"I would like to speak in terms of praise due to the many
brave officers and soldiers who have fought in the cause of the war."
- ABRAHAM LINCOLN

"You know what the papers say Sir," said General Simpson to President Lincoln, "there's more pictures of General Custer out there than you!" They were in his second-floor office overlooking the still green lawn outside the Executive Mansion waiting to greet the Randolphs and Lt. Reynolds.

"True, but the 'flamboyant cavalryman' won't be in this one. These unassuming officers from the First Vermont Cavalry, Seth and John, two heroes from the Gettysburg Battle will stand alone with me. Captain Seth Randolph sure looked majestic on top of that beautiful horse he owns. What's that horse's name again, General?" questioned President Lincoln.

"Brandy, Sir. And that horse, like so many others, are unheralded heroes that serve their masters. Horses perish in man's conflicts and the only things that remain on man's battlefields are their bleaching bones washed by the rainwaters."

"Well," said the President, "water is cleansing but not always pure. You know I only drink water and so do our horses and so do Temperance Committees. One such committee once promised me that water's all they drink. They visited as a group here in July, when the flies were awful and the local waterways smelly, and they assured me that they only drank our terrible Washington water. They insisted that because our army drinks too much whiskey . . . the good Lord surely curses them.

"They challenged me by saying, 'That's why we don't win so much.' I rebutted quickly and whimsically saying, 'Such a curse is unwarranted. It's a known fact that the other side drinks much more and worse whiskey than ours. But their water is reported purer!'"

"I agree Mr. President, but the newspapers are usually kind to you by often reporting in various papers that, 'President Lincoln drinks little or no wine; never truly caring for wine or liquors of any sort, water only, and absolutely never abuses tobacco.'"

"So be it General. The paper writers are a colorful lot. The question is forever debated, 'Water or Whiskey,' but both can be deadly at times. We have the Washington Canal that runs between the White House and the murky Potomac River which has been reported, especially in the heat of summer, in the papers with this byline, 'Any long-term resident of the White House will suffer eventually and not necessarily from the water or whiskey served.'"

"Indeed Mr. President. They glamorize the scenic beauty of the Washington Canal and White House environs in the Spring and Fall, but fail to popularize the fact that the Canal has been suspected to cause the typhoid-like disease that afflicted your beloved Willie, ultimately killing him and now afflicting Tad!"

The two took a moment to watch the arrival of the beautiful Presidential carriage horses that were working in perfect pulling harmony.

The President finished his discourse by saying, "My doctors still don't know the cause of my occasional headaches and my poor wife's often debilitating migraines. Many times when I'm away her telegrams are a constant reminder of her tiredness and headaches . . . and this was often our daily conversations before our boys came down with that dreaded typhoid fever. This is why we often seek our rest and recuperation far away from this city!

"That is why, when we first arrived, Mrs. Lincoln and I often took afternoon rides in the White House carriage to seek the fresh air that our guests are now enjoying as they ride here. Look, they have the window curtains open and I can see their heads popping in and out of the open windows. Oh we know how that feels. Often, even if we are 'under the weather' we readily take a healing, refreshing ride."

"Well Mr. President, just take a look at that scene out front. It sure is encouraging to see those young people who are coming to visit with such a wonderful attitude. One couple is going to have a baby and the other couple just got engaged last night."

"And how do you know all of this General?" inquired the President.

"Sir, I am a general in the War Department; we have a lightning fast telegraph and quick-tongued people and when you told me last night to invite them for lunch I sent off some telegrams and visited their hotel. Quick responses came back including this one I received this morning about Sarah Randolph from a Gettysburg store owner:

ALL THE TOWNSPEOPLE COULD SEE THAT MR. REYN-
OLDS ADMIRED SARAH AND WAS VERY PROUD OF
HER. LATELY, SHE BOUGHT PRETTY FASHIONABLE
CLOTHES IN TOWN TO IMPRESS HIM. SHE ADOPTED
SOME DAINTY LITTLE AIRS AND GRACES AND WAS
VERY GAY AND LIGHTHEARTED. SHE LOOKED HOPE-
FUL AND HAPPY IN HIS PRESENCE.

The President smiled and reflectively said, "She sounds just like my own Mary Todd when I courted her. I can't wait to meet her!"

NOON APPROACHING THE WHITE HOUSE

The matched pair of moving Morgan horses pulling the Presidential carriage lifted their heads high.

"Look honey," said Sarah, "they know they are going home. Look at those majestic Morgans pulling this carriage."

"When we left Vermont enroute to Gettysburg, we noticed so many of the beautiful Currier & Ives prints had Morgan horses depicted in public places. I had thought Morgans were only located in our beloved Vermont," said Betsy as she bounced softly in the well-cushioned carriage.

"Morgans and Currier & Ives prints are everywhere now darling," replied Seth, Jr., as he held her hand tightly. "We have seen them in so many places, even in some of the hostile southern places where we have been fighting."

"We took notice of what was being said about the horses in those prints around those parts. Some argued that a distinct relationship existed in a new breed called a Standardbred and our beloved Morgan breed. I heard officers discussing it, especially those who like 'racing horses,'" added John as the carriage came to a stop next to the walkway leading to a special entrance to the White House.

"Well, that's why I can't wait 'til we can get to our farms and do some serious breeding with the wonderful Vermont Morgan stock we have in our barns," said Seth, Jr., as he stepped out of the carriage door opened by one of the attendants. "Thank you sir," he said as he turned around to assist his stunning Betsy from the carriage while John followed her and turned to aid his equally beautiful Sarah.

They turned and the President of the United States stood there tall, with his hat in his hands saying, "Welcome to the White House. May I address you individually as Seth and Betsy and John and Sarah?" and he walked in front of each addressing them by their first name and shaking their outstretched hands individually with gracious bows and smiles exchanged.

"Oh Mr. President," interjected the General, "what a beautiful picture you all make. And that is why I notified Mr. Matthew Brady's local office and he quickly dispatched one of his aides, a Mr. Gardner, to come over with his traveling darkroom cameras to photograph this meeting. He is here to capture this wonderful event—an Illinois log-splitting President and Vermonters from the first state to abolish slavery in 1777!"

The President and the Vermont party looked at him with a gleeful gaze, and the President said, "Brady once asked me permission to film the battles and I said, 'Ok, but you pay for it!' I thought he was out on the battlefield with his box cameras?"

"Oh no Sir, there are a lot of secrets in this war, but he readily reminds everyone that he rarely visits the battlefields personally—he has many assistants, just like we Washington generals have many assistants—to personally handle the business necessary on the battlefields."

The surprised Lincoln put on his top hat, smiled the biggest grin and gathered them all in front of the Presidential carriage as the photographer loomed overtop his box camera. The cameraman smiled saying, "That is great Mr. President. The carriage is right behind you and you are right between those beautiful Vermont ladies in their colorful dresses and their beaus beside them in their full dress uniforms. That's perfect. I have the Morgan horses in it, too. Now everyone smile and hold that pose. You will see giant flashes but just stay in that pose 'til I say it's ok to move." Then the cameraman ducked his head under the hood and leaned into the camera, "That's perfect hold that pose . . ."

Frequent flashes and pops occurred as the horses whinnied softly. "Perfect . . . this will be a dandy. Ok you can relax."

"Custer's a dandy, Mr. President. But he won't be in this dandier picture!" commented General Simpson.

LATE EVENING AT THE RANDOLPH FARM IN GETTYSBURG

"On March 20, 1748, while on a surveying expedition near a river in Maryland, Washington recorded that 'we swam our horses over,' highlighting the importance that horses were in his early livelihood."
- MT. VERNON

Jake and Seth, Sr., left the porch to go check on the horses before darkness set in.

"Without good Morgans the First Vermont Cavalry is in bad shape. I was informed that only about half of their men have a horse, let alone a good Vermont Morgan mount," said Jake limping to the fence around the open meadow.

"Well, we'll just have to try and help. Sadly it takes a few years for us to make a rideable one. Seth, Jr., will have to find them in the meantime," replied his brother fingering the old leather encased cavalry crop.

"Let's hope the war ends long before that; but if it lasts like the Hundred Years' War they'll be needing what we are breeding!" laughed Jake.

"Oh, let's hope this will end quicker than that; but this wasn't any '90-day war' like they all predicted. Both sides are holding the line; but the Confederates didn't break our lines at Gettysburg like they were doing in the past. Let's hope this horrific battle fought here is the 'course' changer for the North. Oh look at that Brandy. He sure is a spitting image of that picture I have of the first bred Morgan!"

"Yep, sure is brother, just like I told you, 'Put this Morgan in your bloodline . . .' and well," Seth, Sr., chuckled. "Now it's both of our bloodlines down here in Pennsylvania. There are times I get a little tug in my heart for the hills of Vermont when I look at those Round Tops up there. That ever happen to you?"

"Oh yeah! Once a Vermonter—always a Vermonter. Happens a lot more during Winter and Spring when I'm remembering Vermont's sweetest season—maple syrup season! The sweet flow of maple sap only happens for

4-6 weeks a year between Winter and Spring, and I've missed that every year I've been gone."

"Well brother I was reading that Pennsylvania is the Keystone State, being the birthplace of independence and the Constitution. It said the state has a good maple syrup season."

"Oh that's true brother, but mostly up north and west of here. Those sugar maple trees are pretty in the fall no matter where they are!"

"Just like those Morgans, pretty no matter where they are—as long as they are true-blooded Morgans!"

"Brandy is a real looker out there with the mares. Let's check on that younger stallion we have inside the barn," and they both turned and walked carefully towards the barn as the daylight faded into the darkness of the night.

"Let's get the lantern lit," said Jake as he handed it to Seth, Sr.

He held it as Jake struck the tip of the match and made light in the lantern. "Let's see how he looks under the lamplight!"

LATE EVENING ON THE TRAIN
FROM WASHINGTON
TO GETTYSBURG

"I'm so tired Seth," said Betsy, smiling with complete adoration of what she experienced in the Capitol with her handsome and brave husband.

The weary travelers sat in the beautiful passenger car for their 80-mile trip home to Gettysburg, talking in a tired yet excited tone about the whole Capitol experience of meeting President Lincoln, the new baby, and the proposal announcement, as well as General Simpson's parting comments in his patriotic goodbye at the train station in Washington. It was all so overwhelming and to end it all on this special train trip was serendipitous.

"I'll never forget General Simpson's parting words, 'The Baltimore & Ohio Railroad is furnishing the President with a special four-car train for his trip to Gettysburg for the Cemetery ceremony the morning of November 19. I checked yesterday and they set up a trial run for your return home. They are rerouting their hookups from Washington through Maryland to Baltimore, where you will transfer to the Northern Central Railway by a team of horses and meet up with the Gettysburg Railroad for the remainder of the trip that will safely take you to the Gettysburg station. The railroad was glad to do it just to insure it would work for our President! I sent a telegraph to your Randolph relatives. They will be at the train station upon your arrival,'" said Seth.

"Wasn't that the most memorable trip? I won't soon forget General Simpson's marvelous demeanor and words; and no words can describe our President Lincoln," said John.

"He's much taller and much funnier than those pictures. And how about that story he told about water or whiskey? 'I prefer water as long as it's not dipped from that canal over there! I think our Northern rye whiskey is better than their Southern bourbon whiskey. Let's ask General Grant,' he kidded," said Seth. "The President once split logs for a living but he should give comedy a try on that Ford Theater stage. He can split your sides with his subtle jokes and dry sense of humor."

"I'll never forget him. It's a story we can tell our child when it grows up. We can tell it that 'you' were at the White House with President Lincoln, lovingly asleep in mommy's tummy," added Betsy.

"And Betsy," added Sarah as she reached up and softly touched her beau John's red hair, "I can say to my children and grandchildren, 'After daddy proposed to me, the next day President Lincoln shook your dad's hand congratulating him and then he turned and hugged me with a fatherly hug.' I can still smell his coat when he hugged me; he is so tall I felt the soft satin waistband around his mid section."

"Yes and when he laughed saying, 'Just about the same height of my beloved Mary Todd!'" said Seth.

"I am so proud that he is our Commander-in-Chief, knowing he is standing tall behind us and supporting us. When he found out we had just been to a special horse event at Giesboro Point his only comment was, 'I can make more generals, but horses cost money.' That place cost over a million dollars . . . horses are expensive!" replied John.

In the meantime as they chatted quietly and enjoyed the lemonade, the train sped smoothly down the steel rails heading for their destination. The lemonade in the pitcher was reflecting the gaslight from the train car's lights. All were moving side to side softly and delicately.

"Seth, the General told me that he had ordered an extra copy of that picture for us. He said that is why there were so many flashes. He said he is coming to Gettysburg soon and will bring it along. I kidded him and told him about the little framed picture of me that you carry in your pocket at all times. He laughed and said, 'Oh this one will be much bigger. You will show it to your grandchildren and tell them about that day.' I'm just so happy we have been able to do all of this. And to think I didn't want to leave Vermont!" said Betsy.

"The General said he will see me and Brandy in the ceremony and then told me, 'I'm coming to your farm to see that gorgeous horse, and to walk the ground where you Vermonters held the line!'" said Seth.

"It was a trip we will never forget. Too bad it is dark and we can't see outside. Maybe it's best we don't know what's out there . . . it's still not totally safe around these areas. Some Rebels might still be hiding around in some of these wooded areas. This war is long from over," said John.

After a while Betsy said, "Seth I'm tired. Let's retire. I learned to sleep on a train on our travels down from Vermont, but I have never slept in a car that has a 'presidential seal' on it."

"Oh Betsy, that's just a prop they put on. President Lincoln will sleep in the same compartment we will be sleeping in."

"Well then Seth, let's go to bed. I'm sure my feet won't stick out the end of those small beds, but I bet you the President's will!" They all laughed and Seth and Betsy kissed goodnight.

DAY OF THE
GETTYSBURG ADDRESS

It had been a long, hot summer and the task of reburying Union soldiers into the new National Cemetery at Gettysburg was now over. It was an extremely difficult endeavor that had started around October 17th. Now it was November 19th and President Lincoln had finalized his quickly written speech in the same railroad car his Gettysburg guests had travelled in. Upon his arrival he was handed a telegram that his son Tad was doing much better. Now he and General Simpson and Secretary of State Seward and many other dignitaries were getting ready for the day's ceremonies.

Captain Randolph was atop Brandy at the cemetery along with the other solemn paraders. Betsy was in a spring wagon nearby with Seth, Jr.'s, father and uncle on the perimeter in a good place to view the ceremony, but also in an open place to quickly return home if Betsy would have any trouble with her almost mid-term pregnancy.

Sarah sat in the Presidential box hoping to be able to hear the speech and record it in her diary. She couldn't be in two places, the parade ground or here with the President, so she chose here and sat with General Simpson. After all, he had come to the farm the night before to deliver that special picture and then invited the ladies to sit in his specially constructed compartment. They had put a covering over the special seats to block out any rain and they had some lemonade in a special container held in an old whiskey barrel filled with cold water from a nearby spring.

"I see you brought along your diary Miss Randolph. Another favorable memory to record?" asked the General.

"Yes Sir. I have so many since my engagement. We had such a wonderful time with all of you in Washington. I have it all recorded and I'm hoping to be able to copy some bits of President Lincoln's speech to read to everyone. We all can't be here to listen. It will take a few days to get into the local paper and we don't want to wait that long."

"I was watching him write it down on the rail ride here. It's tucked into his pocket. I don't think it will be that long. He was having a very difficult time though. The Emancipation was so special for him and he did get encouraging news on June 20th when West Virginia became the 35th state to enter the Union and the first to enter where the terms 'slave and free' didn't matter! Of course the great triumph here at Gettysburg is monumental, but so costly, so much loss of life and the carnage continues . . ."

"Oh, they are starting the ceremony," whispered Sarah.

Several hours later the sun was waning and the objects all around started to turn grey and misty. The lemonade in the special pail was now cool as the air and the Taps and ceremonial music that was played was now quiet.

Finally amidst the surrounding crowd Sarah and the General saw President Lincoln's well-known top hat appear in the crowd. He moved slowly, making his way somberly to the stand. While sandwiched between all the dignitaries and spectators he began his speech.

It was difficult to hear, even at a short distance. The atmosphere was electric and Sarah got out her diary and started to write.

"Four score and seven years . . ."

She wrote it down in Pitman shorthand, which she learned in her English class at the Daughters of Charity School in Emmitsburg.

"Someday you'll be glad you know this," her teacher said.

Her teacher was correct. It was the perfect occasion to use what she had learned.

EVENING AT THE RANDOLPH
FARM AFTER THE ADDRESS

I t had been a very long day for the Randolph family and John and General Simpson. They sat in the parlor of the old stone farmhouse while Jake started a white oak log fire in the beautiful parlor fireplace to take off the chill in the room. He lit the newer kerosene lamps he had bought from a traveling salesman from the upstate Pennsylvania coal region. They were really a good investment now that the family was growing and they were making more income.

John and Sarah were sitting together on one of the love seats and Seth and Betsy were on the one opposite while Seth, Sr., and General Simpson sat in the high-backed chairs nearest the fire.

Jake finally plopped down at the opposite end and said, "Let's get comfortable. The port and brandy bottles are on the side bar there and the coffee is in the silver decanter and the tea and hot water are there," as he pointed to the silver tray on the mahogany table near the now roaring fire.

"Oh uncle, you think of everything," said Betsy in a loving manner. "It's so cozy here."

"Thanks Betsy. It was Sarah's idea. She wants to read us the President's speech from today. She and the General were there. She told me that she's studied a lot of wonderful speeches at the school in Emmitsburg, but this one is historical!"

"I spoke to the President afterwards," said the General, "and he told me, 'I was a failure today General.'" Even though there was clapping it was a really somber setting but a wonderful tribute to those who fought and died and are now buried there."

"It was so emotional where Seth and John were," added Betsy. "Dad and Uncle Jake and I sat in the open wagon and watched . . . well . . . it was nothing like the other ceremonies he has been in that I have witnessed. Seth, you and Brandy were . . . well the way he carried you followed by all those on horseback was so touching. People all around were bringing out their handkerchiefs, even the children were standing perfectly still. I saw some camera boxes in the crowd and I hope they got pictures. It was so memorable."

145

Jake got up and put another log on the fire. He picked up a tray with empty cups and saucers and walked around the room with the coffee decanter in the other hand, "Coffee for everyone," and he limped around serving them. "Sarah's tea cakes are on that porcelain plate on the sideboard."

Sarah got up quietly and walked to the front after everyone was served by her dad. She opened her diary saying, "I know shorthand so I was able to get the whole speech. I will read it to you in this room not far from where President Lincoln gave it. Not far from that hallowed ground we visited today. I have read it over and over, but most of you will be hearing it for the first time."

She moved one of the kerosene lamps closer and its glow fell onto her scrawled writing in her diary. Everyone set down their cups and stared at her. The fire in the fireplace crackled and sparked as she started to read.

The Gettysburg Address

Four score and seven years ago our fathers brought forth on this continent, a new nation, conceived in Liberty, and dedicated to the proposition that all men are created equal.

Now we are engaged in a great civil war, testing whether that nation, or any nation so conceived and so dedicated, can long endure. We are met on a great battlefield of that war. We have come to dedicate a portion of that field, as a final resting place for those who here gave their lives that that nation might live. It is altogether fitting and proper that we should do this.

But, in a larger sense, we cannot dedicate—we cannot consecrate—we cannot hallow—this ground. The brave men, living and dead, who struggled here, have consecrated it, far above our poor power to add or detract. The world will little note, nor long remember what we say here, but it can never forget what they did here. It is for us the living, rather, to be dedicated here to the unfinished work which they who fought here have thus far so nobly advanced. It is rather for us to be here dedicated to the great task remaining before us—that from these honored dead we take increased devotion to that cause for which they gave the last full measure of devotion—that we here highly resolve that these dead shall not have died in vain—that this nation, under God, shall have a new birth of freedom—and that government of the people, by the people, for the people, shall not perish from the earth.

LATE EVENING AT THE TELE-GRAPH SHOP IN GETTYSBURG

"Mr. Phillips, the line goes all the way out to the barber shop. How are we going to handle all of these people who want to send telegrams?" asked the clerk inside the Gettysburg Train Station.

"We'll just have to stay open until we get all of their messages sent!"

"Yes sir, but it is a bantering bunch; like roosters crowing from the top perch."

"We just have to be polite. They are mostly press people and they all work on deadlines. One tries to beat out the other but they have numbers and will stay in line."

"I felt the President's speech was short but there was some applause in between when he paused. Sometimes it was hard to hear, but overall the crowd seemed to be pleased and afterwards there was strong applause!"

"Well, he is so dignified. He looked like a 'log splitter' and acted like one. I thought it was too short, too," said a bearded older worker in the back.

"You are welcome to your own opinion," said Mr. Phillips as his fingers quickly worked the telegraph machine to finish a message. Handing a receipt to the sender he said, "Next! Please be patient. You'll all get your turn."

The buzz in the room was electric and the comments exchanged between reporters could be heard by all.

" . . . short, to the point, historic," said one.

". . . too short . . . surely he must be embarrassed . . . " came another comment through the air.

" . . . dull and commonplace just like him . . ." said a young man with a pipe.

"Wait until my paper gets my report . . . we'll sell a lot of papers."

One of the local reporters got disgusted and said, "I can ride my full story to my paper faster than this line will move!" So he left the building and climbed on his horse who was drinking from the trough outside. People watched as he sped on down the road out of town.

The next person in line handed his message to the telegraph operator asking, "Can you tell me where the Randolph Farm is located? The one that raises those Vermont Morgan horses."

"Oh that's an easy one to find sir," answered Mr. Phillips. "You take the first right and it's about one-half mile down past the Cemetery. There's a sign out front. Two of the First Vermont Cavalry live there. The family are all Vermonters and some of the nicest people you will find out here!"

Phillips tapped out his message quickly and handed him a receipt.

"Next!"

NEXT MORNING
AT THE RANDOLPH FARM

Brandy watched as the grain was dumped into his feed bin. He felt a strong hand running up his right front leg and then showing his hoof to the other humans around him.

"Look at those feet. He performed so beautifully," Jake said to everyone watching from outside Brandy's stall.

"Remarkable feet. I've never driven a nail into those shiny black walls. And you'll note yesterday I didn't blacken them like those other horses. He's just a natural, like his color. He's starting to get some of his winter hair and I'm so glad he waited until after the Cemetery ceremony."

"The President was right, wanting him out front Seth," said John. "You two added more ceremony and regal pomp; that's what that ceremony was all about. I had a lump in my throat watching, remembering my fellow cavalry members who didn't make it. All are now interred behind those gates they put up around their eternal resting places. Reading their monument stones made me cry. And that speech that Sarah copied and read to us . . ."

"Horses can't talk but Brandy's horse presence was a tribute to all of the dead equines that lie in unmarked graves out in those fields and dales. It was a fitting tribute to how they too served their masters and our country," added Seth, Sr. "They don't have any gravestones but someday they will put up statues and monuments of those who served so gallantly. I'm sure they will have many of those special generals atop statued horses . . . frozen in bronze, forever."

"Mighty powerful words, dad," said Seth, Jr., as a group of men came into the barn.

"Hello Captain! Good morning. Hope we aren't too early," said the bearded man out in front of the large group.

John and the Randolphs turned in surprise, with Jake stepping forward saying, "Good morning. I'm Jake Randolph and we get up early 'round here. Welcome to our farm. This is my brother, Seth, Sr., his son Seth, Jr., and my future son-in-law John Reynolds."

The large group of men smiled and nodded, with the man out front saying, "We know you have your hands full. All of us met in town after the speech. Some of us must see Brandy, that spectacular stallion. Is this him?"

Seth, Jr., looked up smiling proudly, "Yes, this is Brandy. See how excited he is with all of you here. He just keeps on doing his thing and right now, that's eating."

They all laughed and their comments echoed throughout the barn, "Looks better in person. Gorgeous. Really quiet for a stud."

"We came in a group, and they want me to speak their minds and requests."

"Well, what might they be?" asked Jake with a huge smile on his face. Resting his bad leg on the inside rail of the stall he said, "Bad leg needs to rest for a minute."

"Here dad, let me help you," suggested John and he limped over and grabbed an old wooden chair from the corner. "Have a seat."

Jake sat down and one of the guests walked over and grabbed another old barn chair saying, "Here sir, it looks like you need one, too."

Seth, Jr., smiled saying, "Uncle got his in a farm accident and Lieutenant Reynolds got his wound right out there on that battlefield, just in front of this stone barn. Got knocked down when his First Vermont Cavalry held off the Confederates. Helped to stop them from getting 'round the end of the fish hook."

John sat down and his face started to turn the color of his red hair. The men in the crowd all looked in awe at him with one saying, "Wow. I'm sure the President's speech was personal to you yesterday!"

"It was appropriate, and there was a little applause, but it wasn't a time for applause. It was a time to commemorate and appreciate what President Lincoln and those who died out there are doing in service to our Country. I was so proud to be a cavalry officer yesterday . . . some of my fellow cavalrymen are buried there. I was knocked down and taken out of the fight . . . but they managed to get out the shot and save my leg. I'm the lucky survivor!"

All of the men in the room looked at John in appreciation. Seth, Jr., stepped forward, "I see you are carrying a newspaper in your hand sir."

"Oh yes, that's why we are all here together. Some of us are from different parts of the country. Some of us are reporters, and we all love your stallion! Our local papers posted this picture of you and him at a Gala in York. It is a remarkable and patriotic piece. We all raise Morgans, but most of ours don't look like him."

Seth, Jr., interjected with a smile, "My pa and the family are from

Vermont and we Vermonters try to breed to the true Morgan bloodlines, to retain Figure's original look. The Morgan breed was started by a dandy stallion who happened to throw offspring no matter what the mare looked like. And as my dad says, 'This colt looks just like Figure and his famous sons Sherman, Bulrush, and Woodbury . . . just like Justin Morgan said he'd look!'"

The crowd all said noisily, "Sure does," and they watched Brandy lift his head and whinny softly.

They all laughed when Seth, Sr., said, "See how excited he is!"

"See this picture, we're here to see if you would agree to breed to our mares," said the group's spokesperson.

"Sure, that's what were fixin' to do on our farms here. I just bought that one over there, and we brought our stock from Vermont and my son just bought that young black stallion over in that stall. All of our Morgans are Vermont lines and stock, and our studs are Figure look-alikes. Brandy has been bred and the foals look like either Figure or his sons. A good Morgan bloodline will breed true . . . that's what they do!"

"Great," said the leader and the crowd roared their approval.

Jake stood up from his chair and smiled, "I know Winter is coming and I know most want to breed for a Spring foal, but we want to keep breeding year round, especially with the new stallion and a few others we'll be getting. We're just getting started, but what I did here and what my brother did in Vermont we'll be doing together now. We have a lot of bookings for stud from some locals, but we can arrange for early bookings and even offer a breeding discount with an offseason stud fee. Our stallions will be available for breeding all year round. Of course you'll all have to talk it over. If you're not worried much about when your foal hits the ground or your mares having a late foal, we can accommodate all of you.

"John and my daughter Sarah are handling the scheduling. She'll be out here shortly, she's just finishing up breakfast. You can all walk around and check out our horses.

"John, go see if Sarah is ready and please set up the table over there and sign them up. I'd like to get us booked for all of next year!"

"Yes sir!" and John limped out of the barn heading to the farmhouse.

"Enjoy your stay and we are proud to book your mares. We can accommodate keeping them however long is necessary. We now have two Vermont Morgan horse breeding farms here in beautiful Gettysburg!"

PART FIVE

FINALLY A HOME

Betsy smiled at the copy of President Lincoln's Gettysburg Address that she had gotten framed in a local shop. Announcing to Seth who was standing next to her, "That is where it must be Seth, right there so that our children and everyone who comes into our new home can see it."

"That is a perfect spot above the fireplace and when you look at it you can then peer out that window and see where the First Vermont Cavalry made their gallant stand here at Gettysburg."

Seth then got a tiny nail and hammered it exactly into the spot Betsy had pointed to. *Tap, tap, tap.* Then he delicately took the beautifully framed document and hung it.

"Perfect," said Betsy. "Just like the day we all witnessed it."

"Look Betsy, Sarah and John are driving up in their spring wagon. They are arriving early to help us with tonight's dinner. It's a little windy and cold out there and even some light snow is on the ground."

"They are so excited about their wedding plans they won't even feel the cold! Look at the woolen blanket they have around their legs. Brandy's pulling and his head is tucked and he's strutting up the lane. His color blends right in with that 'teasing' snow scene out there."

"Let's go meet them on the front porch, Betsy. Here, let me put my heavy military overcoat over your shoulders. I don't want you to get a chill."

He walked over and picked up his officer's winter coat and carefully placed it over her shoulders. Reaching around trying to button it in the front he said, "Oh look, honey, the baby is getting so big I can't even fasten the coat."

Betsy chuckled. "It won't be long now, the baby is due in the first days of Spring. That is when some of our mares will have foals, too," she laughed and reached up and kissed him. "Oh Seth, this is such a special time, let's meet them at the door."

Seth and Betsy watched as his cousin and her beau John climbed down off the green-colored wagon. Sarah reached back and grabbed some packages from the back while John let Brandy have his head leaving the reins untied.

"Look Seth, he's not tying Brandy to the hitching post."

"Oh, he ground ties! He won't go anywhere. We teach our horses that discipline in the cavalry. It's natural for us Vermont horse people and also a skill that we teach the cavalry recruits in training. It's a must—it can save a cavalryman's life in battle! It's convenient when you have to step away quickly to perform a task. It is a positive tool taught to our horses. They must be obedient and focus on their rider. Some horses have a hard time learning, a few never do and they are then sent down to pull wagons or cannons if they can stand the noise! Brandy picked it up after a few lessons when I trained him. He's a natural and he bonds to his rider."

"Now I have learned another one of your cavalry tricks. You're a good teacher, and honey, I have bonded to you, too." She patted him on the shoulder, and then reached to give Sarah a hug as she came inside.

"*Brrrr* . . . hello . . . you look warm Betsy!" exclaimed Sarah.

"Welcome to you both, quick come inside," welcomed Seth as he hugged Sarah and shook John's hand.

"We've been standing by the open fire and saw you two coming up with that gorgeous Brandy in the lines, that's why I'm still warm. Look at Seth's coat around me, I can't even button it!" They all laughed.

"You are all wrapped up in that woolen overcoat of Seth's and now we have two 'home warming' gifts here that are wrapped up for both of you." Sarah handed them two thin, wide and long packages wrapped in brown paper. "That's why we came early, to help and share these gifts."

"Oh, thank you," said Betsy as she took one and Seth took the other.

"Oh, what a surprise. First let's get our coats off and set next to that cozy fireplace," said Betsy with her blue eyes sparkling.

"That sure is a warm coat," said Betsy as Seth took it off her and placed it neatly on the back of a nearby chair.

He leaned over it and gently smelled the inside of it, "Ahhh . . . smells just like you Betsy. I'm not going to ever get it cleaned."

John and Sarah handed their coats to Seth, who took them into the other room. Upon his return he picked up a huge log and placed it on the fire. "There, that should last for a while!"

They all went to the two matching love seats in front of the huge fireplace and plopped down laughing. "Finally," said Sarah, "we are happily in your new home . . . this is such a special time for all of us. Someday John and I will be plopping down too, as married next door neighbors, and I'll be popping out too just like you Betsy! I can't wait to be married and a mother."

"Now that we are all cozy," said Betsy, "let's unwrap these housewarming gifts. This is so exciting. Seth and I just hung up a copy of President Lincoln's Gettysburg Address above the fireplace. We purchased it in town," and she pointed to the framed image hanging handsomely on the white-washed wall.

"It will be a constant reminder of the day President Lincoln was here. It is so much a part of our lives. What an historical event that Cemetery consecration was," reminded John.

"Now in remembrance of our trip," said Sarah, "Betsy, what you are to unwrap is something that General Simpson promised to us and then gave to me when he visited the farm. I told him I would give it to you both once you were settled in your new home. He thought that would be appropriate. He even had President Lincoln give us a signed note. It's inside the package, go ahead Betsy take off the paper." John and Sarah looked at each other lovingly and watched Betsy carefully take off the outside wrapper.

"This is beautiful!" exclaimed Betsy as the light from the flickering flames of the fireplace played on the glass framed picture. "That was so memorable Sarah and John, we will treasure it."

"Look at the President in the middle, Betsy, he has a special smile on his face," said Seth.

"You ladies are so gorgeous in those gowns," said John.

" . . . and how about those two handsome cavalry officers next to us in those gallant poses?" Betsy got up and held it up in front of her, displaying it proudly. "I know just where to hang it!"

"Compliments of General Simpson," Sarah said. "I know he's coming tonight so I thought you would want it on the wall for him to see. When the photographer's office manager gave him the two copies he asked him, 'Don't you frame pictures?' He took them back and later he returned both to him in these beautiful frames. One is hanging in General Simpson's office and this one is for your new home. He sure knows how to play the audience . . . " and they all started to laugh.

"General Simpson, General Simpson . . . how we love General Simpson," they all started to sing, "and he's coming here for dinner tonight!"

"I know just where this one will go," said Betsy and she got up and held it against the opposite wall. "There, when you look out that window in the morning the light of first day will shine right on it."

"Perfect choice Betsy," said Seth, "but what is in this other package? It's almost the same size."

"John and I were in Gettysburg the day after the Address, and of course, there were so many souvenir searching tourists and they had pictures for sale in many of the stores. There were flags everywhere, some covering the bullet holes in the buildings, and the shops were buzzing with shoppers. We were in the shop at the train station, the one Mr. Phillip's owns. He saw us and said, 'I know Captain Randolph and his lovely wife Betsy are moving into their new home, please give them this housewarming gift. I hope they like it. If not they can bring it back and make an exchange as we have several other wonderful Currier & Ives related prints.'"

"Since we came early to help with all the arrangements for tonight's dinner with General Simpson we better get to it. We are so excited!" said Sarah.

A WINTER COAT

"It is much easier to ride a horse in the direction it is going."
- ABRAHAM LINCOLN

Brandy stood perfectly still outside for a short while as the early winter winds started to blow the loosely laying snow into his face. His legs were locked and he was sleeping and comfortable now that his winter coat was almost fully grown. The Pennsylvania winters were not as cold as the Vermont winters, but a Vermont Morgan horse adapts to any environment. The daily sunlight still diminishes here just as there, and his winter coat grows according to outside temperatures. He now lacked the luxurious color that was superior in the Spring, Summer and Fall seasons, but this dull-colored and shaggy-haired second coat kept him warm.

"Let's put him in the barn. Dinner will be on schedule as planned," said Seth. "I received a telegram from General Simpson. He's due here on the train shortly. It says he has a surprise for me."

"Ok Captain, I hate surprises . . . especially military surprises. I know he wants to discuss the written reports and recommendations we advised. I think we plugged many obvious open holes in that defense line that needed to be filled," said John.

"Yes, I know. I was happy that the War Department was giving noticeable attention to the new cavalry, especially after the heroic deeds at the Battle of Gettysburg. A bright light shined on the cavalry and our War Department is realizing what a valuable arm of the service we have become. General Simpson proudly told me in our meeting in Washington about the gallant General Farnsworth, and how Major Wells and our cavalry pushed through the Rebel lines for nearly a mile against the fierce front fire of five Reb regiments of infantry and two batteries.

"Farnsworth was the only officer killed while in the lines of the enemy. They are aware how we also engaged the enemy's cavalry at Hanover, Hunterstown, Hagerstown, Boonsborough, Falling Waters, and Buckland Mills. The Regiment is now down around Stevensburg, engaged in picketing the line of the Rapidan. They told me to work my magic. General Simpson and the President told me to get more horses to help insure the success of Giesboro!

"General Simpson looked me squarely and sadly in the eyes and lamented to me, 'Your General Farnsworth was only 25 when he was killed!'"

PREPARING FOR EVENING
AT THE CAPTAIN'S HOUSE

Seth, Sr.'s, historic stone farmhouse was softly lit up with his brother Jake's kerosene lamps.

"Don't worry about the expensive fuel, my salesman gets it cheap from his suppliers up in northern Pennsylvania," assured Jake.

"They sure are fancy, Uncle Jake," replied Seth as he heaped more seasoned applewood on the fire in the stone fireplace.

"I just love that applewood smell from a fire. We cut down some dead trees and they dried out all summer on your porch. The burning wood smells almost as homey as Vermont maple syrup!" replied Jake.

"This sure is an older house than yours, Uncle Jake, and we just love that huge walk-in fireplace," said Betsy as she walked into the room carrying a shiny brass candelabra. "This is all I have left from my family's belongings. Mom and dad are both gone now and I wish they could be here!"

"That is so sad Betsy, but we are so glad you are now a member of our Randolph family. I can't wait to see that beautiful baby. Our family is growing, and you are surely lighting up all of our lives," said Jake as he sat on a high-backed chair near the fireplace.

"The owner told me when he sold his house to us that the oldest, most historic house around is in Gettysburg. It is called the Dobbin House and was built in 1776 by the Rev. Alexander Dobbin. It witnessed the Revolutionary War and now is going through the Civil War just like our houses are. He said this house was smaller and built by a farmer who helped build houses. He was a German stone cutter and 1780 is cut into the roof marker!"

"Well it's all stone, but sure needs some work in those outbuildings. It took quite a beating in the battle and I'm glad we didn't have to defend this one," added Seth as he carried in some dinnerware.

"Betsy said the owner left this fine china with the following note:

> When you find this I'll be off to California for some gold. I am too old to enjoy this fine gold-rimmed china that my wife got from a dealer in Philadelphia when we were passing through. We ended up here and she said it was too fancy. She has passed and I'm leaving. I hope it's not too fancy for the new owners. Best Regards, Sam Stoneham, 1863.

"Seth and I found it when we moved in," said Betsy. "The dinner set is a perfect match to our brass candelabra—the fanciest thing we have in our possession."

Seth, Sr., walked back into the room and stood watching the old farmhouse dining room being adorned and turning into a beautiful arrangement. "Looks fit for a king!" he shouted.

"Fit for a general, dad," replied Seth, Jr. "As we discussed, the General is coming to dinner tonight, all the way from Washington! He loves to get away and loves our farms and our Morgan horses. He's going to stay over in the room upstairs. Betsy and Sarah just made it comfortable for him."

"The room that overlooks the meadow where Brandy and the stallions and mares roam?" asked Seth, Sr.

"Yes dad. We chose it because when we were in Washington on military business reviewing the largest horse depot in the world he asked for our recommendations on improving it. The grand opening is next month. When I told him my ideas, General Simpson ordered me to route all my recommendations through him. We've been conversing back and forth with telegrams and letters. He said all are impressed with our write-ups.

"He wanted to know how a young officer like me knew so much more than some of those of higher rank. I wrote back, 'I don't.' I just told him I'm from Vermont and most of it is common sense! He sent me this telegram last night. Here I'll read it."

```
WATER OR WHISKEY. DO YOU REALIZE THAT WE DO
HAVE FAVORED YOUNG OFFICERS SERVING ON STAFFS
OF DIVISION, CORPS AND ARMY COMMANDERS? SOME
HAVE ALREADY EARNED VERY FAST PROMOTIONS TO
BRIGADIER GENERAL FROM CAPTAIN AND FIRST
LIEUTENANT—SOME BEFORE THE AGE OF 25. LOOKING
FORWARD TO OUR DINNER ENGAGEMENT AT YOUR FARM
HONORING FARNSWORTH. GENERAL SIMPSON.
```

"That's so formal and interesting," said Betsy. "It's not his folksy way."

"He was that way in the White House when you ladies were given a quick tour. I spent a few moments alone with him and the President discussing recomendations and he seemed impressed with our plans for horse movements. I told them about the history of our First Vermont Cavalry and how they managed to move from a volunteer unit to an active unit and how our leaders got it all down from Vermont. The President, in his quirky way said, 'And how did they do it?'

"I told him they used one hundred and fifty-three cars, made up into a train of five sections. And that my superiors explained it all to me in my initial officer tactical training.

"He just smiled at me and said, 'You know more than some of my generals. Captain did you know that I can make a General in five minutes but a good horse is hard to replace!'" Everyone in the room laughed.

"Dad, I wish you and Uncle Jake could have met the President like we did. He is so much like you old Vermonters. I can picture an old rail splitter and you two together!"

"Oh that would be an historical event," joked John.

"I can hear it now, Uncle Jake asking, 'Water or Whiskey, Mr. President?' and my dad laughing with a follow-up of, 'Oh he drinks water brother . . . don't you read the papers!'"

"Everything looks perfect. Betsy and I want to thank all of you for all of your help. I'm sure the General will feel relaxed tonight and he will enjoy his stay here. Nothing ceremonial on this trip . . . just a friendly, quiet visit and a special dinner made by the ladies from town."

A GENERAL COMES TO VISIT

"Here he comes up the lane," Betsy said in an excited tone. "Oh my, he has some riders with him and a wagon behind the buggy. It looks like he has come to stay for awhile!"

"Oh, generals always travel with a lot of baggage," said Jake.

"How do you know that brother, you don't know any generals!"

"Well, I read it in the local gazette. And look at what's in that wagon behind the buggy. It's not filled with newspapers!"

The men grabbed their coats and the ladies went to make sure everything was in order.

The men stood on the porch anxious to greet the General, while the ladies peered through the windows, warming themselves near the open fire. The wind was blowing stronger outside and the horses' manes were blowing in the wind.

"Whoa . . . whoa," said the carriage driver and the horses stopped and whinnied, standing perfectly still. The side door flung open and a blue uniformed figure backed down out of the carriage.

"Here Sir, let me help you," said Seth, Jr., as he helped him down and then turned and saluted.

"Thanks Captain, but this is a civilian occasion. I'm just wearing this to keep warm. Nothing warmer than these winter blue uniforms we all have!"

"Welcome to our new home, Sir!" said Seth, Sr., who was standing immediately behind Seth with his brother Jake and John who were extending their hands to greet him.

"That's quite a reception and I'm glad the ladies are inside, it's colder here than in the Capitol. Winds are about the same though!"

"There's always a breeze or wind blowing off those Round Tops down across our place and on into Gettysburg. When it's hot it blows cool, when it's cold, it blows colder," said Jake, adding, "but nothing like a Vermont winter!"

"Come on in Sir. We'll get your bags."

"Oh, don't bother. I hired that buggy and carriage and those drivers will haul in my two trunks. Oh driver," and he pointed to the trunks, "take them onto the front porch and I'll handle them from that point."

The General then fell in line behind Seth, Sr., who courteously led the party up the stairs. At the top the General stopped to catch his breath saying, "Whew, long trip . . . hate trains . . . but they are faster than my horse."

"General, Brandy's out in the barn now. We can see him later. You can see his stall right from that window up there," as Seth, Jr., pointed up. "The girls set you up in that room . . . the room with a view!"

"Oh I love those ladies . . . they love a man in uniform and are always nice to me. Thank you!"

"And Sarah and Betsy love you. They are always talking about you!" said Seth, Sr. "Something about a general . . . especially one wearing blue."

THE LADIES MEET
THE GENERAL

The ladies met the General as he walked into the living room. He bowed and shook Betsy's and Sarah's hands and they both smiled saying in unison, "Welcome back General Simpson."

He smiled gleefully and looked around at the room lit up by all the kerosene lamps saying, "Wow, this is as beautiful as a luxurious Washington hotel. I love it. I'll bet General Washington stayed here!"

"I don't think he was ever this far into Central Pennsylvania, General Simpson. This house was around when there was a standoff by the British generals in the North during the Revolution when Washington was in New York. Those British generals renewed their military ambitions in the southern theater convinced that the southern colonies were full of American Loyalists . . . but they met their demise at Yorktown . . . and Washington moved in for the kill. I hope that our generals push the Confederates to a similar demise in one of those southern towns, just like Washington did," said Seth, Sr.

"That's some history lesson and some visionary thinking, sir. Now I know where your son gets his military intellect!"

"Oh General, that's just some Vermonter common sense!"

"Call it what you want. What a wonderful welcome to this beautifully patriotic household. Thanks for having me back!"

"General, the Lieutenant and I will help you to your room. John and I will carry up your trunks and we will call you for dinner," stated Seth, Jr.

"Oh that would be grand. See that first one with GENL SIMPSON imprinted on it, that's mine. You can take it upstairs. Leave the other one down here. It's for a general friend of mine and he doesn't know he's a general yet. He's being promoted by a special commission from President Lincoln. We've emblazoned his name on it and the name is hidden under the tape!"

"Oh General Simpson," giggled Sarah, "you always have a surprise. I'll bet that man will be shocked."

"Yes he will Sarah, and he deserves the promotion!"

MORGAN HORSES
IN THE BARN

"I'll feed and water and bed down the horses, dad. You keep the fire going and entertain the General if he comes down before we call him for dinner. The ladies from town will be here very soon with the dinner they prepared. They sure are excited to see and serve the General. Ladies like a man in uniform; especially a single one with a white beard like he has. And he loves the attention," instructed Seth.

Seth headed out the front door and noticed a newspaper on top of the trunk the General left behind. He picked it up and saw on the front page a picture like the one he and Betsy had hung on the wall. The headline beneath it read: LOCAL OFFICERS AND WIVES VISIT PRESIDENT LINCOLN.

He sat down on the trunk and flipped the paper out so he could read the article.

GETTYSBURG OFFICERS, Captain Seth and Mrs. Betsy Randolph and Miss Sarah Randolph and her beau Lieutenant John Reynolds were pleasantly surprised on a recent military visit to Washington. General Simpson of the War Department took our local heroes who fought so valiantly at the Battle of Gettysburg with the First Vermont Cavalry to see the President in the Blue Room . . . and were pulled there in classic style by Vermont Morgan horses . . . whose breed is the only horse the First Vermont Cavalrymen ride! Contact General Simpson at War Department about Morgan horses. (full story inside)

Wow, he thought, *this will bring a lot more Morgan horse lovers to our rescue. Wait until everyone reads this!*

He was putting the paper back down when John met up with him asking, "What's caught your eye now Captain? I see your eyes flashing."

"Here John, you read it. I'm heading to the barn to bed the animals."

John sat down on the trunk and opened the newspaper to read the article when the General came up behind him saying, "Oh Lieutenant, you found my paper. I picked up the local gazette passing through the train station and I thought I would read it while I was relaxing before dinner."

"Yes Sir, you left it here on the top of the trunk. Seth happened to notice the picture and told me to read the article."

"I see the article finally made it down to the local cities. It was in the Washington papers and they tell me it's all over the big cities in the North. I had it put in the papers and thought it would be a good advertisement for horses. People don't know how important they are in our military campaign. They are the backbone or shall I say the 'legs under' our war effort."

"That's a great way to put it General," replied John folding the paper and then handing it to the General.

"I saw Captain Randolph in the Ceremony and some of his superior officers have told me that Thomas Jefferson called George Washington 'the best horseman of his age, and the most graceful figure that could be seen on horseback.'" Then he added this comment, "But they never saw Captain Randolph under saddle!"

"Oh Sir, he always has command of the horse under him. Or shall I say they present a beautiful sight in full gallop out front on that battlefield."

"Well, I haven't seen that . . . and . . . well . . . we've had too many generals shot out of their saddles."

"I agree Sir. Captain is only a junior officer and he stays pretty low and obscure when out front so they have a hard time seeing his rank."

The General chuckled, tucked the newspaper under his arm and said, "See you later at dinner Colonel . . . I mean Lieutenant. We will have to change that . . . and tonight I will do that."

"Yes Sir," John answered with a questioning gaze. He turned and headed to the barn.

"John, you have a funny look on your face," said Seth. It was chilly outside but the barn was warm from all the heat from the horses and the humans inside. "It's always warmer in a barn than outside," said Seth, "and this air will take that strange look off your face."

"That look is not from the cold. I just left General Simpson. He came down to get his newspaper, the one you and I were looking at, and we had a very interesting conversation."

"About what?"

"About you and me . . . and he was mumbling something about lieu-tenants, captains, colonels and generals . . . I think he wanted to talk more. He had a gleam in his eyes."

"A gleam?" asked Seth as he stopped brushing Brandy and put the brush back in the wooden tack box.

"Yes, we know him as funny, open-minded and personable and very demanding, but he was different," said John.

"Generals have so much on their minds, especially the head of the War Department. The President had gone through a lot of generals until he settled on General Grant," said Seth.

"When this war started many of those West Point generals sided with their states and the Confederacy, leaving the North very short of West Point talent . . . and leadership!

"Seth, our own state has more generals than most of the other states. Many have made it up through the ranks. Schooling is one thing, but fight-ing in battle more often than not makes the colonels and generals."

"John, can you finish feeding the rest of the mares back there? I want to go in and help Betsy. She's not supposed to be doing much in her condi-tion. But she is so happy being in her own house. She's such a homemaker and she wants everything to be perfect for tonight."

"Sure Seth. This is going to be a special night. I just wonder what the General is holding back?"

"One good thing the General told me, John, was that the town itself looks much better than it did after those battle pictures. He said the road in was a prettier sight than when he was in with President Lincoln for the dedi-cation of the cemetery. He said time and, 'As long as they don't come back again . . . will heal some of the wounds . . . but scars will always remain!'

"It will be an entertaining night, John, with my dad and uncle and the General. I can't wait to hear those old war stories!" and they both laughed as Seth turned and left John with a funny smile on his face.

LIEUTENANTS, CAPTAINS, COLONELS & GENERALS

"My that was a spectacular dinner! My compliments again to those lovely ladies from Gettysburg for preparing and serving us this memorable dinner," announced the General as he sat back and wiped his face with the fancy napkin that was by his plate.

Everyone agreed and passed warm compliments to the ladies from town who smiled. One of the older ladies with grey hair looked at the General and said, "Your hair is as grey as my husband's was. He was only a simple farmer; you are an esteemed general and we are honored to be in your presence. We all want to thank you for your honorable service."

All of the ladies shook their heads up and down in agreement and then started to serve the fine desserts they had prepared.

"Yes General," announced Seth, Sr., who was setting next to him, "this is an honor for all of us. We are simple farmers and we know how much is on your shoulders and on the shoulders of our President Lincoln. When we look out or pass through town or our fields we are constantly reminded and thankful that we have great generals like you."

"Speaking of generals," interrupted General Simpson, "we've had many so far. Now we have General Grant and as we kid, 'Water or Whiskey,' sir . . . mix them please."

Everyone at the table laughed.

"Oh, now that's the General we know from Washington," chided Sarah who sat next to John.

"Yes, we just love your sense of humor, General," flowed from the beautiful lips of Betsy. She curled them softly with a smile, "We have coffee or tea, port or brandy, no whiskey but we do have water. For dessert there's an apple dumpling covered with maple syrup from Vermont, plus many types of local cookies. The apples are from Uncle Jake and the maple syrup is from Dad Randolph. He brought some with him all the way from Vermont!"

"Wonderful," said the General, "that's my favorite . . . and coffee of course."

Seth stood up and said, "Looks like the fire is quieting down, I'll throw some more wood on it. Then we will ask the General what is in that trunk he had us hoist on top of that table over there."

"Yes, I want to do that now," and the General got up and went over to the trunk. He picked up the newspaper that was setting on top and went back to his seat announcing, "I picked this up in town," and he turned it and showed the picture that was on the front page.

"The original of this picture is in my office at the War Department and the other copy I see is hanging over on your wall," and he looked praisingly at Betsy who turned a slight pink.

"General, Seth and I were so pleased to open your 'new home' present today. Sarah and John gave it to us compliments of you and we hung it there. That is a special place. The morning light will shine on it every day."

"Wonderful," the General said with a smile on his face and he nodded his approval.

"Let me remind everyone that I had the maker of it put it into the Washington papers with my comments and it has spread all over the Northern city newspapers. I see your local paper has finally put it in their gazette. Unfortunately newspapers don't fly quite as fast as telegrams, but pictures don't come with telegrams and that picture has become quite popular!

"I have received many inquiries from Morgan horse people. I've organized all of them and will have Captain Randolph follow-up with them on one of his many assigned missions. Right now we feel the most important mission of all is to get more good horses!"

Seth was returning to his seat and interjected, "Can't wait to follow-up on those leads, Sir. Thank you for assisting me in this effort."

"You're welcome Captain. When the President saw the picture he just loved it. He's quite a comedian. He said, 'Everyone's face looked so good but mine . . . I should have worn my other face.' He laughed and followed-up quipping, 'I was ridiculed and called two-faced by a person. But that picture shows that I'm not. If I was two-faced I would not be wearing that one, especially next to those beautiful ladies. I probably should have been standing between the horses.'"

Everyone in the room bust out laughing.

"That was my response to him, too," chimed the General. "Then the President looked at me and said, 'What rank are Seth and John?' I told him Captain and Lieutenant. 'Can't you do something about that?' he said back. So I told him I just got the request approved so one is now a Bvt. Maj. Gen. and the other a Bvt. Col.!"

There was silence in the room. The General got up saying, "Now let's take a look at this trunk everyone is inquiring about." He got up and went to the trunk. "All of our military trunks like this have our names affixed to the outside. This one has tape over the name.

"I came here tonight for many reasons, to enjoy some rest and relaxation and to confer with my new staff officers. But at the top of my agenda is to make this announcement by our War Department—Congratulations to our new officer Brevet Major General Seth Randolph, Jr." and then he tore off the tape revealing the name stamped on the trunk.

Opening it he added, "And inside we have two promotions," and he reached in and pulled out two boxes. While he was opening the boxes everyone in the room sat in awe of what he was doing.

"Captain Randolph please come over here and stand on this side of me and Lieutenant Reynolds you come over here and stand on the other side of me."

Seth and John got up quickly and with surprised looks frozen on their faces they obeyed the General and went and stood by his side.

The General smiled and opened the first box announcing, "Fulfilling the orders of the War Department, Captain Randolph," and he turned towards him, "you are now promoted to the rank of Bvt. Maj. Gen.," and he handed him the box of papers and insignias.

He then turned towards John with the second box and opened it announcing, "Lieutenant Reynolds, you are now promoted to the rank of Bvt. Col.," and he handed him the box of papers and insignias.

"General Randolph you are permanently assigned to the Gettysburg area and you will use the local train station as your headquarters and will coordinate all the rail traffic in and out in accordance with the just approved Military Transportation Equine and Supply to the Army of the Potomac Program and insure the supply of horses for the entire Army of the Potomac.

"Colonel Reynolds, you will report in a week to Giesboro Point, D.C., to the Camp Stoneman Cavalry Depot and hospital to coordinate and insure your program is handled properly and you also are to be treated by a special surgeon to remove the remaining fragments from your wounds."

There was complete silence in the room and then the General smiled, concluding with, "I know that Seth, Sr., brought a special bottle of his best brandy and we are finished with our dessert and the formalities, so I do think it's time for some brandy!"

PART SIX

SERGEANT GLAZIER AT ALDIE.

AN EVENING WITH GENERAL SIMPSON AT THE RANDOLPHS' HOME

After the celebratory congratulations were over, Seth, Sr., announced, "Since we are all trying to digest this wonderful news and that fantastic dinner, and the serving ladies have departed, let's all go into the living room. The General has requested that I light the stone fireplace and create a 'story time' atmosphere. He has a bigger story to tell. I have set up cozy places for our new general and Betsy and our new colonel and Sarah to set in the warm love seats while we old timers share the old cold rockers. I have set the General in the old leather chair with a table in front. He has another yarn to tell."

"Let's tell it the way we used to when we were boys together in Vermont—around a huge campfire!" added Jake.

Seth, Jr., looked at his dad as he led Betsy into the living room. "Dad, I've never heard any of this before today!"

"Oh, son, there is a lot you haven't heard before now. That's why we are telling it tonight. We old timers were young once, too," and he and Jake and General Simpson laughed in a jolly way as they all headed into the living room carrying their drinks.

The General walked over to the old leather chair and plopped down and put a large folder down on the table while Jake and Seth, Sr., went over and dropped the last of the dried apple wood logs on the roaring fire.

"There, that should heat up the room for awhile, now let's have our old time friend color this warm room with his tales."

Sarah cuddled next to John lovingly saying to him, "Colonel Reynolds I'm so proud of you!"

Betsy wiggled and sank deeper into the love seat cushions and her heart swooned almost into a pool of rapture as she gazed proudly at her new General.

John and Seth, Jr., clutched their beloveds, waiting to hear what the General had to say. They all watched as the kerosene lamps glowed and the fireplace released warm currents and added a flickering light source.

General Simpson set back and smiled, his white beard sparkled in the glow of the fireplace. He started his tale, "I am the general who bought Seth Randolph, Sr.'s, Vermont farm! I am the general who will raise Vermont Morgan horses there, too! Seth, Sr., and Jake were my childhood friends!

"We rode Morgan horses together in the hills around our parents' farms. My dad and mom sold ours and moved to New York, much to my sadness; dad and mom wanted to be city people. When I left I told the brothers, 'Someday we will get together!'

"I was an only child and went to West Point with many of the generals now in the Confederate Army. We were cadet friends and they always touted their famous southern families like the Randolphs and their numerous progeny. They were thought of as 'the Adam and Eve of Virginia.' The Randolph family was the wealthiest and most powerful family in Colonial Virginia and presumably still is.

"I always claimed my childhood friends as 'The Randolph Family of Vermont' who were their poorer relatives and still much a part of the back and forth movements in our growing great country of families. I told them the Randolphs I knew never cared about fortune, but they were a huge part of my life and as kids we only cared about Morgan horses!

"When President Lincoln chose me to run the War Department we were chatting one day about Randolphs, Lincolns and Morgan horses! I told him I was from Vermont and loved Morgan horses and often rode one in my early cavalry career. He said he had a favorite Morgan horse that they used to pull the logs to the mill for cutting. He touted that his favorite horse was a smaller Morgan who always out pulled the larger horses.

"We discussed the sadness for all of the West Point officers who decided to fight for the Confederacy. He said that he was relegated to do what Napoleon Bonaparte quoted, 'I made all my generals out of mud.' Then he went one step further and ordered me 'To get out there in the mud and find him those generals.'

"You know how many generals we have gone through? In fact, his reelection campaign is now hanging by a horse hair as the citizens are getting 'war weary' and now one of his fired generals, McClellan, who seemed to hate battle, is running against him for the presidency! Some seem to be 'sick of Abraham Lincoln' and our log-splitting President is now running on a 'horse' theme.

"We Vermonters know how important the horse and especially our beloved Morgan horse has been in this war. We know that a 'mud general'

Sheridan and his Morgan horse Rienzi are riding to our rescue. We all hope that 'mudders' like Grant and Sheridan and horses like Rienzi and Brandy will 'carry the cause.' The President's not as dumb or two-faced as people challenge. He knows how to pick winners and especially if they are riding Morgans.

"When I returned to Vermont and reunited with your dad back in the summertime, I told him about a Lieutenant Seth Randolph who was rising fast in the First Vermont Cavalry and he said, 'That's my son.'

"I met with the President and told him about another potential 'mud general' named Randolph. He said, 'Is he related to that famous Randolph family down South?' I told him, 'I don't know and I don't care. He's from Vermont and he rides a Morgan horse and he'd make a great brevet general! You have to see how he works in the mud! You have to meet him! He's come up from the bottom of the ranks!'

"He agreed with all the other generals who reviewed the files and the President said to me, 'Another mud general . . . named Randolph! Sounds like a winner to me. And he rides a Morgan horse! How wrong can we be?'

"Now you know that story!" General Simpson concluded.

Betsy looked around the room as the heat from the fireplace reddened her cheeks and the amber glow shined on her face. Tiny tears were streaming down her cheeks as she tucked her head into her husband's arm saying, "My hero, my husband . . . General Randolph. How blessed can a woman like me be?"

Sarah looked over at her and smiled, her blonde hair hung loosely over John's clutching arm. "What a tale . . . I am so happy for Seth and Betsy."

The General coughed, and they all looked at him. "There's more, if you all want to hear it."

Betsy exclaimed, "General, we are so cozy and you are so charming, please continue, Sir."

They all shook their heads in agreement while Jake looked at Seth, Sr., and said, "General can sure cast a special spell. Let's hear more."

"Thanks," added the General and he looked lovingly at the ladies saying, "I never had any daughters, but I feel like I have two adopted ones now!"

Sarah smiled and Betsy remarked, "And I now have two generals and a colonel to love!"

"Two generals and a colonel to love . . . we are the luckiest ladies in the world!" Sarah agreed.

GENERAL SIMPSON
TELLS MORE TALES

The flames in the living room fireplace started to die down so Seth, Sr., got up and walked over to the pile of wood. "The apple wood is all gone so let's see how this pine smells and burns," and he dropped on a huge split pine log, saying, "I split this today."

The glowing embers and the low flames quickly ignited the outside of the huge piece. "That should burn for awhile," and he returned to his seat and sat while the General sipped from his glass of brandy ready to start another story.

"Horses have alway been a big part of mankind's conquests and wars. No different now than in the past. I told the President when I took over that we would use the horse to carry us on to a victory in the Civil War and now they may be carrying him on to his reelection victory, too!

"Generals can rally the troops riding out front and some end up presidents like Washington and a few others. Some generals get shot off their horses and die. History records their deeds if they win or lose. The horse never gets mentioned . . . but they always carry the generals, win or lose.

"When we were briefed about the Gettysburg engagement we got all the military details. There were so many holes left open in the lines, some we filled and won; some we didn't and we lost ground. Overall we won the day and Lee is back in the South. But we are now hot in pursuit on horseback with Grant, Sheridan, and Custer and our cavalry chasing Lee and his generals like Stuart.

"They are all out front leading their armies gallantly and getting a lot of press, while we are displaying our heroes on horses as much as possible while they perform against very intelligent and many Confederate West Point erudite officers. Our Northern generals are finally performing well. Custer was last in his class at West Point and was brevetted to brigadier general at age 23, less than a week before the Battle of Gettysburg where he personally led cavalry charges that prevented Confederate troops from attacking the Union rear in support of Pickett's Charge.

"'Little Phil' Sheridan is a rapidly rising star moving from commanding an infantry division to leading the Cavalry Corps of the Army of the Potomac; General Grant was a retired general who reenlisted and moved up quite fast; and your own First Vermont officer Wells, a Private to Major already will probably get the Medal of Honor for actions at Gettysburg and soon another 'mudder brevetted general.'

"So that is just a few of President Lincoln's 'mud generals' and all horse racing people know how well a 'mudder horse' performs and wins on a very sloppy racetrack and this Civil War racetrack is a 'mudder's race!

"All of those generals are out front leading our army in battle, and some are in a different roll on Morgan horses, like you General Randolph. When I was briefed on the Gettysburg campaign and told about all the gallantry I noticed you and the First and followed-up by overriding your leaders and ordering you to go to York and Harrisburg with that horse Brandy.

"We had a horrible morale problem before that battle and I wanted to capitalize on you. A general on a horse leading the charge and winning is a good morale builder. A captain on a horse out in the public and a winner is a good morale builder . . . but making that captain a general on that same horse with the same background is a major morale builder!

"That is your mission, General Randolph, and this will be your outpost headquarters. You will report directly to me. Public relations, horse trading, and special assignments are your new duties. You are not to be in the line of fire. I need you alive and out in public on that Brandy! You are just as important as the generals out front leading the charge in combat! We have a war to win!

"Colonel Reynolds, you will work with the two of us coordinating and assisting us by keeping the overall defense of Washington top priority. The enemy can and will try to penetrate our defenses there and we want you and General Randolph to make sure that doesn't happen by constantly reviewing and reporting to me about any possible holes in our defenses.

"Tomorrow, we will meet privately to discuss all of the plans and missions. Congratulations to both of you and to your family. This has been a long day. I'm going to retire to my room and gaze out at those beautiful horses grazing in your Gettysburg meadows."

BETSY AND SETH

Seth, Sr., banked the fire while Jake, John, and Sarah said goodnight to everyone. They walked the short distance to their farmhouse. The night air was cold but they chatted enthusiastically on their way home. Nothing was going to dampen their spirits. It was a glorious day for the Randolphs and Reynolds. The footprints they left in the light snow on the way home held firm.

"Goodnight General, see you in the morning," said Seth, Sr. "Poor Betsy was so tired Seth carried her to their room. She fell asleep at the end of your talk and he hugged her until you were finished. He said to tell you thank you, and will see you in the morning."

General Simpson and Seth, Sr., both headed for the stairway as the shadows closed in behind them. "That was such a moving moment watching Seth's first act as a new general—lifting up his pregnant wife, kissing her, and then carrying her safely and gently to her bed. We need more generals like him! Goodnight old friend!"

Seth gently carried Betsy to their room, realizing she was not as light as the day he carried her across the threshold in their home in Vermont. She was a little heavier now, but he was now carrying two Randolphs.

"I think it's going to be a boy," said Betsy as she opened her eyes and giggled as Seth gently placed her on their bed.

"You're awake," whispered Seth.

"I'm awake honey. Is this happening or am I awaking from a dream? What a day!"

"It's real Betsy, and boy or girl, I will be the happiest general in the Army of the Potomac! Look at what I have. Look at you. Look how far we have come from that farmhouse in Vermont."

"Yes, the one where I first told you, 'I never want to leave Vermont!'"

"I still carry that picture of you in my pocket close to my heart and soon I'll be carrying the baby you are nourishing in my arms. Providence . . ."

"Oh I think it's a little more than providence. Since I met those angelic sisters on that wide river called the Susquehanna, something really changed in me. Since being around Sarah and now that she is going to be married at St. Mary's in Emmitsburg . . . well, she has really become the sister I never had. But more than that, her *spirituality* has made me feel even closer to you and our baby and to God."

"I feel the same way too, Betsy. Tonight John asked me to be his best man. He is finishing his Catholic conversion next week and they are going to be married by the priest at Emmitsburg."

"A conversion to be Catholic? I didn't know you could do that!" said Betsy and she got up and started to change into her night clothes.

"Oh boy . . . I better turn my head and give you some privacy," Seth laughed.

Betsy giggled, "Don't be silly. Hurry and change too and look at my belly, this must be a boy . . . it's getting so big. It reminds me of how you were too tall for that railroad bed and had to sleep in a chair rather than have your feet stick out. I wonder how President Lincoln slept in that same bed?"

SARAH AND JOHN

John and Sarah held hands as they walked to Jake's farmhouse and Jake trailed behind, both men limping along in the cold evening.

"I'll get a fire going in that old Franklin stove; didn't know Old Ben Franklin invented that in Philadelphia," said Jake. "It's been in the house ever since I bought the place and it just never stops working."

They reached the front door of their historic farmhouse and looked back at Seth's stone farmhouse. "One of the shortest, best walks I've ever had with you," John said to Sarah.

"And I can't wait until I walk with you down the aisle to marry John the week before Christmas!" chirped Jake in a very happy tone.

"That's not faraway dad. Betsy helped me to pick out my bridal gown. She is so excited and she and Seth are so happy to be in the wedding."

They took off their heavy coats and entered the parlor as Jake lit the stove to heat the room. "Your room is right over that pipe John and that should keep you warm."

"Sarah's room and my room are a little colder, but once you two get married it won't make much difference for you two. You will then be in the room my wife and I shared, but since she passed I can't go into it. When you two get married my heart will start to purr again, knowing you two are sharing what we shared. Marriage is a blessing, especially when two people meet and providence is working in their lives."

"Dad, when I told Betsy that our children are going to be educated by the Daughters of Charity like I was, she nodded and said, 'Mine, too!' And then she added, 'Seth and I want to start going to your church here in Gettysburg, just like you and John are doing.' She said they don't belong to a church yet, they didn't really have a chance with the War and moving, but want to start now as their baby will be born soon.

"I told her that our Gettysburg church is still acting as a hospital like so many of the others are since the battle. She told me that those huge white hats the sisters wear are very humbling and spiritual."

"Well, having a baby puts a whole different perspective on marriage and those poor kids just never had a chance to get established as Seth enlisted soon after marriage and they haven't had any time to be together. Now that Seth is a general there probably will be even less time. That is so much responsibility for a young man like him," stated Jake.

Sarah turned lovingly to John saying, "Oh John, and you're now a colonel . . . I'm so happy we are getting married so quickly. Betsy and I will have so much more to worry about!"

"Providence followed us this far Sarah, and since I've been getting instruction in your Catholic faith I trust that God will keep us in the palms of His hands. That story about Mother Seton is so faith based; what you and I have to endure looks to be a much easier task."

"If I learned one thing from those Daughters of Charity and their faith, it's that their future is always today . . . in the Kingdom of God," explained Sarah.

"And in this nasty war General Simpson said General Sheridan would soon be burning crops in the Shenandoah Valley and the 'hades of hell' may be ascending on the South just like it did here in Gettysburg."

"Oh dad, do you think this horrible carnage will ever end?" lamented Sarah.

"Only God knows the answer Sarah, only God knows. Keep praying, keep praying in whatever faith we profess."

THE GENERALS AND COLONEL
MEET IN THE STONE BARN

I t was awkward for both Seth and John to be in their full uniform with their new ranks on their shoulders. Putting star and eagle insignias on their uniforms doesn't help much when someone shoots at you.

Now I'm a bigger target on top of Brandy, thought Seth, but he accepted the rank with complete honor and dignity and would do all he could to live up to this incredible honor.

He and John had both discussed the wonderment of being what the General called "brevet-mudders"—they spent plenty of time on top of horses out in the open and face down in the mud!

They entered the stone barn and there sat General Simpson with a steaming coffee cup next to his briefcase and maps on the table beside him. The smells in the barn brought back the memories of the Battle of Gettysburg and all that transpired. Now it was quiet, peaceful except for the sound of horses' tails swishing back and forth and the sounds of hay and grain being munched by the mares who were now starting to show that they were in foal. Brandy peered over his high stall door and his brown eyes reflected the image he was looking at—a steely, white-bearded general ready for a meeting with his new aides.

General Simpson looked up and returned their salute and directed them to have a seat. "Well General Randolph, the two fellows outside who accompanied me are now assigned as your assistants. They are both sharpshooters and were with you here in this barn during the battle. I'm surprised you didn't recognize them. I've promoted both to Brevet Lieutenants and they are now under your wing for more training. You did such a wonderful job with John and we need a lot more 'mudders.'

"The War Department and the President are finally pleased with the progress of the Union Cavalry. It's rising to the status of the Confederate Cavalry—even with all those smart West Pointers who ride for the Confederacy!

"General Randolph, in a short time you had the quartermasters smartly purchasing many more good Morgans with your new techniques, warding off the crooked traders. Your galas in York and Harrisburg got notice-able press coverage and many more are finding that the Morgan is a unique American breed strong on endurance, unique with versatility, and loved for their heart and courage, especially under point-blank and cannon fire.

"We know how good Morgans can be like Old Clem, ridden by Colonel Lemuel Platt; General Phil Sheridan's Winchester or old Rienzi; and Charlemagne, the noted Morgan mount of General Joshua Chamberlin now famous after the Little Round Top battle. Now they are reading about you and seeing you atop that beautiful stallion Brandy. Everyone is getting more and more press coverage.

"I want you to keep it going and now that you are a general you will get even more press coverage. They love generals . . . especially our 'mud generals' . . . brevets—up from the ranks and brilliant under fire!

"We have an Open Purchase Order Agreement, just like you suggested, set up in so many states where they are now forming Morgan Horse Breeder Groups. They will get money up-front before their horses hit the ground. We're still working on a separate and long needed proposal for a new U.S. Government Morgan Farm Breeding Program. We want to call them Government Morgans! Congress works so slow in all things that cost money. It could take years but we're whispering in their ears. The President and now Congress and more importantly the public, all know that horses cost money!

"Pull in your chairs and let's discuss this mission. I have brought this map . . . it's one of two. One hangs in the War Room in Washington and this one is for you two to study and keep secretly hidden. You have both been to Washington and reviewed the defenses. A U.S. President has not come under enemy fire during wartime since the War of 1812 and we want to keep it that way!

"In '61 McClellan set the lines—a complete 33-mile circle of entrenchments and fortifications with closed forts on high ground around the city, adding well-protected field artillery batteries in the gaps and many heavy guns pointed to the south. Rifle pits were dug for troops. They say it's foolproof . . . impregnable!

"I don't believe them and I want you two to think like Jubal Early or J.E.B. Stuart and find a way to get in. If we don't, they will . . . and we will have failed.

"The President lost trust in McClellan when he didn't go after Lee after Antietam . . . and he's lost his trust in his defenses around Washington! McClellan is a civilian now and running against him for President.

"Mudders know how to get anything done and if they get through, it can be very problematic for the War cause and also for his reelection. If they get through it's easy for politicians to blame it on McClellan's Plan or Buchanan's War but the President does not see it that way . . . he's the President!

"I'll leave this map with you two to conceal in a safe place and to study every conceivable way one can break the safety seal! I'll be leaving in the morning. I'll send you more orders but in the meantime celebrate your promotions with your wives and family—you both deserve it. I know you're not on the battlefield with your unit, but your mission is extremely vital to the success of us winning this war!"

They all got up and saluted and then General Simpson remarked, "Now let's talk horses!"

THE CHRISTMAS SEASON—1863

Sarah and Betsy saw the postman coming up the lane in his sleigh as the snow blew softly in the afternoon sunshine.

They quickly put on their shawls to go out to meet him, but Sarah turned and said, "You stay here Betsy. We don't want you falling in your condition."

Betsy reined in her childlike fervor that always came out in the Christmas season and obeyed. She stood by the decorated parlor window watching the postman hand Sarah some packages and then wave goodbye. He then guided the decorated sleigh around the small circular driveway and slid out on the road with his horse prancing and kicking up the snow in their wake.

"I'm so glad we are getting snow in Gettysburg for the holiday season! We always had it in Vermont," Betsy said to Sarah as she was coming back inside.

"Sure is cold out there, but much warmer in here," Sarah said as she closed the door making the holly and pine cone decoration that they had made for each of their farmhouse doors bounce on the wire hanger.

"Early gifts," said Sarah. "Let's take them in by the fire," and they strolled girlishly past the small decorated Christmas tree setting on the side table. They both stopped and picked off a small sugared fruit.

They giggled like schoolchildren and Betsy said, "Mistletoe for my Seth right up there."

"And another one over there for my John," kidded Sarah.

"Added for good luck," said Betsy, "and to the merriment of this special season for the Randolphs. We'll swap our own old homemade decorations tonight at the Eve party and we'll pop corn and string it with some of those Vermont and Pennsylvania pine cones and dried cranberries we have saved from past seasons."

"And once we see what is inside these packages we'll finish placing the candles, pine bows and holly on the fireplace mantels just like we did to your farmhouse yesterday," added Sarah in her holiday mood.

"Don't forget to decorate the barn, ladies," joked John.

"Brandy and his mares celebrate Christmas, too," added Seth as they both came through the back door one after another from the barn, laughing and in good spirits.

"When we both left Vermont, we didn't know if we'd see Christmas in Vermont again. So far this is perfect, we are celebrating it all together in these quaint, bullet-holed farmhouses in Gettysburg," said Seth.

Betsy watched Seth as he moved and then said, "You are so perfect, stop right there!"

Seth stopped. "What's wrong honey? Are you ok?"

"I'll come over there and you can check my forehead. I might have a fever," and she slowly walked over and stopped in front of him under the mistletoe above him. He bent over to check her forehead and she threw her arms around him and kissed him! "A good luck kiss on the Eve of Christmas—you are standing right under my mistletoe honey!" and she laughed and Sarah laughed, too.

"You ladies are full of good cheer," said John.

"We are two of the happiest and luckiest ladies under the protection of two cavalrymen. Innocent ladies like men in uniform at Christmas," said Betsy as she released Seth from her romantic exchange.

"Sarah has a big package from the other cavalryman in our life, General Simpson. Let's go over by the fire and see what he sent. The postman just delivered it," chimed Betsy in a giddy way.

They all went over and sat in the separate love seats. The fire in the fireplace smelled good from the pine cones they had thrown in before, adding a festive Christmas touch to the old house charm.

"It smells so good, a little better than the inside of that cold barn. Glad horses can stand the cold, because it would be hard to create this atmosphere in one," said John.

"We'll decorate in there later, no fire of course, but we have some apples and treats we got in town yesterday to give to the horses for Christmas morning. Betsy bought some dried apples from the old German Christmas Shop in town," said Sarah.

"Our Lord was born in a stable. At the convent the Daughters of Charity set up a crèche scene every Christmas. They said it came from their Mother House in France. You'll see one in town at midnight mass tonight in our church. I'll explain it all then."

"We can't wait," said Betsy, "now let's see what's in that package."

"Packages," exclaimed Sarah in surprise, "there are two small packages with this Christmas card." She handed one of the packages to Betsy. "This one has your name on it, and this one has my name on it," and she giggled with delight.

"I'm like a child at Christmas full of serendipity. The Sisters taught me the meaning of that word. The Earl of Orford in England wrote a play called 'The Three Princes of Serendip.' It's a fairy tale where the heroes always make accidental discoveries of things that make them happy. This Christmas is serendipitous!"

"We're going to send our children to the Sisters' school for their education, too, Sarah."

"You did receive a beautiful and special education," came a rough voice from her father approaching from behind carrying glasses and a big pitcher of egg nog on a silver tray. "Here, we must sample this before our party."

Walking in behind him was Seth, Sr., with a beautiful spruce topped Martin parlor guitar in his hands.

"Dad, what's that?" asked Seth, Jr., as the girls delighted in their packages.

"This is our gift to General Simpson. He plays the guitar."

"So do John and I," offered Seth, Jr.

"After the girls open their presents we'll talk guitars." Seth, Sr., handed the guitar to Seth, Jr., and then sat down on the rocker after grabbing a glass from the silver tray. Seth sat next to Betsy strumming the guitar lightly.

"Out of tune," chimed John. "I'll get my pitch pipe later."

"First we have to open the Christmas card from General Simpson."

> *Train due in on Christmas Eve at 4 p.m. Looking forward to spending the Holiday Season with the Randolphs, Reynolds and the Morgans. Merry Christmas and Love, The General*

Betsy and Sarah opened their packages delicately, and both announced excitedly, "*Godey's Lady's Book—Special Christmas Edition!*"

"Look, inside it has a story about America's most beloved symbol of the American family Christmas—the Christmas tree. It tells the tale of Queen Victoria and Prince Albert and England's Christmas tree. That is quite a love story about Prince Albert and the queen. Their love story reminds me of my Cousin Seth and his beloved Betsy's love story. This is such a special gift from the General. I love it!" exclaimed Sarah.

Betsy held her copy to her heart and started to cry.

"Are you ok Betsy?" asked Sarah.

Betsy sat back in the love seat and looked at Seth who was cradling her with his arm and speaking in a soft voice she explained, "These are tears of joy . . . utter joy. Being an expectant mother adds to the emotions, too."

Betsy began telling her own tale, "One day last summer Dad took me to Brattleboro to the photo shop of a man who left home and went off to the Civil War. He was a professional Civil War photographer and the folks in his office made a picture of me and I sent it to Seth as a sign of my love.

"On the way out of town I stopped and bought a copy of the summer edition of *Godey's Lady's Book* with dainty pictures and a lemonade recipe. I still have it in my hope chest. I was praying that picture would get safely to him.

"When Seth and I met again for the first time since he enlisted, he pulled it out and showed me and then kissed me. That is my little love story!

"Setting here with all of you around and in this family Christmas scene . . . I just am overwhelmed. I don't know Prince Albert and Queen Victoria's love story, but my love story with my Prince and General is truly the finest love story I know!"

Everyone in the room started to tear up. "That was the time and trip that changed both of our lives, Betsy. I was suffering so much grief at the loss of my wife and what you gave to me on that trip has filled my heart with such a love for you. And with a grandchild on the way . . . I am a part of that love story," declared Seth, Sr.

CHRISTMAS EVE
AT THE RANDOLPH FARM

The Randolphs and John and General Simpson all sat in the old stone farmhouse of Jake Randolph. Sarah savored the scene. When they all toasted with Jake's egg nog Sarah got up and politely asked, "May I also add a toast? I am reminded of last year when Dad and I were alone lamenting the loss of my mom and Sister Kate was away with the Daughters of Charity. But now look at who is here. I want to toast the Daughters of Charity for teaching me this special prayer of their Foundress Mother Elizabeth Ann Seton, 'Look up, look, and we will all get to Heaven on horseback!'"

"Amens" came gleefully and happily out of all those present.

General Simpson got up and tipped his glass and added, "Of course she was speaking of a Vermont Morgan horse!"

Everyone burst into laughter and then they all thanked Sarah for the beautiful, prayerful toast.

"Now General, it is the Randolph tradition to open our holiday gifts on Christmas Eve. The ladies got your's today and have been swooning over them all day. You gave quite a dandy! It is also our tradition to light the candles on our tree and afterwards to pop corn over the fire and the guys and girls string it and hang it on the tree. Afterwards my wife would play our piano and we always had music. Kate can play but she is gone and Sarah plays, too, but we haven't had many happy occasions for her to play. You told me you play parlor guitar," stated Jake.

The General was sipping on his wine and looked up to see them all staring at him. "Yes I do play, but sadly my old guitar is being repaired in a tiny shop in Washington along with so many others. The shopkeeper is overwhelmed trying to repair so many instruments. My problem is we are waiting for the French 'Jerome' tuners to be shipped in from Paris, France.

"Many don't realize that when the War started countless soldiers brought their musical instruments with them to pass the time in camps. They had their own banjos and fiddles, but mostly guitars. And I think most of them are now *in repair* in the same shop in Washington," chuckled the General as he put his glass down on the table next to him.

190

"Here are some boring facts from this old general. When the War started, our War Department officially approved of every regiment of infantry and artillery having a brass band with two dozen members, and a cavalry regiment with sixteen members!

"When General Randolph and Colonel Reynolds visited last week to discuss military matters, after our meeting we left my house and visited Tudor Place overlooking the Potomac River. We were entertained in the special gardens by wonderful parlor guitar players. We had a grand time and I wanted them to see the house that was built by a granddaughter of Martha Washington with an inheritance from George Washington. We had an opportunity to stay in its rooms—a favorite of the leading politicians, military leaders, and dignitaries visiting the Capitol—but the boys had to catch an early return train so we didn't stay.

"We had a splendid time and we all got a chance to play those magnificent instruments. We were not as good as those professionals but we had a good laugh," said the General.

Sarah and Betsy, who were totally intrigued by the General's story, both sat up and looked right in the eyes of their beloveds and said in unison, "I didn't know you played the guitar!"

Both looked sheepish and chuckled. "I only pick a little," said John.

"I only poke it a little," kidded Seth.

"Oh no ladies, they are better than me now! I told them that there is a general who told me he gives his cavalry bands the best horses and special uniforms. We generals all agree, 'Music helps to win a war!' Don't believe me, check out our drummers and buglers. Music moves the momentum of the troops on the battlefield. How about that, *Battle Hymn of the Republic*?

"But they don't carry guitars into battle like fifes, bugles and drums . . . that's why they call them parlor guitars! And when those boys get around the ladies in the parlors, oh the ladies always love a man in uniform, and playing a parlor guitar is a bonus!" exclaimed the General.

Sarah and Betsy just sat there in complete fascination and looked at John and Seth with complete adoration. Jake got up and announced, "Well it's time to give our special guest his present." He got up and went into the other room and came back with a beautiful off-white colored guitar and handed it to the General. The General went white and then red with blushing.

"Thank you. Where did you find this beautiful instrument?"

"They had only one in the Gettysburg music shop. The storekeeper had hidden it in the cellar during the battle. He said it was made by a Martin Company up in northern Pennsylvania," said Jake.

"I know about them. They used to be in New York. Martin started there after immigrating to the U.S. Then he moved to a religious community in Nazareth. We all know about Nazareth—that's what our Christmas is all about! Oh my, how providence comes into play in my life, too! A Martin parlor guitar made in Nazareth . . . a gift to me on Christmas . . . a gift to me . . . Jesus of Nazareth."

The old general started to tear up, stuck in a moment of nostalgia. "Thank you. Thank you. This is a special gift on a special Christmas."

"General," said Seth, Sr., "I'm sorry it didn't come with a tuning instrument. The boys told me it was out of tune. John said he has a pitch pipe, but no guitar!"

"Oh I have perfect pitch. I don't need a pipe," and he took it gently and started to pluck and simultaneously tighten the strings. While he was tuning he kept talking and everyone was fascinated watching his stubby hands move in meticulous movements while his lips moved the words out, "You know what they say about parlor guitar players?"

"What?" asked Seth, Sr.

"Well there are three types of guitar players."

"Only three?" chimed in Betsy and she giggled while tasting the egg nog in her glass.

As he moved across the frets tuning each of the strings, E A D G B E, mumbling and tuning each string to his perfect pitch, he continued, "One can play a guitar and can't sing. One can sing, but can't play the guitar. And finally, one can play the guitar and sing at the same time."

"Really," interjected Sarah, "and which one are you, Sir?"

"I used to be the third one, but old age, paralysis in the knuckles, and hard of hearing throws off my voice. I'm now the first one. But I can still play!"

He plucked each string and then strummed softly. "Perfect!" echoed John and Seth. "Perfect Sir. You are amazing!"

"Now I can play *Oh Little Town of Bethlehem*," and he started to play.

"Wait General, let's go over to our piano. I know that one, too. Can you play that in the key of C?"

"Oh that's an easy one," and he got up and went over and sat down in a chair opposite the piano as Sarah came over in her pine green satin dress with fluffy holly adorned sleeves.

"The piano is in tune. I do play it when I have time, but lately not so much. Can you sing General?"

"I'll let everyone in the room do that," he said and laughed.

"Wait," remarked Seth, Sr., "we'll all come over and sing together." Everyone got up and grabbed their glasses of egg nog and gathered around the piano. It was a mixture of Christmas colors and holiday decorations. Then Sarah and the General started playing as all started to sing,

"O little town of Bethlehem
How still we see thee lie
Above thy deep and dreamless sleep
The silent stars go by
Yet in thy dark streets shineth
The everlasting Light
The hopes and fears of all the years
Are met in thee tonight

For Christ is born of Mary . . ."

PART SEVEN

THE YEAR OF 1864 IN REVIEW

The Battle of Gettysburg and Christmas 1863 were past and the Randolph farms in Gettysburg were finally out of the action. The town was mending and the locals were very fortunate to have peace and a quiet time to celebrate the Christmas traditions of the 19th century. General Simpson and the War Department had added a Brevet Colonel and General to their host of "Mudder Generals." All were adding to the Union war efforts and to their own personal Christmas traditions.

The four seasons of 1864 passed quickly with many colorful events. In the Spring, Betsy had her baby boy and the Randolphs named him Simpson Randolph, after General Simpson. John and Sarah were married in the chapel at the Daughters of Charity Convent in Emmitsburg where they first met.

Brandy was running around the meadows with his mares who now all had a foal on the ground, including his old mother. Some were cookie-cutter images of him, some of his mother; some were black, some bay and one even showed his color of brandy. The meadows were alive and in constant movement with equine life and Seth and Betsy were alive with the newborn in their life. Ulysses S. Grant was on the move, too. After President Lincoln promoted him to Lieutenant General in command of all the Union Armies, the following day he started his "Red River Campaign"—the overall Union strategy to strike deep into the Confederacy.

In the Summer and Fall the Union Army raided the South by assaulting Petersburg, Virginia, and raging forward into September when Atlanta fell and the Confederate troops under General Hood evacuated the city of Atlanta. General Sherman and his Army of Georgia now occupied the city and began their "March to the Sea," all riding into the Winter as another Christmas approached.

Three Medals of Honor for the capture of three flags of Southern regiments had been awarded to the First Vermont Cavalry and President Lincoln campaigned with his reelection slogan, "Don't Change Horses in Midstream!"

CHRISTMAS EVE 1864
AT THE RANDOLPHS'
IN GETTYSBURG

Overall it had been a wonderful year for the Union Army and the Randolphs and Reynolds. Colonel Reynolds and General Randolph were successful in filling open holes in the Capitol's defenses, deterring the Confederate Army from attacking except for what General Simpson had feared—Cavalry Lt. Gen. Jubal A. Early's unsuccessful and only attack on Washington. It was the first and last time since the British burned the Capitol in the War of 1812 where a U.S. President had come under attack. Now the war would be fought exclusively in the South.

On Christmas Eve, General Simpson sat lamenting the generals lost by both sides as he paged through his diary of clipped obituary notices. Despite Stuart being a Confederate General he mulled over his obituary:

OBITUARY OF J.E.B. STUART
Died at The Battle of Yellow Tavern
May 12, 1864 (aged 31)
Richmond, Virginia

The "flower of Cavaliers"—No death, since the fall of Stonewall Jackson, caused more painful regret than the demise of Major-Gen. J.E.B. Stuart. A Virginia made model cavalier and dashing chieftain, whose name alone once struck terror into the Union Army. Dead is a legend, a name known on two continents. Hit by a last bullet from a volley of shots fired at him striking the General in the left side of the stomach. He did not fall, gallantly avoiding capture if fallen, he reined his horse's head and spurred for the protection of his comrades. His severe stomach wound ruptured but he fell into the arms of his gallant troopers, and was carried to safety. He breathed out his gallant spirit before death, and in the full possession of his faculties of mind and body.

He put it away and sat in the same leather chair as last year. He took in all of the Christmas decorations and the wonderful Randolphs and Reynolds around him. Everyone was sipping egg nog waiting for his "grandfatherly" holiday tales.

Instead of having a guitar in his hands he held his namesake, Simpson Randolph, who was holding a tiny flag and waving it in his face trying to touch his beard. The General lifted Simpson up in front with a huge smile on his face announcing, "My parents were from North Yorkshire, England, and my mother taught me the custom when visiting a new baby for the first time, to place a silver coin in its hand! So I am placing this 1861 George Washington silver coin in his hand," then quickly he handed it to Betsy.

Betsy took it and smiled at the General. She looked curiously at it, and turned it over several times and then read out loud, "The front reads, 'The Constitution is sacredly obligatory on all.' The back side says, 'U.S. Mint Oath of Allegiance Taken by the Officers and Workmen Sept. 9, 1861. Jas. Pollock, Dir.'"

"And now I've made my mother happy; those coins were handed out at the start of the Civil War," remarked the General.

"Thank you General," said Betsy. "We will put it in his baby trunk and I know he will cherish it later. Sarah made his little blue suit for him. She said now he looks like all the officers in our family."

"You look beautiful too, Betsy, in your peppermint-striped holiday dress. Did Sarah make that too?"

"Yes, we both did. We got the patterns from the special Christmas edition of *Godey's Lady's Book* you gave to us last Christmas. This matching hairstyle was in, too," and she turned and smiled at her husband Seth. "Seth likes the style." Her hair was tied back revealing her beautiful face glowing with a soft patina of happiness.

"I wish I had a box camera to capture both of them in their outfits and hairstyle. I would carry that picture next to my heart forever," said Seth softly.

"Next time you are in Washington with the family we'll see my friend, he has a shop down in Georgetown. He hires out to Matthew Brady at times. He's getting more arthritis like this old general and he prefers now to take only family pictures in his home studio."

"That's a wonderful idea, Sir. Brandy and I are going to be leading President Lincoln's Inaugural Parade March 4th."

"That will be a dandy," answered the General. "I'll arrange it."

Betsy got up and said with a huge grin, "I'm expecting another child next Spring. I do hope I will be able to make that trip! And if it's a boy Seth wants to name him John, after Colonel Reynolds. He said he doesn't want a Seth the 3rd!"

Seth, Sr., burst out laughing and lifted his wine glass and toasted, "Congratulations, that is wonderful news on Christmas Eve! I'm going to be a grandfather again!"

Jake piped in and tipped his glass of wine saying, "Congratulations brother, that will give you two grandchildren. What a glorious Christmas present. Our houses are only half full like our glasses, but they are starting to fill up again," and everyone laughed.

Everyone raised their glasses and toasted and Sarah got up in her pine green Christmas dress to say, "And I'm due in the Spring, too!"

John got up with a start, "Sarah, I didn't know that!"

Sarah giggled, "Since you captured my heart with your romantic proposal in Washington on a moonlit night, I wanted to seal our hearts together in front of this special family Christmas celebration!"

CHRISTMAS MORNING
AT THE RANDOLPH HOUSE

The Randolphs and the Reynolds left early for church in Gettysburg and the old farmhouse was very quiet. The General watched out the window as snowflakes feathered the landscape and Brandy and his mares and their growing young ones were getting a light dusting out in the meadow. Snow and winter air was good for the herd.

Being out of their stalls and in the fresh air of the fields was good for them. Their winter coats were there to protect them. Gettysburg winters were nothing like a winter in Vermont. Vermont had much deeper snows and colder temperatures, but Gettysburg was a fine place to raise horses.

There was ice forming on the window panes but the iron stove was sending out a fine heat source. General Simpson sat at the huge table with his large portfolio of papers with lined and numbered pages.

On the front page of his dossier type manuscript the words "Mudders and Morgans" appeared in black ink . . . including a small, underlined subtitle "The Backbone of the Civil War." It was his memoir of the war. Someday he would set down and write his version of it—after the many skilled historians wrote their first histories—he would then write his!

The copper pot filled with water was now steaming on top of the old Franklin stove. Would he have tea or coffee? Musing out loud he said to himself, "The pundits write a funny story about the President when he said, 'If this is coffee, please bring me some tea; but if this is tea, please bring me some coffee.'"

He chuckled as the tea steeped in the small porcelain container. "Is it tea or coffee?" and he laughed out loud. Looking out again at the horses he waited a few minutes then finally poured the liquid into the china cup saying, "By jove, it's *tea* Mr. Lincoln."

"Who are you talking to?" shot out a barking voice from the entrance to the farm kitchen.

The General turned abruptly, startled and red-faced, his white beard moving up and down. Almost dropping his cup, recognizing Seth, Sr., he said, "To myself, Seth. I do it a lot as I'm usually alone. I thought you were at church?"

"I went to the midnight service after you all retired last night. I've been doing that since my wife died. It's more serene for me."

"Well then set down, there's plenty of 'tea or is it coffee,'" and he chuckled and sat down at the table. There were paper items strewn across the pine table.

"Here," said the General, "let me clear some of those papers."

"Looks like you are writing a book," joked Seth, Sr.

"I am! It's called *Mudders and Morgans*."

"What's it about?"

"Lincoln's generals and Morgan horses!"

"What's the 'mudders?'"

"When the war started over thirty percent of our officers resigned their commissions, standing firm with their own states' part in the Confederacy. That included their own Confederate President Jefferson Davis. He welcomed those prize officers, and of course the biggest gift—General Lee's choice to join the Confederacy. Many were given immediate positions of authority and responsibility and they formed a formidable adversary. Many of them had formal military training at the United States Military Academy at West Point.

"Our War Department records show that about fifteen percent of our original officers have been made generals. Their big prize General Lee has been formidable. He has been an adept, fearsome battlefield commander, beating our far superior Union Armies until Gettysburg We feel that his overly aggressive tactics are depleting his available manpower. At the same time we too have losses and have lost many of our leaders, but their losses of Jackson and then Stuart at Yellow Tavern have caused severe Southern morale problems in addition to their depleting manpower and dwindling resources.

"This is a war of mudders, horses and attrition and what you see in front of me are many obituaries cut out from newspapers. I collect them and add them to my resource dossier for my eventual manuscript. I feel confident that our 'mudders' and horses will carry the day for our army. Time will tell. I had some time here this morning to put this bundle of clippings and notes in some order for a later read.

"The South lost their famous cavalry leader J.E.B. Stuart this year, but we lost Colonel Preston of the First Vermont Cavalry and our 'mudder' General Custer said of him 'the best cavalry colonel in the Army of the Potomac!'

"Stuart is a legend in the South and cavalry officers on horses are the types of heroes that Walt Whitman writes about in his verses of, 'Ashes of Soldiers.' He eloquently refines my 'Mudders and Morgans' topic in this serene excerpt that I have clipped out of a newspaper article. Here, read it."

"Ashes of Soldiers" by Walt Whitman
. . . the head of my cavalry, parading on spirited horses,
With sabres drawn and glist'ning, and carbines by their thighs
—(ah, my brave horsemen!
My handsome, tan-faced horsemen! What life,
what joy and pride,
With all the perils were yours.)

"Old time friend, you have filled my kitchen table with historic clips of well-known military heroes' obituaries, all who have paid the ultimate sacrifice to date. We set here with tea and when we look out the windows we can see the Gettysburg Battlefield where countless future tales will fill books telling of heroes who lie buried in marked and unmarked graves out in the vast environs that surround us.

"It's Christmas for us and graves and eternity for them. It is an honor to have you alive and setting at my table. I look forward to your book. Document those who aren't so well known . . . especially our horses whose bones lie strewn over the battlefields of mankind!"

"Well spoken, friend," added General Simpson. "I better clean up. I see the buggies coming in from church. If little Simpson sees all these cutouts my book writing will be finished!"

They both laughed and hurriedly gathered the documents and put everything into the General's portfolio and then into his huge trunk that was in the corner.

"Merry Christmas!" rang in as the front door opened.

"Merry Christmas!" replied Seth, Sr., and the General.

The Randolphs and the Reynolds came wistfully in the front door in their colorful outfits. Seth, Jr., was carrying little Simpson who was fast asleep in his arms.

"Too much singing," laughed Betsy.

"Too much church," laughed the General.

"Oh, you can never have too much church," came out of the mouth of a smiling Kate who was dressed in black with a soft black hat.

"Never too much church General Simpson when my daughter Kate is here. You have never met her. Kate this is General Simpson!"

Kate smiled and walked over to the General and he bowed slightly and shook her hand graciously saying, "So you are Kate? You are the nun?"

"I'm a Daughter of Charity, General."

The General teased, "Is there a difference?"

"I can explain later. Dad and Sarah have told me about your storytime at last Christmas; and that you will be having it again today on Christmas. I like to tell stories, too. We will talk later."

"That we will."

Jake chuckled, "Oh we all want to hear your stories. It's now a tradition down here on the farm. Let's all get this place ready for a celebration this afternoon!"

"This should be a great storytime tonight—a general and a Daughter of Charity entertaining us on Christmas," Betsy said with a cute laugh.

"It should be a fun evening," chimed in John, "a very fine evening and I am looking forward to it!"

Seth, Jr., returned from putting Simpson in his bed while Betsy went to change into a more comfortable dress. Sarah walked over to the General and pinched his beard saying, "One of the older ladies at church said she saw you coming off the train in town. She said to me, 'He looks like that Santa Claus on the card we got from our cousin in Boston!' and one of the other ladies inquired, 'Is there a Mrs. Claus?'"

Betsy, holding a sugared fig she had picked off the Christmas tree offered it to the General with a smile saying, "Try this Sir. All of the ladies from our church have made you a special Christmas dinner for six tonight and they want to serve it to all of us. We accepted. They said it was an honor from the parish to our 'General' who keeps everyone safe."

"That is sure nice of them," said Seth, Sr.

"This town has suffered so much, and I thank them," said the General.

CHRISTMAS AFTERNOON
AT THE RANDOLPH FARM

The General saw the colorfully dressed church ladies exiting their buggies with their husbands carrying the covered dishes. He opened the back door and they all quickly assembled in the huge kitchen.

Their designated spokesperson said politely, "General, we weren't sure what the dinner menu should be . . . beef, ham, turkey, or oysters, with gingerbread and cakes, pickles, apples, cheese, and mince pie. We couldn't make up our mind so we decided to do it all!

"We are here to serve all of you dinner and clean up afterwards. Our husbands will be attending a church service with Father Matty at seven o'clock and then be back to pick us up around eight fifteen."

The General was overwhelmed when an inviting voice from behind him said, "We are truly blessed this holy Christmas day, please come in." It was Kate, dressed in her simple black Daughter of Charity attire.

"Thank you," said the leader.

"God bless all of you," said the accompanying priest who was carrying a mince meat pie. "What an honor for our group to be greeted by a General and Sister Kate!" announced Father Matty in a soft voice. "We are truly blessed this Christmas Day."

"And so are we Father Matty. We all want to thank you and your parish for this splendid feast. We will surely enjoy it," said Seth, Sr. Betsy, Seth, Jr., Sarah, and John took the dishes of food from the men and walked them to the tables in the back of the kitchen.

"We all wanted to treat your special War Department General Simpson," said Father Matty. "We know what a difficult task he has. It's like being one of our Cardinals always out on the front lines. Only cardinals don't get shot at with bullets!"

The General graciously and firmly shook the hands of the husbands, thanking them as they stopped to greet him on their way out.

"This sure is an honor and a special Christmas for me," he said. "I don't get to church much and thank you Father, for bringing church to me!"

"We keep you and your generals in our prayers everyday along with our Cardinals. We know how difficult our superiors have it. Have a blessed Christmas, General. We will be having a special mass at eight o'clock to pray for all who are suffering in this terrible war."

"Amen . . . and thank you Sir," said the General. As he closed the door there stood little Simpson holding a toy horse. The General bent over and picked him up gently asking him, "What is the horse's name?"

"Brandy!"

Betsy came in, smelling like turkey. "Let me take him General." She put a small piece of turkey in her mouth, adding, "A little cool, so we are going to warm up everything for dinner soon."

"It's ok, Betsy. You go back and help the ladies. Can I take Simpson out to see Brandy and the horses?"

"Sure, let me get his coat. That's all of our favorite place to go. When I'm finished Seth and I will be out in a few minutes."

–––––––– ––––––––

The General carried Simpson out to the barn. He wasn't much heavier than his filled traveling bag but he sure could talk a lot more! They laughed and talked all the way to the barn but once the General opened the barn door and stepped inside Simpson said, "Don't talk loud."

"Why not?" whispered the General.

"Daddy said we can scare the horses."

"I taught him that," echoed Seth, Jr., coming in behind with Betsy.

"This is our favorite place, even on Christmas," echoed Betsy as she sat down on a stack of aromatic hay bales. "I soon found out that it's not as cold in our barns down here as it was in Vermont. We don't need to go underground like up there with all the bank barns. It was warmer down under but I always felt more closed in. Look at those vents up there. During the day the sun shines through."

"Good for snipers to shoot out of honey," teased Seth.

"I know Seth," said Betsy, "and I'll concede that you will always think of those snipers up there and the enemy out there."

"Not when you are around," and he picked up some hay and doused her with it.

She coughed and giggled. "Careful honey, Simpson always copies what you do."

"Water daddy, water daddy," said Simpson softly.

"He wants to help feed and water the horses," said Seth.

"Watch him General, he already gets the hay first and smells it for mold. Then he'll get that stool and put it front of the feed bin and lift it and . . ." Betsy ran to him as he opened the bin and almost fell in.

"Don't fret honey, he'll bang his head once and he won't do that again. He's a quick learner just like Brandy!" and they all laughed.

"There goes the dinner bell," decreed Betsy. "Dad's doing his thing again. We all better get in and cleaned up . . . this is going to be some evening down on the Randolph farm!"

CHRISTMAS DINNER 1864
AT THE RANDOLPH FARM

"We have two more now for Christmas dinner than last year," announced Jake Randolph. "And next year we are expecting two more grandchildren, which makes a total of three. Our family is growing more each year."

"Three is a very spiritual number," spoke Kate in a soft voice. "It pictures completeness."

"And our neighbors have completed our meal with three main dishes of beef, ham, and turkey," added Sarah with John at her side.

"We are truly blessed and thank you Lord for blessing us with little Simpson and may He grant us two more grandchildren this time next year," proclaimed Kate.

"Now if we will all hold hands and bow our heads in prayer, daughter Kate will say grace," announced Jake.

The room grew silent while the crackling embers in the fireplace reigned supreme and the kerosene lights and candles in the candelabra on the table glowed like the angelic smile on Sister Kate's face.

"Bless us, O Lord,
and these thy gifts,
which we are about to receive
from thy bounty,
through Christ our Lord.
Amen."

"That was beautiful Sister. I like the one in the edition of *Harpers*," said General Simpson as he started to recite it.

"Oh Lord, we have so much to bless thee for,
we must refer it to eternity, for time is too short;
so bless our food and fellowship for Christ's sake."

"That is indeed beautiful, too," said Seth, Jr., as the village ladies started to serve the food all around the table.

"They recite that at some formal military functions. I believe it may be the Episcopalian version," added the General

"Are you Episcopalian, General?" inquired Kate as she took some turkey and passed the plate to Sarah.

"I was," answered the General as he stopped the ham and took two slices. "This smells good! Better than what our military serves!"

"Our Foundress Mother Seton was Episcopalian," replied Kate as they engaged in an exchange of conversation while everyone else smiled and took what they liked from all the wonderful food that was being served by the gracious servers.

"And what is she now, Kate?" asked the General when he finally stopped taking food and reached for his glass of wine and drank.

"Oh, Sir, she converted to Catholicism."

"Why would she do that?" asked the General as he picked up his utensils and in his English manner used both while most of the others watched how he ate.

"She was married to William Magee Seton, a wealthy New York City businessman. They were blessed with five children and were friends and neighbors of Alexander Hamilton, and once hosted a reception for George Washington . . . but they fell on bad times. It's a sad story, Sir. "

"Kate that is a fascinating story. I know about the Setons of New York and some naval officers. Your dad told me you are a wonderful storyteller and I can't wait to hear you finish it. That is truly fascinating and as my Welsh grandfather would say, 'It's got a *wee bit* of Providence in it for me!'"

"I told you General that you and Kate would fascinate each other," echoed Jake.

"Honey, Simpson needs a new bib. He has spilled his milk all over this one . . . I'll hold it up while you get another one," said Betsy as she rolled the bib up keeping it off the linen tablecloth. "Soon we'll be having three little ones at the table and we'll all be holding a bib."

Sarah giggled, "I can't wait Betsy and that will mean more children's gifts. Christmas is for kids."

"Oh we're all still kids," chided John. "I may be a Colonel but there's nothing like exchanging gifts like we did last year."

Seth, Jr., came back holding a clean bib and handing it to Betsy said,

"Here honey, give me that one." Betsy untied the soiled one and handed it to Seth and then she put on the clean bib.

John smiled and said, "They are a good baby team."

"He's not such a good cavalryman when it comes to changing diapers," said Betsy and she laughed out loud and blew Seth a kiss.

As he came back and sat down next to her he affectionately patted her hand saying, "Next baby I'll do better honey. I'm learning to 'down tie' a diaper."

Everyone laughed and someone inside the parlor started to play "What Child Is This" on the family piano. Everyone looked up and Kate said, "That is Mrs. Murdock. She plays the organ at the church. I told her that I would cue her to play that when we were getting finished with dinner."

"That is so beautiful Kate. What a wonderful way to end our dinner and to prepare for our 'gift giving' and special storytelling in the living room by the Christmas tree," said her father Jake.

"Just perfect," said Sarah. "You see why she always has been a loving role model for me."

Kate blushed and then Jake put down his napkin and announced, "It looks like we are finished with this lovely dinner. I know the ladies need to clean up and get ready for their husbands to pick them up." He looked at the antique clock adding, "It's seven thirty and they will be here in about forty-five minutes."

"Betsy, Sarah and I will help them Dad. You go set up the living room and we'll clean up. There are plenty of leftovers and we will keep some in the pantry and let the ladies take home the rest. We can all share God's wonderful gifts!"

CHRISTMAS EVENING
IN THE BARN

Seth rose and said, "John, you and I can make sure the horses are ok."
Upon hearing that, the General readily remarked, "I think I will
follow the cavalry on this mission with a chance on Christmas to see all those
foals and their mothers as well as Brandy and that gorgeous black stallion."

Seth, John and the General headed for the barn, first stopping to put
on their winter military overcoats.

"There goes the cavalry," chided Betsy as they went out the back door
and trudged through the snowdrifts that were piling up from a winter storm
that was blowing in off the Round Tops. Seth stopped to get a lantern and
then John lit the wick.

"Not far from here in 1776, George Washington and his troops crossed
the Delaware and saved the 'cause,'" decreed the General. As they entered the
barn the light from the lantern reflected off all the objects inside. Overhead
some moonlight from the full moon was filtering through the barn vents.

"It's a lot warmer in here than in those Vermont barns," said John.

"Oh this barn is like a fortress and not far from here our Revolutionary
Army was camped at Valley Forge. There's a lot of history in this state," exclaimed Seth as he walked down the long alley between the closed stalls and
into the wide open area where the mothers and foals were gathered.

"We still haven't gotten word from 'Little Phil' and his mission. He's
been quiet. He and Rienzi were a big help and the President credits them for
helping him to win the reelection," said the General. "I have some newspaper clippings saved in my 'book folder' and there's one article about Sherman's final charge at the Third Battle of Winchester explaining why Sheridan changed the name of his black Morgan from Rienzi to Winchester. If
my memory is correct it read something like this: 'General Philip Sheridan's
Morgan horse was presented to him by the officers of the Second Michigan
Cavalry in 1862. The horse was three years old.' That's about the age you
started to ride Brandy, right Seth? Am I correct?"

"Yes Sir, close," answered Seth as they stopped in front of Brandy's
stall. He nickered quietly raising his head and peering at them.

"Now that black stallion over there is a copy of Rienzi—jet black with three white fetlocks," added the General.

"Yes Sir," said John as he approached their young black stallion's stall. "Rienzi is 16 hands and our boy 'Midnight' is only 15 hands."

"We named our boy after some of the blackest nights after our Gettysburg battle and General Sheridan named his Morgan, Rienzi, after the town of Rienzi, Mississippi," added Seth as he approached the young stallion who was eating some hay. "He's gonna be a winner. When he's ready Major Wells is gonna get him. I promised him!"

"Major Wells of the First Vermont Cavalry is a real hero, too, and he's down there in the South now leaving a trail of history. Who knows if he'll change Midnight's name after some battle," said the General as he sat down on a chair by the white pine table where Seth and his troops had discussed their strategy for their Gettysburg battle that transpired right outside.

"General Sheridan changed Rienzi's name to 'Winchester' after he carried him on his back during that famous ride from Winchester, Virginia, to Cedar Creek, Virginia in, October just in time to rally his troops and turn a certain loss into a gallant victory. While Cedar Creek was his most famous engagement . . ." continued the General as Seth and John sat down beside him.

"This is where we sat General, planning our defense when those Rebs were attacking with their charges all around. Brandy was as calm then as he is now," said Seth, ". . . and John was on the battlefield outside."

John lifted his leg saying, "And out there is where I got this leg injury while Major Wells and the rest of our Cavalry won the day! . . . I'll never forget it."

"Oh I doubt the War Department will forget any of the heroics here at Gettysburg. Medals of Honor are being given for so many tales of glory. I think the First Vermont already has three recipients. I'm sure a fourth will be coming soon from what I know occurred outside these walls," said the General.

Getting up he said, "Everything and everybody looks peaceful here. Let's head in for storytime. I can't wait to hear Kate's story. She sure casts an angelic spell whenever she talks, and surely being in her presence makes one feel the presence of our God. I love her soft black bonnet and matching dress. She's in her black uniform that represents her Order and we are in our blue ones!"

"She and the Daughters of Charity all radiate that Sir. They can take the sting out of war merely with their presence. We are so fortunate to be here in peace, for we know that out there battles are still going on as this war is not showing any signs of being over!" stated Seth.

PART EIGHT

COMING DOWN
THE HOME STRETCH

Cavalry Soldier on Horseback
by Winslow Homer

CHRISTMAS EVENING
IN THE PARLOR

"We did the traditional lighting of the candles on the tree and after we all popped corn over the fireplace the guys and girls, and Simpson, all strung it and hung it on the tree. Then Sarah played the piano and we all passed another Christmas Eve, but saved a new tradition for Christmas Night," announced Jake.

The General smiled with everyone else as he sipped on his port wine and others drank egg nog. Looking up he said, "I do believe we *missed* a guitarist or should I say three guitarists last night!"

They all looked perplexed. Sarah and John were snuggled on their love seat, Seth and Betsy were comfortable on theirs, and little Simpson was nestled on Seth, Sr.'s, lap fondling a toy horse. His head was in constant motion as the holiday colors and images in the room flashed in his eyes.

Kate sat on a hard chair near the blazing fireplace and Jake kept busy filling the fireplace and glasses with drinks a plenty and offering desserts made by the church ladies.

"That was some parlor guitar scene last Christmas Eve," reminisced the General.

"Did you get your guitar back from your friend's repair shop? The one that was waiting for parts from Paris?" asked Jake as he threw a large white oak log onto the fire.

"We were in France in the summer on a special trip to visit Vincent de Paul's area where our Order was established," interjected Kate. "He is known as 'The Father of the Poor.' He started our first religious group of women with this decree, 'Whatever you do to the least of my brothers and sisters you do it to me.' Today I mentioned Paris and the General told me his story about his parlor guitar and we were amused by the coincidences."

"Yes," added the General with a big grin on his face, "and I now have Kate as another 'adopted' daughter. I love her stories. She is a delicate soul and she reminds me of what's in my big trunk over there. We all shared our Christmas gifts last night and yes, they all were wonderful, and indeed Jake my parts from Paris arrived and finally my antique guitar was fixed.

"I visited the shop and when I was there I was involved in something very special to me. I have saved special gifts for tonight to be given to our beloved Cavalry officers."

John and Seth sat up straight and their wives hugged them lovingly. "They are so special," said Betsy adoringly.

"John, you and Seth please carry my trunk over here and place it in front of me," said the General in a polite tone.

Seth and John obeyed and brought over the General's travel trunk and laid it at his booted feet.

"When I went to pick up my repaired guitar there was a beggar nearby the shop holding a sign that read: '*Whatever you do to the least of my brothers and sisters you do it to me.*'

"It was touching. He was collecting for the poor in one of the richest parts of Georgetown. I just could not pass without dropping in a donation. He was right next to the music shop.

"I then went into the music shop and my friend happily got my guitar. When he was putting it in my case he told me, 'General, look at those two Martin guitars I just got in here. Two war widows brought them saying they had belonged to their dead husbands who were killed in the war. They needed money and wanted to sell them, sadly saying it was the right thing to do as it was their husbands' wishes left in their wills that if they were killed to sell their guitars to other soldiers, so they would have money to survive and to insure other soldiers would own them.

"I was so heartened by that and moved by the sign I had read out front. I asked my friend how much they wanted for them. He said, 'Whatever the soldier could afford.' I asked him what they would cost if they were brand new. He told me a lot and it would probably take at least a year to get as Martins are made in a little town called Nazareth, Pennsylvania.

"I then asked how much my bill was for my repaired guitar and he replied, 'Veterans are free!' I wrote him a check and told him I would take all three and for him to deduct his fee for handling the sale for the widows and then give the balance equally to each widow. He looked at me with a grin saying, 'No fee. Veterans' widows are free. Surely this is just too much to pay. You can get new ones for less.'

"I told him, 'These guitars are priceless and no amount of money will compensate for the loss of their husbands. Tell them that a General and a Colonel will be playing their husbands' guitars . . . with an old general. There will be three of us playing this Christmas!'"

Betsy stood up saying, "General that is one of the most heartwarming stories I've ever heard."

Sarah got up too adding, "That is so touching General . . . my stomach is churning or maybe the baby in my belly is turning over?"

The General put down his glass of wine and bent over and opened his huge trunk. He lifted out the first long box and said, "Here Betsy this is for your General." Betsy walked over and held the plain box as Seth came over.

"Here Sarah this is for your Colonel." Sarah walked over and held it as John came over.

"I know those war widows will be smiling every time you officers play for your wives," concluded the General.

Betsy and Sarah, in their colorful Christmas dresses, held out the light boxes, balancing them on the top of their protruding bellies as Seth and John both took out honey-toned Martin parlor guitars and started to play them.

Kate got up and silently moved to the piano announcing, "Here is the General's guitar behind our piano. All three of you come here. I want you officers to join me in playing Mendelssohn's 'Hark the Herald Angels Sing' in C."

Seth, John, and the General smiled and gathered around Kate at the piano. Kate added, "The General's instructions to me for tonight is 'Just one song and then it's storytime.'" She giggled and sat down and started to play. "Everyone join in singing please."

After they played, Jake announced, "That is a new tradition."

"That was beautiful," said Seth, Sr.

"Oh, there is more," said Kate. "Now we can all go to our seats and the General wants me to tell my part of our story. It seems we have some things in common and we found it very comforting in these war torn times." She went and sat next to the General telling all, "I was in Paris, France, this summer. The General's guitar parts were sent from there this summer. We both felt that providence put him in that shop to help those war widows, and providence put me in another shop to help two officers' wives.

"We Daughters of Charity were on religious retreat and visiting our founding home in France. We stopped in a tiny shop and they had two Christmas crèches on a shelf. I paused to admire them. The owner told me that two local widows had passed leaving her the crèches with the instructions to give them both to the first person who understood their meaning in the St. Francis tradition. She asked me questions and I told her of the smaller crèche I had. The owner said, 'If I gave them to you what are your intentions? They are not to be separated.' I told her if I had them then I would have three, but I would give one to my sister and one to my cousin-in-law who live next door to each other. The owner said, 'Three crèches! Perfect! We want you to have them' and she wrapped them up and gave them to me."

She stopped talking and went over to a package that was atop the piano. She picked it up and went back and sat next to the General continuing her story, "We Sisters take vows of poverty, and so I want to add 'my gifts of love.' One to my beautiful sister Sarah and her husband John as a wedding present; and one to my cavalry officer Cousin Seth and his wife, Betsy, as a present for the birth of their first son.

Sarah and Betsy, emotionally moved, both went over to Kate; all faces in the room were aglow. Kate handed each a plain package and Betsy and Sarah carefully opened them to reveal two beautiful handmade crèches.

John quickly went over and carefully took the crèche out of the box and handed it to Sarah while Seth took out the other one and handed it to Betsy.

"Now you all know why the General and I are so moved by these stories, and we wanted to tell them this way tonight!"

Betsy and Sarah both were gleeful and Betsy said, "I am so blessed to be a part of this wonderful family!"

Sarah replied, "Amen! Amen! Amen!"

"And three is a very spiritual number," spoke Kate in a soft voice. "It pictures completeness."

Everyone was silent as the glow from the roaring fire in the stone fireplace and lighted kerosene lights illuminated the living room.

"We are expecting and we must set awhile before we burst with love from these special gifts given to all of us tonight," said Betsy and they all returned to their seats.

Kate then bent over and kissed the General on his cheek saying, "One of the best parts is that General Simpson grew up in the same part of New York where our Foundress Mother Seton had once lived. He also had previously attended her historic Trinity Church and while he was at West Point he read all about her military sons William Seton and Richard Seton who were midshipmen in the Navy. He also shared her Episcopal faith."

The General patted her on her hand and smiled saying, "And Kate is now one of my 'adopted' daughters. I now have three wonderful 'adopted' daughters here in Gettysburg—Betsy, Sarah and Kate. It pictures completeness for me!"

DAY AFTER CHRISTMAS
IN THE BARN

"I want to congratulate you General and Colonel for your assistance in the defenses around Washington . . . pictures completeness for me. I told you when you were both promoted of our trepidation about McClellan's early defense plan. McClellan set up the original defense but when the President replaced him from command of the Army of the Potomac he didn't trust the defensive posture he had left behind him.

"What I didn't tell you was our other deeper concern at the same time. In November '62, our Secret Service Chief Pinkerton resigned too in support of McClellan's release. We weren't that upset because his intelligence reports during the Peninsula Campaign were shoddy about Confederate troop situations. He seemed to overestimate enemy army strengths as much as McClellan complained of being outmanned—thus pausing when the President wanted him to move . . . this was his demise and caused his removal!

"We never had central intelligence in our army. Most generals use our own agents to assist, which is why I assigned you those two scouts General Randolph. Do you realize that President Lincoln fields his own 'spies!' That has always terrified me. No combined overall control like our military Chain of Command! The South has a central command.

"Southern General John Mosby was the only one who infiltrated our lines after we got involved. We are positive that he had inside Washington 'spy' help. He is an effective guerrilla and we know he has his own phantom spies. Many call him the 'Gray Ghost.'

"J.E.B. Stuart was General Robert E. Lee's 'eyes of the army' and he had his own spies in both armies. We now realize that because his 'eyes' were confused by a lot of our own sporadic cavalry engagements with him he was kept moving and was little if any help to Lee at Gettysburg. Stuart is dead now, but spies don't stop being spies even when the general they spied for is killed. They just spy for another and Jefferson Davis has good intelligence— 'a secret line.'

"Both sides of this Civil War have their share of spies. We have caught some of their spies and they are in our jails. They have caught some of ours

. . . and they hung our spy, Webster, despite President Lincoln's message of retaliation to Jefferson Davis.

"The North and the South obtain crucial intelligence from spies. I have always felt that the Confederacy has had a better spy network, especially in our Capitol. We know there are many southern sympathizers in the Capitol. Lately we have been informed that Jefferson Davis has had a Confederate Signal Corps getting covert intelligence along an unknown word of mouth 'Secret Line' from Washington to Richmond.

"We have the telegraph but they have a network of human spies! We have come to realize that they have some good female spies, and eventually we will find out more. We know that their Stonewall Jackson had some very good intelligence on us during his Shenandoah Valley campaign in '62. Who was the spy? We also use female spies and they all risk their lives for whatever cause they serve.

"I am deeply concerned that as this war rages in the South, sympathizers may get more aggressive. That is why I would like you two to keep your 'cavalry eyes' open when you are doing business in Washington. Watch closely those who are suspicious to you. Cavalry eyes can pick up more than civilian eyes can. I ask you to submit to me, just like you did on your perusal of our defensive plan, any suspicions you may have. Be careful around female admirers, women like a man in uniform and female spies like generals in uniform."

The General kept talking and the heat from the many horses in the barn kept the air inside the barn comfortable.

"Nothing like our special meetings out here, Sir," said Seth as he and John took notes in their mission books.

Brandy suddenly looked up and whinnied. "I bet there is someone coming," said Seth as he got up. "That's his warning . . . he knows someone is coming before we humans do."

"That's probably Mr. Phillips from the train station. I asked him to bring all my messages to our meeting in the barn this morning," explained the General.

"He knows about our meeting in the barn?" asked John with a frown on his face as Seth opened the barn door and in walked Mr. Phillips.

"It's ok, he's one of my spies," he chuckled.

Seth looked with astonishment saying, "It's old Mr. Phillips! He brings out message sometimes."

"That's only when he's snooping around for information," said the General. But today he's here with all my messages. I want to introduce you to

Mr. Boggs, which is his real name. He's one in my own shadow of spies and thank God we had him during the Gettysburg siege. He was very helpful. He actually changed some messages sent out and we are sure it helped."

"I'm confused General," said Seth while John looked astonished. They all sat down around the table.

"First let me have my dispatches Mr. Boggs!" exclaimed the General. The messenger dug them out of his mail pouch.

The General opened one of two. "Look, this one came in from the President on Christmas Day. Can you decipher it for me Mr. Boggs?"

"Sure General it reads:

GENERAL SIMPSON—GOT A GREAT CHRISTMAS TELE-
GRAM TODAY FROM LITTLE PHIL: "I BEG TO PRES-
ENT YOU, AS A CHRISTMAS GIFT, THE CITY OF
SAVANNAH, WITH 150 HEAVY GUNS AND PLENTY OF
AMMUNITION, AND ALSO ABOUT 25,000 BALES OF
COTTON." PLEASE RETURN JANUARY 2ND FOR WAR
MEETING. HAPPY HOLIDAYS LINCOLN."

The General laughed explaining, "We have our 'perimeter defenses around Washington' in great shape and now I'm concerned about the increase in spy activity. Mr. Boggs has been masquerading as Mr. Phillips since '61 and he's one in my line of spies all the way down to Jefferson Davis' back door neighbor woman. Sadly they suspected something and she is being interrogated now, but she won't crack. She was a 'freed slave' in our underground railroad through the Lancaster pipeline. When the war broke out she let herself be recaptured and they returned her to her owner who is Davis' neighbor. She told them she was homesick for her family. They had originally taught her to write because she was a nanny and well trusted. She got us a lot of good intelligence.

"Mr. Boggs or Mr. Phillips as the townspeople know him is a trusted and likable employee and everyone confides in him. We now know that there are a lot of southern sympathizers in the area. Mr. Boggs, tell the General and Colonel who some of them are!"

"Mrs. James Withers . . ."

"Mrs. Withers!" exclaimed Seth. "She's one of the nice ladies that helped the town group that cooked and served our food for our dinner yesterday!"

"She's also the one that wanted to know if General Simpson is married.

He isn't, and we know that, and now she does too! Old generals like him are lonely and need some companionship and who better than she? She's a retired actress from Savannah who just happens to now live in Gettysburg. She'll probably make a move on you General," warned Mr. Boggs.

"There's more here," said the General, "and Mr. Boggs keeps me informed. He's intercepted some of their messages."

"But I didn't think that Davis is as 'telegraph operational as our Lincoln," commented Seth, adding, "he communicates with us generals instantly, even to the battlefield."

"Davis is at a disadvantage, they lack the technological and industrial ability to conduct such a high-scale communication system like our U.S. Military Telegraph Corps, but they do improvise where they can. We've trained thousands of telegraph operators, and we've unknowingly trained some of their spies who are in our system. They communicate back and forth to their operatives in our system and then get the info into their message system to avert suspicion. Mr. Boggs has caught a few and we have a few we just let alone and intercept their messages. There are times we even give them bad information. Sometimes what they think is good intelligence is really bad intelligence.

"I wanted you to know Mr. Boggs, trust Mr. Boggs, and use Mr. Boggs as part of our messaging. He'll stay the night as a holiday guest and he will inform you of all that he knows. I have to leave in the morning for an urgent meeting on the 28th."

"The 28th Sir? The President's message says the 2nd."

"That reads the 2nd but it is the 28th."

"I don't understand General," said Seth.

"That's why I want Mr. Boggs, or is it Mr. Phillips, to explain it all! Now let's see what my second message is."

GENERAL—GALA NEW YEAR'S EVE BALL IN THE BLUE ROOM TO CELEBRATE LITTLE PHIL'S CHRISTMAS GIFT TO THE UNION. PLEASE INVITE SETH AND BETSY, JOHN AND SARAH AND LITTLE SIMPSON. PRESIDENT LINCOLN

NEW YEAR'S 1865
IN THE WHITE HOUSE

The New Year's Eve Gala at the White House was in the Blue Room and there were blue uniforms everywhere. News reports of the Union Army's glorious victories were flowing just like the liquid from the brandy bottles to attendees' glasses.

Sherman had just taken Savannah in his "March to the Sea." John Bell Hood's Confederate Army was soundly defeated, ending a threat to Tennessee. The Union Army was on the move.

So too were all those attending the President's New Year's Gala. Diplomats were socializing in their colorful uniforms, and all the army and dignitaries who were in Washington attended in their full dress uniforms, including General Randolph and Colonel Reynolds, and even Tad Lincoln had his cavalry sword.

Because Sarah and Betsy were in the later stages of their pregnancies, General Simpson had set up a special reclining area for them in the huge room. You couldn't tell from the gorgeous satin gowns that captured their radiance and matched the blue and gold-trimmed uniforms of their husbands.

General Simpson ushered them in separately and as they entered there was a hush in the room, all eyes watched. Those in the rear could be heard saying in hushed voices, "That's not the President . . ."

The General smiled as he escorted Betsy dressed in a royal blue floral Victorian dress with subtle golden stars and white gloves matching her husband's uniform. She was elegant alongside her husband who was carrying little Simpson dressed in a child's cavalry uniform (a present of General Simpson). Everyone in the room stood in amazement as the General guided them to the separate area housing two golden love seats.

The General seated them and then went back to the enterance and escorted Sarah who was dressed in a raspberry-colored Victorian satin dress with embroidered gold linen eagles. She was stunning and on her arm was her husband John with his golden eagles handsomely embroidered on his uniform. The crowd was astonished as the General escorted them to the resting area, seating them beside Betsy, Seth and little Simpson.

Then the General smiled, turned to the crowd and strolled back and looked out through the doorway. His white bearded head bobbed up and down. He turned back to the crowd, stood at attention and nodded to the small segment of the Marine Band on the side of the room and they started to play, "Hail to the President" as General Simpson announced, "Ladies and Gentlemen. The President, Mr. Abraham Lincoln."

The President stepped gracefully in, dressed in black with a clawhammer style coat and white kid gloves. He stopped and turned randomly, duty bound shaking hands; the look on his face was obvious—he would like to be somewhere else. General Simpson quickly approached saying, "Come with me Sir, I have your special guests that you invited over here." They walked ceremoniously over to where Betsy and General Seth were standing. "This is my namesake *Simpson*, Sir, dressed in blue for you!"

The President bent down with a huge smile on his face and he quickly straightened up with little Simpson going up higher than anyone in the room. Little Simpson laughed and kicked his feet and giggled.

The President laughed out loud and with a deep voice announced, "Someday you will be riding that beautiful horse Brandy, just like your Dad!"

A cheer went up in the room and in the back his Assistant Secretary applauded and whispered to the Vice President who was next to him, "His love for children always shines through in all occasions."

PART NINE

1865

Capture of Ricketts' Battery, depicting action during the First Battle of Bull Run, one of the early battles in the American Civil War. The painting is oil on plywood, and is displayed in the Henry Hill Visitor Center at Manassas National Battlefield Park.

NEW YEAR'S DAY
AT THE WILLARD

The Civil War was still going on three and three-quarter years after it was supposed to end. The slaughter was continuing between the North and South, but the carnage had been shifted to the southern states, far away from Brandy's peaceful Adams County community.

Brandy and his Morgan mares had managed to survive. They were the progeny of Justin Morgan and would continue to carry on the Morgan breed as well as the First Vermont Cavalry exclusive battle cry, "We ride Vermont Morgan horses!"

The inside of the Randolphs' stone barn was their haven and the fields and the Randolphs' pastures around Gettysburg were, again, a safe sanctuary for them. Beneath the earth lay dead combatants and their equine supporters decaying and becoming part of nature's process of re-generation. They were now the fertilizer for the new generations of living things.

General Lee and Jefferson Davis somehow managed to be high on the South's military posture when Lincoln sent a Presidential emissary to try to negotiate a Southern surrender. Davis responded to Lincoln a willingness to discuss ending actions but with the gusto provision—the South must remain *independent!*

The Union Army then moved and overtook Fort Fisher, North Caro-lina, occupying Cape Fear River and then closed the last southern seaport of Wilmington. The east coast supply route to the South for blockade runners and commercial shipping was now closed to the South!

The term of enlistment for many of the original members of the First Vermont Cavalry had expired in late 1864. A lot of officers and about 300 men returned home to be mustered out, leaving about 500 enlistees and recruits under the command of Maj. William G. Cummings readying for more encounters but still needing Morgan horses!

General Randolph and Colonel Reynolds advised General Simpson that they were staying until the war ended and started off the New Year as Presidential guests with their wives. They were guests again at the Historic

Willard Hotel. There they sat on New Year's morning with a cozy fire toasting the chilled air in the breakfast room when General Simpson walked in and approached their table. "Good morning, General Simpson," said Seth as the General walked over to their breakfast table and sat down with a giant smile on his face.

"Happy New Year to all! That was some Gala last night. Little Simpson and your party seemed to be the 'main attraction.'"

Betsy and Sarah smiled while little Simpson's face shined with his rosy cheeks covered in milk and oatmeal. "General," said Betsy, "yesterday was so special that we've been talking about it all morning."

". . . and we'll be talking about it for years to come," acknowledged Sarah.

"I can't wait for the picture to show up in the newspaper—the one where the President lifted little Simpson high over his head!" said the General. "He is most comfortable in those 'homey' situations."

"Did they take a picture?" asked Seth.

"I saw a pop and flash about the time President Lincoln lifted little Simpson up above his head . . . so perfect . . . and we'll know soon. The dignitaries in the room were affixed on you two couples. I heard some of the politicians talking about how they have seen you all in the Willard and at the Ford Theater and some of the dignitaries from your area were saying, 'Those two look like good candidates for future political seats.'"

"Oh, not me," said John. "Can you see me limping up to a podium?"

"Now that would be a real plus for you Colonel, a military hero that doesn't need to talk about his actions—they can see it in your movements—especially after they read about the gallant efforts of your First Vermont Cavalry."

"Thanks Sir, but no politics for me. I've fought my last battle and that was at Gettysburg."

"I am intrigued by the stories from our room attendants. One never knows which is true. This morning my attendant said, 'General did you know that when General Grant came here he was quickly called to the White House with a special invitation from President Lincoln, and shortly thereafter he was made Commander in Chief.' So one never knows who or why someone approaches your table here!"

"We all were glad you once approached our table, General," said Betsy.

A smiling waitress came over asking the General, "Would you like to try our famous breakfast?"

He smiled and politely said, "I'll have some of your black tea, toast and scrambled eggs."

He turned to his party informing them, "The well-known writer Nathaniel Hawthorne had visited here once, among other writers. That is why I have always booked your rooms here."

The General straightened his chair and started to tell a questionable love story about one of the owners of the Willard, "I am very much enamored by the love stories of both of you and it seems this place is filled with many love stories to tell. It is said that one of the owners was an officer and he resigned his commission recently and married his love who he met during the war. They were married last year and the gossip was that the lady was one of General J.E.B. Stuart's spies for the Confederate Army. Rumor was that she did help change the outcome of a major battle and was thought to have aided in the capture of a Union general, horses, men, and supplies and that she had been a family friend of Colonel John S. Mosby. She was arrested and confined to Old Capitol Prison in Washington.

"John and Sarah, I do know your moonlight proposal love story is true, and Seth and Betsy, your baby announcement is a lovely tale of love here at the Willard.

"I have many newspaper clippings in my portfolio and continue to add them to my Civil War manuscript. One clipping I remember goes like this:

"Clipping from Washington Post
Quote in Tom Winship column
        'Famed Hotel Is Worth Its Weight in Tradition'
        You are mixed up here with office seekers, wire pullers, inventors, artists, poets, editors, Army correspondents, attachés of foreign journals, long-winded talkers, clerks, diplomatists, mail contractors, railway directors—until your identity is lost among them.
        One wag joked that there were so many VIPs at Willard's that 'a gentleman passing by threw his stick at a dog. The stick missed the dog but hit six generals.'"

Everyone in the group laughed out loud and Seth commented, "General, might you have been one of those six generals?"

"I don't remember being hit by a stick!" He laughed and added, "It has been such a pleasure for me to have met all of you here and for all of you to include me as a part of your family!"

Betsy smiled lovingly and reached over and picked up little Simpson saying in a soft, gentle voice, "General, someday little Simpson will ask why we named him Simpson. It will be one of the sweetest love stories that Seth and I will ever tell him!"

TRAIN RIDE
BACK TO GETTYSBURG

S eth holding Simpson, and Betsy by his side in step with John and Sarah finally boarded the black four-car Baltimore and Ohio Railroad for the eighty-mile trip back home. The ladies were tired and the extra weight of the babies growing in their bellies made for a tiresome trip.

"We don't need a ticket for our two secret travelers," kidded Sarah.

Betsy smiled saying, "And they aren't even as heavy as the travel bags we have in our hands."

They slept comfortably leaning up against their husbands' uniformed shoulders. The smell of their woolen uniforms made them feel warm and cozy.

They all laughed later when railroad personnel had to bring in a team of horses to pull the train through city streets to reach the Bolton Station, the depot of the Northern Central Railway and Seth remarked, "Still need horses . . ."

Eventually a dinner was served to them. When the train finally pulled into the Hanover Junction, John remarked to Seth, "General I will never forget the First Vermont Cavalry regiment fought Stuart's Cavalry here at Hanover, Pa., June 3rd of '63 and at Hunterstown July 2nd, and then July 3rd at Gettysburg led by our Gen. Elon J. Farnsworth, where he perished. He led us in a charge through the First Texas Infantry and to the line of Law's Brigade, in a point-blank barrage of fire from the Confederate regiments and two batteries. Major Wells later told us we lost 67 men. We both are so honored to be on this train with our beautiful pregnant wives and little Simpson. Providence has shined in our lives."

Seth looked at him saying, "There isn't a day that goes by that I don't thank God for what we have!"

They all got out and were stretching their legs when Betsy noticed a picture on the wall. "Look at that picture over there." They walked over to it and Betsy read out loud the printing underneath.

They stood in front of it and Seth commented, "General Simpson has a cut out of that same picture from a newspaper. I remember the General telling me it was taken at Hanover Station and as the President boarded the train he flashed the dry humor we all know and love by saying, 'Well, you have seen me, and, according to general experience, you have seen less than you expected to see.'"

They all laughed and quickly boarded the train as the conductor announced, "*All aboard for Gettysburg!*"

The ladies had been sleeping as the train pulled in to the Gettysburg Station just before dark. Seth nudged Betsy and John nudged Sarah and both awoke with a surprise.

"We're in Gettysburg, honey," said Seth as he still cradled sleeping Simpson.

Betsy awoke and looked out the window and exclaimed, "Oh there still is one coffin on the platform . . . that is so sad!"

They all looked and Sarah remarked, "Betsy, there are no coffins on the platform."

John agreed and started to get up as Sarah followed.

"Betsy, there were still a lot of coffins on the platform when we first came through town on the way back from Harrisburg. But there aren't any coffins there now. You must have had a bad dream," said Seth.

"Seth, when I awoke and looked out that window I had a terrible feeling inside and I saw a coffin. I don't see it now . . . but it could be just a mother's pain from all the sorrow that has passed through this beautiful train station."

"That's probably what it is, honey. There has been so much ugliness that has passed through our little town . . . let' just hope we've seen the last of it!"

MORNING AT THE RANDOLPH FARM

"Sarah, you make the best biscuits," said Betsy as the family sat around the table at Jake Randolph's farm.

"I agree Betsy. Sarah's biscuits are great and these eggs . . . " countered Seth.

"Are not as good as the breakfast they serve in the Willard in Washington," joked Sarah as they all sat back and discussed the wonderful trip they had all just experienced.

"The President wants Brandy and me, and John and a Morgan horse all in full regalia, out front leading the military portion at his Inauguration, and then he wants all of us to be in the reviewing stand later! And he said that includes our whole family!" exclaimed Seth.

"You mean he wants your dad and me, too?" asked Jake as he sipped from his coffee cup. "Where would we all stay?"

"The General said he'll handle it," said John.

"They know Betsy and Sarah are due and joke that the hospitals in Washington can handle baby births, too! They said many more babies are born there than this little town of Gettysburg. That's their dry sense of humor and besides, it's just not easy to say NO to the President of the United States!"

"Then it's a must," decreed Seth, Sr., "I want to see the man who I voted for face to face—the face he wears for his best occasions—and hopefully shake his hand."

"That would be a great picture for Brady's photographers to take," said Betsy. "I know the President would love that one . . . a log splitter and a real Vermonter on the cover of *Harper's Weekly*," said Betsy as she looked at Simpson next to her eating his scrambled eggs. "Look, even Simpson loves the eggs Aunt Sarah served!"

Sarah laughed and dumped the last of the eggs she had in the pan onto John's plate. "Looks like everyone is done," said Sarah as she went and finally sat down next to John.

"We may be done, but there is a rider coming up the lane on a fancy

Morgan stallion and he's dressed in a First Vermont cavalry uniform," said Jake. "I thought he might be from a local Pennsylvania Unit, but they don't ride fancy Morgans like that fellow!"

Seth got up and looked out the window exclaiming, "I don't believe it! That's my old Vermont friend Brett Macinrow. Look at him now, a fancy Lieutenant!"

"Seth, he came to visit us just before we left Vermont when he was on leave. Let's meet him on the porch," said Betsy.

"Too cold out there honey. You and Sarah stay in here and John and I will greet him. He looks pretty tired out, and I'm sure he'll be hungry. If you don't mind Sarah, let's fix another plate. This will be a great reunion!"

Seth, Jr., John, Jake and Seth, Sr., went out on the front porch just as Brett dismounted and ground tied his horse. When he looked up all four were waving and acknowledging him.

"Hello Brett. Hello Lieutenant!"

"Sure am glad I found the right house. Folks in town told me two Randolph families live out here side by side. I couldn't believe it. The last time I was in Vermont, I was setting on your porch Mr. Randolph, with you and Betsy drinking lemonade."

"Well come on in, no lemonade today but plenty of coffee and brandy, too," replied Seth, Sr., adding, "my brother and I will take care of your horse. I'm sure he'll be glad to see all of our Vermont Morgans in the barn. He'll have a reunion and we'll all have a reunion."

"Thank you all. I've been riding for days. The First allowed me to leave early as my enlistment is up."

"Come on inside, Dad and uncle will take care of your horse. We were just having breakfast and our wives have set another plate for you. They saw you coming."

They went inside and Seth made the introductions and Sarah told Brett where to wash up and then to join them for breakfast.

"I'll make him some scrambled eggs and there are plenty of biscuits left and Betsy is making more coffee," said Sarah. "This sure is a surprise, another Vermonter in Gettysburg."

———————

"Have a seat here, Brett," said Seth, "and while you are relaxing let me explain that Dad sold the Vermont farm and he and Betsy moved down here right after you left. My uncle owns this farm and my dad owns the one next door. John was injured at a battle here but was promoted to a Brevet Colonel and I was promoted to a Brevet General. We're still a part of the First but actually report to General Simpson in the War Department with special assignments. Now we want to hear all about you and the First Vermont Cavalry!"

"I've been in so many battles and was made a Brevet Lieutenant right after our battle here at Gettysburg. My horse, Charger, and I rode with the First harassing the enemy all over different points in the South and finally camped for the winter at Stevensburg, Va.

"We rode in a raid at Richmond with Gen. Kilpatrick and my horse took a hit and we went down. He got up and it was only a slight graze above his right eye. As our Spring campaign opened this year we were attached to the 2nd Brigade, 3rd Division Cavalry Corps. In the Battle of the Wilderness we lost so many brave officers and men.

"After Gettysburg my depression got really bad after watching Gen. Kilpatrick and Gen. Farnsworth mixed in a fray to make a charge with our brigade against Confederate positions south of the Devil's Den area of the battlefield, below Little Round Top. I was there and saw no hope. Major Wells and a lot of us made it but Farnsworth didn't. My horse saved me by executing my low charging Morgan routine.

"Charger and I were at the Battle of Yellow Tavern under Maj. Gen. Philip Sheridan in a raid on Richmond. I was so proud of my horse and when I looked over there was General Sheridan on Rienzi leading the charge. Charger followed him right into the face of the enemy. I wasn't as brave as the General and stayed low in the saddle . . . my rank not visible. It was a bloody fight.

"We then joined a group of about 10,000 troopers to combat Stuart, and we did. We ran many pickets disrupting their supply lines and railroad tracks, but the real challenge was to move on the Confederate capital of Richmond. The Rebel troopers held us firm along a ridge line and a counterattack by the 1st Virginia Cavalry at the Battle of Yellow Tavern was pushed back by the 5th Michigan Cavalry. One of their Union sharpshooters shot Stuart off his horse with a pistol from a short distance and he died in Richmond the following day.

"Charger and I were also near Custer on his Morgan horse Dandy who also participated in the Battle at Yellow Tavern where J.E.B. Stuart was mortally wounded."

Brett stopped to drink the coffee that Betsy had placed in front of him while Sarah handed him a plate of fried eggs and some of her biscuits.

"You deserve a lot more than this breakfast for what you and your horse have been through," said Sarah.

"This is the best food I've had in months, Sarah. I'm so glad to be here with fellow Vermonters. I've been so depressed it's just awful. Talking about what I've been through does help."

"Then continue," said Seth, Jr.

Jake and Seth, Sr., came back in from the barn with Seth, Sr., saying, "That's one fine Morgan you have there Brett. I see he has some battle scars. He and Brandy are becoming friends. I see he is still a stallion."

"Oh yes sir. I raised him from a colt; never cut him . . . he's just too handsome. I was going to breed him but my wife and I live in a little house up in Vermont. We have a little stable and my wife has a quiet mare while I'm away with Charger. That's another reason I'm so depressed. I saw so many dead horses . . . good horses. My horse has been through it all and he's just stuck with me.

"I'm not a hero, but he is. He saved my life so many times. Now I have to put him on a train and get him back to my home. He'll probably catch some shipping disease and die on the way and after all he did for me and the First Vermont Cavalry! Better he die in battle! It's just not fair."

Sarah went over and put her hand gently on his shoulder. "I'm sure your wife will be happy to see you and him."

"She sure will, but we only have room for one horse, and we'll have to decide what to do with Charger when I get home. He deserves a better ending than to be stuck in a small stall."

John got up and grabbed the coffee kettle and limped back and poured more into Brett's cup. "Good Vermont Morgans are hard to find. Good Vermont stallions with Charger's blood are in high demand. Good Vermont stallions with Charger's bloodline and military history are legends; they just can't talk about what they have been through . . . but we humans can!"

He grabbed his cup and drank while Brett and everyone listened. "Seth and I will be riding in President Lincoln's Inaugural Parade. Seth will be on Brandy and they will assign me a Morgan from Giesboro."

John then turned and watched some snow start to kick up outside the window. "You made it just in time, looks like a storm is brewing!"

"That's another problem, the winters are so cold in Vermont and Charger's spent most of his life in some warmer climates. I will adjust but I just worry about him," said Brett. "I'll always be a cavalryman, but I'll always care about my horse *first!*"

"Then we'll have to do something about that Brett. I too was at that Battle where Farnsworth died. I was shot off my horse and almost killed, but I survived with this limp. But my beloved horse was killed and is buried out there in that field past the old stone barn. Seth and I will be out front in the President's Inaugural Parade in March. He'll be on Brandy and folks know him and love him. My horse is dead and I'd like to be on your brave horse Charger for the whole world to see him!"

"That would be wonderful Sir, but I can't stay here that long. I'm heading home to be mustered out."

"I'm not asking you to stay. We raise Vermont Morgans here. Brandy and our other stallions are lined back to Figure's famous sons Sherman, Bulrush, and Woodbury and we're booked solid with so many mares being serviced. Charger looks to me like he's lined back to Sherman Morgan, am I correct?"

"Yes Sir, direct line, got him when he was six months old!"

"Here's an offer for you and Charger. You leave him in my care and keep. We'll shelter and favor him for the rest of his life and use him for stud. We'll send you half his stud fees every six months and if somewhere down the road you would want him back we'll ship him to you. You and your family will always be free to come and visit and stay here at your convenience. If you agree, I want you to set down with Sarah and tell her his whole story and where and in what battles he has served. Sarah takes shorthand and it won't take you long. We will make sure it gets in a breeding pamphlet and also wherever I take him they will know who he is. And if we are lucky we'll have his picture out there in the newspapers just like Rienzi, Dandy and Figure are."

Brett looked up from his plate with a smile. "Will you send me pictures when you can?"

"Every time he's posted! We cavalrymen always take care of our horses!"

"Well then," he decreed and stood up and reached across the table to shake John's hand, "from a Vermonter to a Vermonter . . . that's a deal!"

PART TEN

THE FINAL TRAIN RIDE

The National Hotel is shown on the left (north) side of Pennsylvania Avenue. The unfinished Capitol dome is in the background. This view is courtesy of the Library of Congress. This view was painted facing southeast circa 1860.

SAYING GOODBYE
TO CHARGER

"A dog may be man's best friend, but the horse wrote history."
- UNKNOWN

Charger watched as his master entered the place that he had long missed . . . a stable like the Randolph stable. He had spent the night in here with their herd, calmed by all their nighttime equine noises. It made him feel safe and the snoring creature next to him just added more security to his herd instincts.

He was in a calmer place and it smelled like the enclosure where it was always safer. It was different, but comforting. He watched as his master walked over and opened his stall door, standing there with the other human beside him. The horse they called Brandy munched hay nearby.

"What do you say to a cavalryman's best friend when he has to leave his horse?" asked Brett as he and John stood in front of Charger.

"I can't answer that Brett, but at least you have a chance to hug him and say goodbye. My beloved horse was shot out from under me. I tried to get to him and then I, too, took a bullet and went down near him. I rolled and crawled back to him. I looked him in the eyes and he tried to get up but blood was running from his neck. I grabbed for my kerchief but he let out a scream and died. I rolled to safety under him as other horses and riders jumped over top of us; I felt the hooves glance off of him. One last time he was protecting me and he saved my life—again!"

Brett looked at him with tears in his eyes. "Colonel . . . he's yours now. Take care of him like he took care of me! . . . I know he'll take care of you. After spending time with your sweet wife Sarah and watching her lovingly write down all of Charger's war history I just know that this is the right thing to do."

"I'll leave you alone with him Lieutenant and want you to know that the best thing now in my cavalry life is your horse! We won't be riding into battle, but we will be riding in ceremonies in honor of horses who fought in battles!"

John left the stone barn and encountered Seth coming up the farm lane. "Will you and Sarah take Brett to the station to get his train? Also please get any of our messages from Mr. Phillips. Betsy is not feeling well," said Seth.

"Sure we will. I hope she'll be alright."

"And before you leave the Gettysburg Station check with the adjutant to see if there were any coffins in the depot yesterday when we arrived. Betsy still insists that she saw one and that she was not dreaming. I don't want her to go back to the train station today. She either had a dream or a premonition. Pregnant ladies are known to have spiritual experiences, but I do hope it was just a dream!"

"Will do, Sir," answered John as they both turned and went into the house; John to fetch Sarah who was in the bedroom and Seth to go upstairs to see if Betsy was feeling any better.

When Seth reached the top of the stairs Betsy was coming down the hallway holding Simpson's hand. She let go of his hand and he went running to Seth who picked him up and hugged him.

"I'm feeling better Seth. I want to say goodbye to Brett. I feel so bad for him. I remember traveling down here with Dad and with all the different stops it was so long and worrisome and frustrating."

"His trip will be a lot better, but he'll travel alone. He'll surely hook up with other Vermonters heading home as many enlistments ended at the year end."

"He was suffering from depression when he visited us in Vermont and he seems to be worse now."

"He's seen so much death and destruction . . . the human heart can only take so much. We spoke in great lengths with him last night after you and Sarah went to bed. Dad, Uncle Jake, and John and I had some brandy and we all told some really heartwarming tales of old time Vermont.

"Brett informed us that his dad owns a little hardware store. His wife and kids live upstairs and that's where he'll end up, too. His dad wants him to take it over, as it's been in the family for a long time. Brett will do well, and he knows if things change he can get his horse back at any time. That is comforting in itself. He is really happy to hear what we have planned and said Charger will love the crowds and deserves the attention.

"He knows Charger is a gorgeous stallion like Brandy and that they both will be head turners and good stallions for the breed. He agreed that Morgans had been inbred with so many other horses they were losing their real image. He, too, wants to maintain the 'original' Vermont Morgan and Figure image."

"How was he this morning? I saw him and John going into the barn earlier," said Betsy.

"I'm sure it was difficult, but John is pretty good at saying goodbyes, too. Don't forget, he lost his beloved Morgan in a tragic situation. He and Brett are cavalry officers and Charger will be a good match for John at this time. He and Sarah will be having their first child at about the same time we will have our second; and a new horse will help him carry out our mission. We still need a lot more Morgans, but Brandy and Charger out there together should make quite a picture."

Seth hugged Betsy and Simpson grabbed his mother's hand as they went down the steps and into the living room, just in time to see Brett climbing into the carriage to go to the train station.

"I feel terrible for him. I've been having a few 'funny' moments with this pregnancy. When I was at the Willard, General Simpson showed me some tickets for the Ford Theater that he had in his case. He had tickets with quite a few available dates. He said he carries them with him to give out to dignitaries who come to Washington. He wanted us to go to a performance while we are attending the March Inauguration so he was going through the tickets and one fell out and I made a terrible sound.

"He looked at me and said, 'Oh, I agree you wouldn't like that performance with Booth. He's a Lincoln hater. Besides, it's not until late in March. I cringe too when I see his name.'

"Enough about my whimsical premonitions. Let's get dressed and jump into a carriage and send Brett off with a hug and a kiss from all of us Randolphs!"

SAYING GOODBYE
TO BRETT AT GETTYSBURG
TRAIN STATION

Brett sat between Sarah and John drinking coffee in the Gettysburg Train Station. It was crowded and the train was late so John continued to tell Brett about what he and Seth were doing in the Morgan Program.

"Our First Vermont Cavalry is not the only unit using the Morgan," said John as he sipped and talked, trying to boost Brett's morale. He continued as Sarah took more notes for her own "Morgans in the Civil War" book she was considering for publication at the end of the war.

"General Randolph and I have catalogued and have a separate register on Civil War Morgan horses. One hundred Morgan horses were bought from upper NY and from our Champlain Valley area and most were papered to Black Hawk through a Bridgeport, Vermont, breeder. They served at Gettysburg with the 5th New York Cavalry and when Sarah was working with the Daughters of Charity she rescued two of their mares who were shot up pretty bad. She wouldn't let them put them down so she brought them back to the barn and they are now a part of our herd.

"The 5th's Colonel John Hammond has a beloved Morgan named Pink that is a grandson of Black Hawk and who hails from Crown Point, Vermont. I saw the horse and met and talked to Colonel Hammond at an engagement in Gettysburg. He enlisted as a private, like all of us, and made Colonel and is rising through the ranks and will probably be a General before this war is over.

"Morgans are serving in other units such as the 1st Maine Cavalry, 2nd and 3rd Michigan Cavalry, 14th Pennsylvania Cavalry, and the 1st Rhode Island Cavalry.

"There are many well-known Morgans carrying generals, like Phil Sheridan's Morgan horse Winchester or Rienzi, a black gelding Morgan of Black Hawk lineage; Charlemagne is the Morgan mount of Joshua Chamberlain, who we met at Gettysburg before the hotly contested action at Little Round Top; and even Confederate States officer General Stonewall Jackson rode a Morgan named Little Sorrel. Little Sorrel carried General Jackson in

241

many engagements until Stonewall was mortally wounded at Chancellorsville in 1863.

"We have a few other Morgans that some of the fellows who mustered out sold at a local auction here because they were too frail to ship home; we bought them up quickly. Now we have your beautiful stallion and we have a wonderful line of Morgans to breed at our farms here in Gettysburg. With the stallions and mares Seth, Sr., brought from Vermont and our Dad's own prime Morgan stock we will produce the best Morgans available."

Brett smiled and managed a laugh, "You've convinced me that he's among some of the finest Morgans still alive."

John sat back and watched as the smoking train came noisly into the station. He finished by saying, "Charger is one of the finest, Brett! He doesn't come much better than our Black Hawk bloodlines. He and our lined mares, which are the foundation to our breeding program, from the 5th and Brandy's bloodline and some others we got who survived the war have everything we are looking for from Black Hawk and Figure lineage. They have beautiful heads, quiet dispositions and perfect conformation. They are great cavalry horses! Seth and I will call it the 'Calvary Golden Cross' and they will become the cornerstones of our breeding program here in Gettysburg. Also, our leader General Simpson is working on getting a permanent Government Breeding Program approved through Congress."

Brett got up and John and Sarah walked him over to the train as the conductor called, *"All aboard!"*

"Wait! We want to say goodbye!" came a yell from Betsy as she with Seth carrying Simpson, rushed onto the boarding platform.

Brett's face lit up and he said, "Thank you Randolphs for coming. Thank you all for everything you've done for me and Charger. I'm now leaving knowing that Vermonters are going to take care of my beloved Vermont Morgan horse, Charger."

JANUARY TO
MARCH 1ST, 1865

As the Union Army cut its way through the South, the Randolphs and Reynolds were busy with their military schedules and breeding schedules.

In February, Sherman's Army marched through the Carolinas capturing Columbia, South Carolina, while North Carolina defenders bowed to Union troops and the last significant southern port on the east coast for the South was closed. Betsy and Sarah were nearing their delivery dates in early April as the Randolph and Reynolds' families were preparing to go celebrate President Abraham Lincoln's Inauguration in Washington, D.C., on March 4, 1865.

"Three telegrams from General Simpson today," Seth said to John as they prepared Brandy and Charger for their journey to Washington, D.C.

"This one reads, 'Sheridan on the move. Columbia, S.C., is burning. Your reservations at the White House are confirmed as arranged. Horses will be stabled nearby for your convenience. Will advise when they arrive here. You will be at front of troops participating in the march.'"

"Betsy is going to be very happy. She did not want to stay at the Willard this time," said Seth.

"Just as well, Sarah is happy, especially since they both are expecting in early April," said John.

"General Simpson said that the White House physicians are always on call for any Presidential emergency and having a baby at such an exciting time would be a 'homespun' tale for the President to tell later on if it happens. You know his sense of humor," said Seth.

"Can you imagine if our children were born in the White House or nearby? That would certainly make the papers!" exclaimed John.

"Brett will be thrilled if he sees us out in front with the African-American troops. He's such an anti-slavery Vermonter. I do hope the Brady photographer people get a picture of both of us out in front and then it makes it into the Vermont papers and *The Burlington Times*. Sarah wrote up a little piece for me to give the reporters."

John and Seth finished grooming their horses and then the government grooms took them to a waiting vehicle.

"They leave this evening and will arrive tomorrow, while we leave tomorrow at eight in the morning and arrive at about the same time," said John. They both left the barn and headed to their own houses.

Betsy greeted Seth at the door with a big hug and little Simpson hugged his right leg. Seth leaned over and picked him up saying, "Not as high up as President Lincoln takes you!"

"He's so excited Seth. He has been hearing us talk and when I mention the President he looks at me and puts his arms out like he wants to be picked up. He'll be doing that 'til he's married," kidded Betsy.

Climbing the stairs to start packing Betsy said, "This reminds me of that staircase we had to climb to the second floor the first time we stayed at the Willard. I really loved that place until one evening when a lady was assisting me down with Simpson she told me, 'I was mistreated by an actor on this staircase here a while back. He was nasty when I told him slavery was abolished here in April 1862—months before President Lincoln issued the Emancipation Proclamation—and that Washington is a very popular place for we freed slaves to mingle . . . and he slapped me and told me *we'll change that!*'

"She told me it was John Wilkes Booth and she helped him carry down his actor's case. She said it smelled like perfume and when she told him that he slapped her again!"

They reached the top of the staircase and headed to their bedroom and sat down on the bed, with Simpson playing with a toy horse between them.

"I tried to comfort her by saying maybe he was just acting. She looked at me with those big brown eyes and said, 'Oh he wasn't kidding, ma'am!'

"I did discuss this with General Simpson and he said that Booth may have been there but his security people report that he often frequents the National Hotel, which is a known hangout for Southerners visiting Washington. They have an open investigation concerning former President Buchanan and a 'National Hotel sickness' where several patrons became ill. Some believe it was an assassination attempt against Buchanan. It's still under investigation!"

"You should have been an investigator, Betsy. I didn't know you had discussed this with General Simpson."

"I did the last time we talked. He laughed and said the same thing, 'We need you as a Union Lady spy!' I laughed and told him being a mother and a wife is a tough job."

"You are so sweet, Betsy. I am so fortunate to have you as my wife."

"That's what General Simpson said, too! He was so humbled we named Simpson after him. He doesn't have any children and I know he is so thankful. I told him it was a good excuse not to name him Seth the Third. He laughed when I said that!"

"We better get finished packing. They will be here early in the morning for our trunks. You can pack more of your wrappings in my trunk. I'm just taking one other uniform besides the one I'll be wearing."

As they packed Seth, Sr., knocked on the door announcing, "Seth, Betsy . . . Kate just came in downstairs and she wants to talk. She's very excited. John, Sarah, and Jake are with her and they are all in a very good mood."

"What a pleasant surprise," called out Betsy in a folksy mood. "Tell them we are finishing packing and will be right down."

KATE COMES
TO VISIT

"**H**ello!" exclaimed Kate as she swiftly moved around the old pine floor living room greeting everyone—her tiny black-soled shoes hardly touching the honey-colored wooden planks—dancing like an angel on dust that sparkled beneath her feet.

"I have wonderful news! I am here to attend the Inauguration with all of you!"

"Let's all set down and I'll get some coffee brewing and then Kate can tell us all about it," said Jake.

"And I'll get some more wood on the fire to keep it going," said Seth Sr. "We are so glad to see you Kate!"

Betsy and Sarah encircled Kate and little Simpson tugged at her soft black dress.

"You two are getting so much bigger and you too, Simpson," as she bent down and kissed him. They all went and sat down around the now cozy fire.

"General Simpson set it all up. He sent me a telegram saying that he wanted me to accompany you ladies to Washington just for his own peace of mind. He knows they have doctors there but he knows I've delivered babies in my hospital experiences."

"We sure feel better, too, that you are coming with us," said John.

"The General came to visit us in Emmitsburg and he was very impressed."

"He came to Emmitsburg?" questioned Seth, Sr.

"Yes, he came and stayed in the Moritz Tavern nearby. It once was Headquarters for General J. Reynolds. He came to collect old newspaper clippings for his book portfolio from the local Emmitsburg newspapers. He also came to see our White House!"

Sarah and John sat back with big smiles on their faces. Sarah said, "That explains why he was inquiring about the many instances of providence in play for the Randolph and Reynolds family at Emmitsburg. He asked me a lot of questions. Many I couldn't answer."

"That's what he asked me Sarah. He said since no one could answer him he had to come and see for himself. He said he had spent so much time in the White House in Washington, he had to see the little White House in Emmitsburg people talked about," said Kate.

She went on to explain, "He even wanted to go to church with us on Sunday at the Mountain. It was so funny, I told him we had to walk across a stream to get up to the Mountain Church and he didn't mind. When we got there the creek was too high but Father brought along our new horse and we crossed one by one on his back. When it came to the General's turn to ride he asked Father about the horse. Father told him it was the one Sarah had found wandering the roadway after the Big Battle and no one claimed him. The horse was so frightened Sarah caught him and tied him to the back of the wagon and he trailed behind the wagon to our sanctuary. He was pretty scarred from the battle and frightened and Sarah took care of him in our tiny stable. The General told Father that it looked like one of those long-legged Confederate Cavalry horses. Father told him it was just a poor creature of God who needed our help and we were glad to now have him in our peaceful place. He is a lovely horse—Confederate or Union."

"Did the General go to church?" asked Jake.

"Oh yes, he sat in back of us. I looked back at him at times and he was looking all around. When mass was over he asked if we were going up the mountain for a walk to the top where we saw the battle. We said we had a picnic and some of us were going with our priest. He asked to come along and he did. He made it all the way to the top and we all sat and looked down at the town of Gettysburg. It was all peaceful at that time.

"We all trekked back down the mountain and he thanked everyone and then went back to town. He said I would hear from him in the future. He asked if he could borrow my book on Mother Seton to read. I gave it to him and he mailed it back a few weeks later with a note thanking me. He said he had a surprise for everyone and would let everyone know when Betsy and Sarah's babies were baptized at their church in Gettysburg."

"That's the General. He always loves his intrigue. He keeps us all in the dark and then he surprises us!" said Betsy laughing and reaching for the coffee that Jake handed her.

"We are sure happy that you are coming," said Seth, Sr. "It will be a fun trip on the train."

"I'm not very comfortable on those smoking machines. At least it's not like that tugboat ride we had across the Susquehanna—that was scary!"

"I didn't mind that trip," said Betsy. "The flowing water made me feel safer, especially when Dad and I were in the company of you and your Sisters."

"Yes, that was some wild ride," said Seth, Sr. "We had such a long and interesting trip down here from Vermont. We even saw that bridge that was burned. There is a bridge near here called Sauck's that we cross. The bridge was used by a part of Lee's retreating Confederates out of Gettysburg. They didn't burn that bridge, thankfully."

"We got an encrypted message from the General this morning and we have an urgent meeting tomorrow at 2 p.m.!" stated Seth, Jr.

"Confederates tried to burn the bridge at Shenandoah to stop Sheridan's two cavalry divisions moving south to join up where Custer's men put out the bridge fire. They need more horses. There still is a war going on around Washington and Saturday is the Inauguration. We all better get to bed!" said Seth, Jr.

TO THE WHITE HOUSE

"He always had more horses than oats."
- WILLIAM H. HERNDON and JESSE WEIK,
Herndon's Life of Lincoln, p. 429

The matching black pair of Morgan horses pulling the Presidential carriage lifted their heads regally as they approached the entrance to the new stable. The coachman inside the Presidential carriage had a somber look on his face telling them, "I have only been here about a year. They had a fire here last year and the stable was destroyed. It's rumored that the prior coachman was under suspicion. They told me that the President ran out of the White House when he smelled the smoke from the stable. The fire department and a crowd of people were outside saying the horses were still inside. They told me they had to stop the President from breaking open a stall door to rescue them. Sadly all of the animals and even the kids' ponies were lost. The President lost two of his horses but most sadly his son had recently been buried and now his pony had perished. General Simpson awarded the President these two beautiful Morgans from . . ."

"Oh how sad," said Betsy as she cradled little Simpson in her arms. I can't imagine that grief, and to be the President with all the terrible things going on in this war."

"Yet he's concerned about our welfare and invited us to watch here with Kate . . . it makes me love him all the more," said Sarah.

"I will hold him special in my daily prayers," said Kate.

As they approached the White House there was a group of men setting outside in a tent next to a wagon. The coachman explained, "Those are the photographers General Simpson has set up. President Lincoln has the first African Americans to ever march in an inaugural parade. The procession will end back here at the White House. That's where your husbands and their horses will end up and you will be able to see them with the President and his hosting committee.

"The General wants them in the picture with their Morgan horses and that is just one of the many newspapers who will be here. You ladies must be really proud to be special guests here. You will be able to watch and wave from those windows up there.

"General Simpson does not want you to attend the Presidential Ball at the Patent Office. He said it would be much too hectic so they have arranged a small party in the Blue Room for you and your husbands and special military guests. They will serve the same buffet menu that is being served at the Ball and each of you will take home an autographed menu with the President's Seal and picture on it. I have been advised to hand you off to the President's valet and he will escort you ladies to a special reviewing room.

"After the parade is over your husbands will be escorted back here and their horses will be taken back to the train to be shipped back to your home. You will attend the Blue Room Ball with the guests and then General Simpson will have a carriage ready to take you to his personal home where you all will be housed for the evening. The officers will then have a War Department special staff meeting and then will join you at General Simpson's residence afterwards.

"In the morning the General will have you escorted back to the train station for your return home. The carriage ride is over and there is the valet waiting at the door. The General said he will join all of you ladies at the little Ball tonight and that there is a doctor on call if you need one."

REVIEWING THE PARADE
INSIDE THE WHITE HOUSE

Kate, Sarah, Betsy and little Simpson watched the Inauguration from an upstairs window inside the White House. Kate brought along some of the opera glasses the Daughters of Charity had used when they viewed the Gettysburg Battle scene from up on Look Out Mountain.

"This reminds me of the day up on the mountain and the horrible battle scenes we watched in far off Gettysburg. I will never forget it . . . those scenes are forever painted in my mind. It was just awful," said Sarah.

"Hello ladies," spoke a mustached man standing next to them with a sketching pad and images drawn on the top parchment.

"Hello, sir, are you an artist?" asked Betsy. "That is a beautiful scene on your board."

"Yes I am ma'am and a friend of Winslow Homer. He illustrated Abraham Lincoln's first inaugural address in March 1861 for *Harper's Weekly* and has spent the last four years recording the war with his paintings and drawings. I'm just an apprentice and am here doing a story. He is now a famous painter and artist. I came over because I noticed you, ma'am," addressing Kate. "Are you a Daughter of Charity?"

Kate smiled. "Yes I am sir, how do you know that?"

"This is one of Mr. Homer's sketches from the magazine," and he pulled out a picture. "This looks just like you. I have it in my portfolio as a sample. I'm learning his techniques . . . we are both self taught. I work for a different newspaper and am here to capture 'human interest stories.' Why are you lovely ladies here in this special setting?"

"My husband is General Randolph and Sarah's husband is Colonel Reynolds. They will be leading the soldiers who are participating in the parade. General Simpson said that it will end right out there in front of the White House."

"This is my sister Kate," added Sarah. "She is a Daughter of Charity and we are all friends of General Simpson. My sister is here to 'look after' us as we are both due to have babies in a few weeks. The General is so kind to us. We also raise Morgan horses in Gettysburg. Our husbands are a part of the Quartermaster Department and they are in charge of horse acquisitions."

"Now, that's a really interesting story! Do you have anymore details?"

"My husband rides a Morgan horse named Brandy and Colonel Reynolds rides a Morgan horse named Charger. Both horses and our husbands were at the Battle of Gettysburg in the First Vermont Cavalry skirmishes."

"Your husbands are going to be right out front when the parade ends here?" questioned the reporter.

"Yes, sir. "

"This is a great story. I will work my way down to the front and capture their images in my drawings for the paper. I will be at the Ball here in the Blue Room tonight interviewing General Simpson. Will you all be here?"

"Oh yes," said Sarah, "and with our handsome husbands."

"This is going to make a terrific story. Thank you for all the information and I will see you all tonight with my drawings. Just imagine—horses and officers and African-American U.S. troops participating in the march at Lincoln's second inauguration—what a byline! Everyone in the Union Army will be celebrating this Inauguration today!"

TRAIN RIDE HOME

Everyone was used to getting up early on their Gettysburg farms so this 'up early in D.C.' was an advantage because most of the Inauguration partygoers were still in bed and taking later departures.

The Randolphs and the Reynolds were impressed as the sun appeared through the windows of the horse-drawn streetcar that ran on a track from their location to the depot.

"What will they think of next?" exclaimed Kate as she looked out the back window at the Capitol moving farther away in the distance.

The New Jersey Avenue Station was always jammed. It was the foremost embarkation site for hundreds of thousands of Union troops during the Civil War. The day after President Abraham Lincoln's Inauguration it was raining and not too crowded at the station, but General Simpson had managed to get General Randolph and his party in through a special entrance and onto the train heading for Gettysburg.

They were quickly assigned their special car compartments and the porter came and took their breakfast request saying, "The General has asked me to get breakfast items from the Soldiers' Rest Area and bring them back to you. He wants to thank you ladies for making the trip for the President in your precarious conditions."

"Thank you," said Seth. "Do you know if our horses are on board?"

"Yes they are Sir, the General arranged that, too. They are in the transportation car right behind this one. The General doesn't want the ladies or your horses to get any travel sickness—the closer to the engine the smoother the ride."

The train started to move and Seth sat next to Betsy with Simpson between them and John sat next to Sarah with Kate between them.

"See John, Kate fits between us just like Simpson fits between Seth and Betsy," giggled Sarah.

"Pretty soon we might have to set alone, if we get any bigger. I have felt my baby moving a lot this trip," said Betsy.

"Me too," said Sarah. "This is so exciting. Now we can go home and just set back and wait for our babies to be born."

"Just think about what we have experienced," said Kate. "God sure does move in mysterious ways."

"And He has moved us in many forms of transportation—horses, trains, coaches, buggies, Presidential carriages, tugboats—we've done a lot of walking, too. Who knows what means of transportation providence will provide next or where we will go," said Sarah.

"Right now this train ride feels good. Look, here comes the porter with some breakfast!" exclaimed Betsy.

"Compliments of the sergeant running the Soldiers' Rest Area," said the porter as his assistant placed a serving table between them. He said, "To-night they will be having a group of soldiers playing guitars entertaining the troops. There will be full moon over the Capitol and the White House and many of the local veterans bring their loved ones to listen to the music and watch the moon. It's a grand sight and he is sorry you all will miss it."

Betsy and Sarah smiled as they accepted the trays of delicacies and placed the coffee cups on the table between them.

"We both know how romantic that scene can be," said Sarah.

"We sure do, and you thank the sergeant for his concern for us. That is so nice of him to think about us," said John as he took the lid off a plate full of eggs, bacon and toast.

"That sure smells good," said Seth, "but it doesn't smell like the smoked ham that was on our menu last night."

"I don't think we'll ever be served a menu like that again," said Kate. "I loved the jellies and crèmes and especially the Crème Neapolitane. It re-minded me of my trip to France."

"My favorite was the White Coffee Ice Cream," said John.

"The General was so gracious. He packed copies of the menu and signed invitations by the President in our bags. What wonderful souvenirs," said Betsy.

"He did discuss one situation he was not happy about," said Seth.

"What was that?" asked John eating his eggs.

"He said that there were a lot of shady characters at the speech. One of his security men thought they even saw Booth. Washington is full of Southern sympathizers even now that the war is going so well for us in the North!" said Seth.

"Isn't it fitting that shortly after the President's first Inauguration, there was a call to arms with the advantage going to the South and odds makers were bet-ting on all the leadership the South had to an early Union defeat," said John.

"Now two days before his second Inauguration, President Lincoln appoints Ulysses S. Grant, a Lieutenant General, a rank revived at *his* request, to take command of all Union Armies in the field. President Lincoln's leadership and wisdom and his dauntless stand of 'give me death in the cause of liberty for all' along with his 'mud generals' turned the tide of this terrible conflict. A win of freedom for all is coming!" added Seth.

"General Simpson rallied us yesterday with his speech that the Civil War is coming to an end. Much of the Southern landscape has been burned and altered, their economy is limping into a death spiral, and the Southern morale is in decline, especially after the loss of some of their top leadership and generals and Lee's defeat at Gettysburg," said John. "His conclusion that with the President reviving and bestowing the rank of Lieutenant General to Grant, which only George Washington was given that rank before, that a Northern victory is inevitable . . . and coming soon!"

SPRING 1865 AT
THE RANDOLPH FARM

"It's a boy!" shouted Jake to all the family members assembled in the living room.

"Mom and baby are doing fine. The doctor, Kate, John and Betsy are at her side."

"Congratulations, brother," said Seth, Sr., as he clasped his brother's hand and shook it. "Now we are even—we both have a grandson!"

Jake was so excited his left leg started to give out so he sat down quickly and said, "The doctor said Betsy will have her baby soon. He wants Seth to take her home. All the excitement could make her go into labor. He doesn't want to birth another baby right now. He's joking of course, but he said it would save Seth, Jr., his fee. He has a great sense of humor."

"The vet is out there in your barn helping deliver three foals," said Seth, Sr., as he sat down next to him. "Yesterday he delivered six in my barn, one right after another. Three gave birth in the wee hours. Poor fellow hasn't been to bed all night."

"We didn't get much sleep either and poor Sarah was up most of the night. This is her first child and it was a little rough. Baby has red hair just like his father."

"We have some red-haired foals too," joked Seth, "and of course Brandy's bred mares dropped two colts. One looks just like him when I first saw him in the morning after he was born."

"Come on into the kitchen brother, I'll make some of George Washington's Hoe Cakes. Got the recipe from a traveling salesman from Philadelphia. I've tried them and I still have plenty of your Vermont maple syrup you gave me when you came. What a way to celebrate this event—the old 'sweet' Vermont way."

"Grandkids and Morgan foals, brother," said Jake as they headed out to the kitchen. "Soon we will have enough of both to fill up our houses and our barns."

Seth, Sr., laughed as his voice trailed their trip to the kitchen, "Two of a kind brother . . . that's what we want . . . a stallion and a mare . . . and a boy and a girl grandchild each!"

Jake opened the fire box on the cooking stove and threw in a few pieces of dried maple firewood. "That smokey maple smell will go along with the maple syrup smell. Now let me mix up this recipe, it's so simple. I have it on this piece of paper tacked up in the cupboard."

Fifteen minutes later the kitchen smelled like someone was 'maple sugaring in Vermont,' and the aroma wafted down the hall and into the upstairs bedrooms. It wasn't long before Betsy, John and Seth, Jr., showed up in the kitchen. Jake and Seth, Sr., were eating their hoe cakes with the maple syrup and drinking coffee and chatting. "Look at those mares and foals out there brother. I told you that you would love this place."

"I told you that was a maple syrup smell," announced Betsy as she and John and Seth and Simpson came into the kitchen.

"Look at those two . . . " said John.

"Nothing will draw a Vermonter faster than maple wood in the cook stove and maple syrup on hoe cakes on a spring morning," decreed Jake.

"We old timers have been through a lot and it's now time to celebrate," said Seth, Sr.

"Any left?" asked Seth, Jr.

"Sure, there's plenty of batter left. I mixed up a triple batch . . . I knew you'd be down. There's enough for everyone. Let me cook them up. Sarah is taking care of my grandson, so I'll take care of the cooking," laughed Jake.

"Betsy, you set right down in my seat. It's warmed up. I'll get the plates, everyone have a seat. Look out that big window at all of those foals and mares in our combined meadows. Did you ever see a prettier sight?"

"Dad, we sent Brett Macinrow a copy of the drawing the artist made for us at the White House. His Charger is in it with John in the saddle and Brandy and me beside them at the Inauguration. We also sent him a copy of the Washington paper with our pictures and his Charger and the whole story that the young reporter got from Sarah. He should have received them by now."

"General Simpson also sent him a letter about Charger. We would all love to see that 'Vermont scene' in his home when he gets his mail!"

SPRING 1865 WITH BRETT IN VERMONT

The spring nights were still cold but the days were now warm, and Vermonters were finishing up another great maple syrup season.

Brett sat in his father's hardware store and watched as the "sugar makers" came and delivered his Spring supply of pure Vermont maple syrup he was to sell.

He was setting with his dad and the local mayor who stopped in for an afternoon visit. The mayor listened as suppliers were dropping off their syrups saying, "We are the nation's leading producer of maple syrup . . . now about half the maple syrup in the States. More sugar houses are popping up every year."

"Wish we could say that about our Morgan horses. We don't sell off our maple trees but we sell off our Vermont Morgan horse stock," said Brett in a sad mood.

"Soon as this war ends we'll get a lot back. Our cavalry will return and hopefully we'll have some good stallions left," said the mayor. "What happened to Charger?"

Brett got up and a huge smile crossed his face.

"Go ahead, son," said his dad, "show the mayor. Show him that your wonderful horse was in President Lincoln's Inauguration!"

"What!" exclaimed the mayor.

Brett walked over and removed a framed picture from the wall behind the main counter. He handed the picture to the mayor explaining, "Now that's Charger on the right with my friend Colonel Reynolds on his back and on the left is my friend General Randolph on his horse Brandy. The picture is signed by President Lincoln with a thank you note from him."

The mayor held the picture out in front of him and a huge smile crossed his face.

"Now there is also a drawing of Charger with my friends and his horse. This artist works for a famous newspaper and they sent me a copy of it. Here let me get it." He got up and went to the counter and reached underneath and pulled out a newspaper.

The mayor sat there and held out the framed picture and looked at Brett holding the newspaper and his chest puffed like a peacock. "We produce almost half the maple sugar in the country—we also produce some of the finest Morgan horses in the country. These are proud looking Vermont Morgans. Bet they are out of Black Hawk."

Brett walked over and handed the newspaper to the mayor. "Mayor if you want to puff up your chest more, puff it up on this 'cause they mention our town, our Vermont Morgan horses, and a General, Colonel and me, a Lieutenant in the First Vermont Cavalry, and tell all about our State having sent about 10 percent of its population to this Civil War. The writer also mentions that the horses and officers in the picture were at the Battle of Gettysburg, and the original owner of Charger is Lieutenant Brett Macinrow who served with Charger in many other battles!"

"Brett this such wonderful news."

"Sure got me out of my depressed mood. I've packed up a case of our maple syrup and I'm sending it to the Randolphs and Reynolds in Gettysburg."

"That's terrific," said the mayor, "and now I want to present to you a letter from General Simpson in the War Department. He wanted me to come and present it to you so that you know it's official!"

"Official? They don't want me back do they?"

"Oh no. Here, let me read it to you. It's a letter sent to me to present you his *official notification!*"

Dear Lieutenant Macinrow.

I will be retiring after this war is over and I don't think that will be long!

I will be returning to my Vermont Morgan horse farm that I purchased from your friend and once neighbor, Seth Randolph, Sr.

We are shipping your Vermont Morgan horse named Charger home to my farm near you! He is now retired to my farm under your ownership.

They tell me you are close and will take care of him. He should arrive by the end of this month. I am also offering you a job as my herd manager.

I sent this official letter to your mayor to present it to you in tribute to you and your horse's outstanding service.

G Simpson, War Dept. USA

APRIL 10, 1865
AT THE RANDOLPH FARM

"It's a girl!" shouted Seth, Sr., to all the family members assembled in the living room.

"Mom and baby are doing fine. The doctor, Kate, Seth and Sarah are at her side."

"Congratulations, brother," said Jake as he clasped his brother's hand and shook it. "Now you are one up on me as you now have a granddaughter."

Seth, Sr., was so calm and collected. He went into the parlor and sat down. Outside he saw a rider in a full gallop coming up the lane.

"John, it looks like Mr. Phillips is in a real hurry. He's yelling something. Go get Seth and we'll see him at the door."

John hurried up the stairs as Seth, Sr., and Jake both walked calmly to the front porch. Mr. Phillips had a smile on his face and his horse was lathered. He pulled up close to the picket fence and quickly jumped off his horse just as Seth, Jr., and John came out.

As they stood on the porch Mr. Phillips yelled out to them, "The war is over! The war is over! Here's General Simpson's message."

WAR IS OVER. LEE AND GRANT MADE A GENTLEMEN'S AGREEMENT. LEE ASKED THAT HIS MEN KEEP THEIR OWN HORSES TO RETURN HOME TO FARM. GRANT ALLOWED ANY CONFEDERATE CLAIMING A HORSE OR MULE BE ALLOWED TO KEEP IT! THANK GOD FOR OUR HORSES! G. SIMPSON.

– THE END –

TIMELINE

April 14, 1865 - President Abraham Lincoln is assassinated by actor John Wilkes Booth at Ford's Theater in Washington, D.C. On the same day, Fort Sumter, South Carolina, is reoccupied by Union troops.

April 26, 1865 - General Joseph Johnston signs the surrender document for the Confederate Army of Tennessee and miscellaneous southern troops attached to his command at Bennett's Place near Durham, North Carolina.

May 4, 1865 - General Richard Taylor surrenders Confederate forces in Alabama and Mississippi.

May 10, 1865 - Confederate President Jefferson Davis is captured near Irwinville, Georgia.

May 12, 1865 - The final battle of the Civil War takes place at Palmito Ranch, Texas. It is a Confederate victory.

May 23, 1865 - The Grand Review of the Army of the Potomac in Washington, D.C.

May 24, 1865 - The Grand Review of General Sherman's Army in Washington, D.C.

May 26, 1865 - General Simon Bolivar Buckner enters into terms for surrender of the Army of the Trans-Mississippi, which are agreed to on June 2, 1865. The Civil War officially ends.

THE BACK STORY

About the First Vermont Cavalry at Gettysburg

The First Vermont Cavalry commander at the Battle of Gettysburg was Lt. Colonel Addison W. Preston. They had 687 men in the field; 13 were killed, 25 wounded, and 27 went missing.

Major William Wells (later Major General) earned the Medal of Honor for his actions on July 3rd for "extraordinary heroism while serving with 2nd Battalion, 1st Vermont Cavalry, in action at Gettysburg, Pennsylvania. Major Wells led the second battalion of his regiment in a daring charge."

Front of the Slyder Field Monument:

FIRST REGIMENT VERMONT CAVALRY
FIRST BRIG. THIRD DIV. CAVALRY CORPS

———————

IN THE GETTYSBURG CAMPAIGN THIS REGIMENT FOUGHT STUART'S CAVALRY AT HANOVER, PA. JUNE 30, AND AT HUNTERSTOWN JULY 2; AND ON THIS FIELD JULY 3, LED BY GEN. ELON J. FARNSWORTH, WHO FELL NEAR THIS SPOT, CHARGED THROUGH THE FIRST TEXAS INFANTRY AND TO THE LINE OF LAW'S BRIGADE, RECEIVING THE FIRE OF FIVE CONFEDERATE REGIMENTS AND TWO BATTERIES, AND LOSING 67 MEN.

Rear of the Monument:

ENTERED THE UNITED STATES SERVICE NOV. 19, 1861. MUSTERED OUT AUG. 9, 1865. TOOK PART IN THE BAT- TLES OF GETTYSBURG, WILDERNESS, YELLOW TAVERN, WINCHESTER, CEDAR CREEK, WAYNESBORO, FIVE FORKS, APPOMATTOX STATION AND 67 OTHER BATTLES AND ENGAGEMENTS. AGGREGATE 2297 OFFICERS AND MEN. KILLED AND MORTALLY WOUNDED IN ACTION 102; DIED OF DISEASE AND BY ACCIDENTS 123; DIED IN CONFED- ERATE PRISONS 172, – TOTAL 397. TOTAL WOUNDED IN ACTION 275.

Slyder Field Monument. Gettysburg National Park.

MEDAL OF HONOR FACTS

The Medal of Honor was first awarded in the American Civil War by President Abraham Lincoln with a bill containing a provision for the medal for the Navy on December 21, 1861.

1,522 were awarded during the American Civil War. The first Medals of Honor were given to many of the participants of the Andrews' Raid, some posthumously. Mary Edwards Walker, a surgeon, became the only woman (and one of only eight civilians) awarded a Medal of Honor. Twenty-five were awarded to African Americans, including seven sailors of the Union Navy, fifteen soldiers of the United States Colored Troops, and three soldiers of other Army units. It was common for Civil War Medals of Honor to be awarded decades after the conflict ended and in one case, Andrew Jackson Smith's Medal was not awarded until 2001, 137 years after the action in which he earned it. Smith's wait, caused by a missing battle report, was the longest delay of the award for any recipient, until November 6, 2014, when President Obama awarded the Medal of Honor to Union Army First Lieutenant Alonzo Cushing for his actions at the Battle of Gettysburg, taking the longest delay of the award to 151 years.

ABOUT THE AUTHOR

Ray and his wife, Megan, are Second- and First-generation Americans as well as history buffs.

Ray proudly served in the USAF with the 366th Tactical Fighter Wing during the Vietnam Era. He met and married Megan and they moved into an old farmhouse in historical Bucks County, Pa., raising three children and enjoying their Morgan horses. Ray worked as an executive for Sears and MAB PAINTS and was a "Ghost" writer while Megan was a stay-at-home mom and watercolor artist with the local Art Leagues.

Ray played Washington's second-in-command for almost 20 years in the Washington Crossing the Delaware Re-enactment and both he and Megan at times have played George and Martha Washington at non-profit events.

Ray and Megan are retired and now live in Lancaster County, Pa., on their beloved "Shepherd Too" home base that's also a National Wildlife Backyard Habitat and once were featured in a one-hour video highlighting bluebirds and the National Wildlife Backyard Habitat Program on their local Blue Ridge Cable network. They have also been featured in two *Lancaster County Magazine* articles.

Ray publishes his stories, books, and photographs selectively and has stories published with other authors from around the world in three *Dog/ Horse Tales for the Soul* books that support many charities. He is also the proud author of the *Four Seasons of Lancaster County* series by Masthof Press.

His stories and scenes have been in *Bucks County Panorama, Bucks County* and *Lancaster County Magazines, The Franciscan Tau, The Franciscan Way* publications, *The Horse and Dog Tales* series and other magazines and periodicals.

His photographs have won grand, first and honorable mention awards in *Amish Country News* and many are featured on the Discover Lancaster Tourist Facebook Fan Club.

Megan loves to watercolor and create things with her busy hands and Ray is often busy with the animals, playing guitar, writing his short stories and books, or taking photos.

Ray and Megan love living among the Plain Folk with their many rescued animals and they spend most of their free time enjoying their family of three grown children and seven grandchildren. They both hope you enjoy this book.

Author's wife and Brandy at their Shepherd Too Farm.